Love by Design

The Lilac Lake Inn Series
Book 1

Judith Keim

Wild Quail Publishing

BOOKS BY JUDITH KEIM

THE HARTWELL WOMEN SERIES:
The Talking Tree – 1
Sweet Talk – 2
Straight Talk – 3
Baby Talk – 4
The Hartwell Women – Boxed Set

THE BEACH HOUSE HOTEL SERIES:
Breakfast at The Beach House Hotel – 1
Lunch at The Beach House Hotel – 2
Dinner at The Beach House Hotel – 3
Christmas at The Beach House Hotel – 4
Margaritas at The Beach House Hotel – 5
Dessert at The Beach House Hotel – 6
Coffee at The Beach House Hotel – 7
High Tea at The Beach House Hotel – 8 (2024}

THE FAT FRIDAYS GROUP:
Fat Fridays – 1
Sassy Saturdays – 2
Secret Sundays – 3

THE SALTY KEY INN SERIES:
Finding Me – 1
Finding My Way – 2
Finding Love – 3
Finding Family – 4
The Salty Key Inn Series – Boxed Set

SEASHELL COTTAGE BOOKS:
A Christmas Star

Change of Heart
A Summer of Surprises
A Road Trip to Remember
The Beach Babes

THE CHANDLER HILL INN SERIES:
Going Home – 1
Coming Home – 2
Home at Last – 3
The Chandler Hill Inn Series – Boxed Set

THE DESERT SAGE INN SERIES:
The Desert Flowers – Rose – 1
The Desert Flowers – Lily – 2
The Desert Flowers – Willow – 3
The Desert Flowers – Mistletoe & Holly – 4

SOUL SISTERS AT CEDAR MOUNTAIN LODGE:
Christmas Sisters – Anthology
Christmas Kisses
Christmas Castles
Christmas Stories – Soul Sisters Anthology
Christmas Joy

THE SANDERLING COVE INN SERIES:
Waves of Hope
Sandy Wishes
Salty Kisses

THE LILAC LAKE INN SERIES
Love by Design
Love Between the Lines – (2024)
Love Under the Stars – (2024)

OTHER BOOKS:

The ABC's of Living With a Dachshund
Once Upon a Friendship – Anthology
Winning BIG – a little love story for all ages
Holiday Hopes
The Winning Tickets

For more information: **www.judithkeim.com**

PRAISE FOR JUDITH KEIM'S NOVELS

THE BEACH HOUSE HOTEL SERIES – Books 1 – 6:

"Love the characters in this series. This series was my first introduction to Judith Keim. She is now one of my favorites. Looking forward to reading more of her books."

BREAKFAST AT THE BEACH HOUSE HOTEL is an easy, delightful read that offers romance, family relationships, and strong women learning to be stronger. Real life situations filter through the pages. Enjoy!"

LUNCH AT THE BEACH HOUSE HOTEL – "This series is such a joy to read. You feel you are actually living with them. Can't wait to read the latest one."

DINNER AT THE BEACH HOUSE HOTEL – "A Terrific Read! As usual, Judith Keim did it again. Enjoyed immensely. Continue writing such pleasantly reading books for all of us readers."

CHRISTMAS AT THE BEACH HOUSE HOTEL – "Not Just Another Christmas Novel. This is book number four in the series and my introduction to Judith Keim's writing. I wasn't disappointed. The characters are dimensional and engaging. The plot is well crafted and advances at a pleasing pace. The Florida location is interesting and warming. It was a delight to read a romance novel with mature female protagonists. Ann and Rhoda have life experiences that enrich the story. It's a clever book about friends and extended family. Buy copies for your book group pals and enjoy this seasonal read."

MARGARITAS AT THE BEACH HOUSE HOTEL – "What a wonderful series. I absolutely loved this book and can't wait for the next book to come out. There was even suspense in it. Thanks Judith for the great stories."

"Overall, Margaritas at the Beach House Hotel is another

wonderful addition to the series. Judith Keim takes the reader on a journey told through the voices of these amazing characters we have all come to love through the years! I truly cannot stress enough how good this book is, and I hope you enjoy it as much as I have!"

THE HARTWELL WOMEN SERIES – Books 1 – 4:
"This was an EXCELLENT series. When I discovered Judith Keim, I read all of her books back to back. I thoroughly enjoyed the women Keim has written about. They are believable and you want to just jump into their lives and be their friends! I can't wait for any upcoming books!"

"I fell into Judith Keim's Hartwell Women series and have read & enjoyed all of her books in every series. Each centers around a strong & interesting woman character and their family interaction. Good reads that leave you wanting more."

THE FAT FRIDAYS GROUP – Books 1 – 3:
"Excellent story line for each character, and an insightful representation of situations which deal with some of the contemporary issues women are faced with today."

"I love this author's books. Her characters and their lives are realistic. The power of women's friendships is a common and beautiful theme that is threaded throughout this story."

THE SALTY KEY INN SERIES – Books 1 – 4:
FINDING ME – "I thoroughly enjoyed the first book in this series and cannot wait for the others! The characters are endearing with the same struggles we all encounter. The setting makes me feel like I am a guest at The Salty Key Inn...relaxed, happy & light-hearted! The men are yummy and the women strong. You can't get better than that! Happy

Reading!"

FINDING MY WAY- "Loved the family dynamics as well as uncertain emotions of dating and falling in love. Appreciated the morals and strength of parenting throughout. Just couldn't put this book down."

FINDING LOVE – "I waited for this book because the first two was such good reads. This one didn't disappoint.... Judith Keim always puts substance into her books. This book was no different, I learned about PTSD, accepting oneself, there is always going to be problems but stick it out and make it work. Just the way life is. In some ways a lot like my life. Judith is right, it needs another book and I will definitely be reading it. Hope you choose to read this series, you will get so much out of it."

FINDING FAMILY – "Completing this series is like eating the last chip. Love Judith's writing, and her female characters are always smart, strong, vulnerable to life and love experiences."

"This was a refreshing book. Bringing the heart and soul of the family to us."

THE CHANDLER HILL INN SERIES – Books 1 – 3:

GOING HOME – "I absolutely could not put this book down. Started at night and read late into the middle of the night. As a child of the '60s, the Vietnam war was front and center so this resonated with me. All the characters in the book were so well developed that the reader felt like they were friends of the family."

"I was completely immersed in this book, with the beautiful descriptive writing, and the authors' way of bringing her characters to life. I felt like I was right inside her story."

COMING HOME – "Coming Home is a winner. The

characters are well-developed, nuanced and likable. Enjoyed the vineyard setting, learning about wine growing and seeing the challenges Cami faces in running and growing a business. I look forward to the next book in this series!"

"Coming Home was such a wonderful story. The author has such a gift for getting the reader right to the heart of things."

HOME AT LAST – "In this wonderful conclusion, to a heartfelt and emotional trilogy set in Oregon's stunning wine country, Judith Keim has tied up the Chandler Hill series with the perfect bow."

"Overall, this is truly a wonderful addition to the Chandler Hill Inn series. Judith Keim definitely knows how to perfectly weave together a beautiful and heartfelt story."

"The storyline has some beautiful scenes along with family drama. Judith Keim has created characters with interactions that are believable and some of the subjects the story deals with are poignant."

SEASHELL COTTAGE BOOKS:

A CHRISTMAS STAR – "Love, laughter, sadness, great food, and hope for the future, all in one book. It doesn't get any better than this stunning read."

"A Christmas Star is a heartwarming Christmas story featuring endearing characters. So many Christmas books are set in snowbound places...it was a nice change to read a Christmas story that takes place on a warm sandy beach!" Susan Peterson

CHANGE OF HEART – "CHANGE OF HEART is the summer read we've all been waiting for. Judith Keim is a master at creating fascinating characters that are simply irresistible. Her stories leave you with a big smile on your face and a heart bursting with love."

~Kellie Coates Gilbert, author of the popular Sun Valley Series

A SUMMER OF SURPRISES – "The story is filled with a roller coaster of emotions and self-discovery. Finding love again and rebuilding family relationships."

"Ms. Keim uses this book as an amazing platform to show that with hard emotional work, belief in yourself and love, the scars of abuse can be conquered. It in no way preaches, it's a lovely story with a happy ending."

"The character development was excellent. I felt I knew these people my whole life. The story development was very well thought out I was drawn [in] from the beginning."

A ROAD TRIP TO REMEMBER – "I LOVED this book! Love the character development, the fun, the challenges and the ending. My favorite books are about strong, competent women finding their own path to success and happiness and this is a winner. It's one of those books you just can't put down."

"The characters are so real that they jump off the page. Such a fun, HAPPY book at the perfect time. It will lift your spirits and even remind you of your own grandmother. Spirited and hopeful Aggie gets a second chance at love and she takes the steering wheel and drives straight for it."

THE DESERT SAGE INN SERIES – Books 1 – 4:

THE DESERT FLOWERS – ROSE – "The Desert Flowers - Rose, is the first book in the new series by Judith Keim. I always look forward to new books by Judith Keim, and this one is definitely a wonderful way to begin The Desert Sage Inn Series!"

"In this first of a series, we see each woman come into her own and view new beginnings even as they must take this tearful journey as they slowly lose a dear friend. This is a *very well written book with well-developed and likable main characters. It was interesting and enlightening as the first portion of this saga unfolded. I very much enjoyed this book and I do recommend it"*

"Judith Keim is one of those authors that you can always depend on to give you a great story with fantastic characters. I'm excited to know that she is writing a new series and after reading book 1 in the series, I can't wait to read the rest of the books."!

THE DESERT FLOWERS – LILY – *"The second book in the Desert Flowers series is just as wonderful as the first. Judith Keim is a brilliant storyteller. Her characters are truly lovely and people that you want to be friends with as soon as you start reading. Judith Keim is not afraid to weave real life conflict and loss into her stories. I loved reading Lily's story and can't wait for Willow's!*

"The Desert Flowers Lily is the second book in The Desert Sage Inn Series by author Judith Keim. When I read the first book in the series, The Desert Flowers-Rose, I knew this series would exceed all of my expectations and then some. Judith Keim is an amazing author, and this series is a testament to her writing skills and her ability to completely draw a reader into the world of her characters."

THE DESERT FLOWERS – WILLOW – *"The feelings of love, joy, happiness, friendship, family and the pain of loss are deeply felt by Willow Sanchez and her two cohorts Rose and Lily. The Desert Flowers met because of their deep feelings for Alec Thurston, a man who touched their lives in different ways.*

Once again, Judith Keim has written the story of a strong, competent, confident and independent woman. Willow, like Rose and Lily can handle tough situations. All the characters are written so that the reader gets to know them but not all the characters will give the reader warm and fuzzy feelings.

The story is well written and from the start you will be pulled in. There is enough backstory that a reader can start here but I assure you, you'll want to learn more. There is an ocean of emotions that will make you smile, cringe, tear up or out right cry. I loved this book as I loved books one and two. I am thrilled that the Desert Flowers story will continue. I highly recommend this book to anyone who enjoys books with strong women."

Love by Design

The Lilac Lake Inn Series
Book 1

Judith Keim

Wild Quail Publishing

Wild Quail Publishing
PO Box 171332
Boise, ID 83717-1332

DEDICATION

In loving memory of my grandmother

PROLOGUE

GG

Eugenia Wittner had always hated her name until the day her doting father said, "Well, then, why don't we call you Genie?"

"Like the magical character in the bottle who grants wishes?" she'd said, feeling a thrill go through her five-year-old body. She loved the idea of magic.

"I don't see why not?" A known philanthropist who adored her, her father hugged her to his broad chest. "You'll see how gratifying it is."

From that moment on, Genie's life took on a special kind of purpose.

At eighty-two, she still loved to fulfill the wishes of others. She'd had the money to do so until recently when her financial advisor in Boston took off with most of her funds and those of others too. She'd panicked until her usual, sharp financial instincts took over, and she did the best she could to come up with a way to meet her father's wishes to save the family property in the Lakes Region of central New Hampshire.

For generations, the Wittner family had owned just over ten acres on the shore of Lilac Lake, the house that stood on it that had been expanded into a lovely inn, and the little cottage at the southern-most tip of their land where a large sun-bathing rock nearby emerged from the lake water like a gift from the rocky shore.

Genie, or GG as her granddaughters called her, knew she

couldn't continue maintaining the property, paying the taxes, and running the inn. In addition, she needed a place to live for the rest of her life.

She found buyers for the inn and most of the land surrounding it, reserving a section of the acreage and the cottage for her family. But there was a catch. If after the cottage was renovated, it was unoccupied for more than six months of any year, it and the land would be sold to the new owners for a fair price. Genie understood. The cottage and the land were too valuable to go unused or to be unappreciated. It wasn't ideal, but it was a plan that might work if her granddaughters were willing to help her keep her promise to her father to hold onto the family property. Their mother had never had any interest in it. Genie hoped this plan would work because it was probably the last opportunity that she'd have to bestow such a generous gift.

Now, Genie was about to make a request of those beloved granddaughters—three strong, independent women. She hoped her request would fulfill a wish of theirs always to be able to come to the lake and be the impetus to make some changes in their lives, that more than the property would be her gift to them. How she loved each one!

Whitney, a real beauty with blond hair and blue eyes, was the oldest of the three at thirty-two and was adored by everyone who followed the television series in which she starred. The show, called *The Hopefuls*, was about a young woman named Hope and other young people trying to break into the movie business. It gave Whitney a chance to showcase her ability to sing and dance, something she'd loved to do since she was a small child. Viewers were all cheering for her. Of all her granddaughters, Whitney was the one least like her, which may be why GG adored her.

Danielle, or Dani as she liked to be called, was the most

outgoing of the three girls with a pleasant nature that people welcomed. With honey-colored hair and bright-blue eyes, she wasn't the least bit musical like Whitney. But she was talented when it came to drawing. That, and helping her adoptive father build a playhouse when she was young had led her to the field of architecture. Dani's independence and determination matched GG's own. Both Whitney and Dani had been adopted by their mother's second husband, Taylor's father, whom they all adored.

Taylor was the youngest at twenty-five and the quietest. Pretty, with long black hair and dark eyes, she sometimes felt left out by her older half-sisters who looked nothing like her, making her feel different because they had different birth fathers. Books were her way of coping from a young age. Taylor wrote romance novels under the pen name Taylor Castle and was very good at it. GG had read and loved every page of them, delighted Taylor shared a romantic streak with her.

Regardless of what they were doing, GG hoped the girls would honor her wishes and help keep a promise to her father to hold onto the family land—something she herself wasn't able to do as she'd wanted. She'd never considered aging a problem. But now, suffering from congestive heart failure, she was forced to acknowledge that life, indeed, was one big circle.

DANI

Danielle "Dani" Gilford drove to Lilac Lake from Boston, where she lived in her downtown condo, wondering why her grandmother had insisted that she come there for this specific weekend. It wasn't a long trip, though, and one she was happy to make in late May before the summer crowds hit the Lakes Region of New Hampshire *en masse*. She needed this break. She'd fought hard for a degree in Architectural Studies from

MIT, and until recently, she'd enjoyed her job with a respected firm in Boston. But lately, she'd begun to realize that she was never going to shake off the unspoken discrimination she endured because she was a woman. Oh, the men were trained enough to be careful of how they said things. Jobs used to be assigned fairly. But that was changing, and she didn't like it. No doubt they thought she'd be married and gone by now.

As she drove, her thoughts flew to her grandmother. Some people thought GG was eccentric for having kept her maiden name after marriage and becoming a widow after her husband's death in the Vietnam War years ago. But GG had always been a free spirit. People often said Dani reminded them of GG, something that pleased her. Dani had always considered GG a fairy godmother who somehow knew when she needed to talk or feel loved. Her own mother, Laura, was not a cuddly person, and they often were at odds. Summers spent in New Hampshire either with GG or at summer camp had been a reprieve from the life Dani couldn't fit into in Atlanta. No matter how much her mother tried, Dani was not interested in a social life there. She'd rather be doing a project or two in a workshop. The feel of a piece of smooth wood under her hand gave her more pleasure than a new dress or, heaven forbid, a hairdo that was way too fussy for her.

GG had told Dani she loved that she was different from many young women her age. She was proud that Dani marched to her own tune. The fact that Dani had earned a master's degree in architecture was proof she went after what she wanted.

Her mother had worried with all that hard work studying, Dani wouldn't have time to meet any eligible men. Thinking of that now, Dani chuckled softly. She worked with men all the time. But at thirty, she was growing tired of competing with them to get the same recognition and opportunities. She hoped a visit to Lilac Lake would help put things in perspective. If the time came when she could pull in one last big project at the firm to prove herself, she'd complete the job and leave.

TAYLOR

Taylor Gilford wended her way through the traffic at Boston's Logan International Airport, into the Sumner Tunnel under Boston Harbor, and onto I-93 to head north to New Hampshire. The trip to Lilac Lake would take a little over two and a half hours—time she intended to use to try and plot a scene in her next book. At twenty-five, she had a growing readership demanding more and more of her sweet romance stories. She'd been surprised when people loved her first book. But then, she'd been a reader and a romantic from the time she was young, turning to books for the companionship she lacked in her life. As the younger half-sister of two beautiful, strong, independent girls, she hadn't always felt as if she fit in. Whitney, the dramatic one with a ton of friends, and Dani, the tomboy who loved sports, weren't mean to her; they sometimes simply forgot she was around.

There was nothing worse to Taylor than having her mother prompt others to notice her or ask them to include her in their activities. Rather than irritate them, Taylor chose to lose herself in a book. GG had always understood Taylor's need to be independent in a different, quiet way and had encouraged her to write from an early age. Taylor would always be grateful. Now if she could only have the courage to go after love like the heroines in her books, she'd be truly happy.

More than that, she needed to believe she could write another book. It wasn't a case of not knowing what to write; she had plenty of ideas. But she, like some authors experienced, didn't think she could get through the tedious process required to take another book from beginning to a satisfying end. Caught in this insecure time, she worried that everyone might think her earlier books were just flukes, that she had no talent. She gripped the steering wheel until her knuckles turned white. Just think of it as one more book with a beginning, a middle, and an end, she scolded herself, feeling the knot in her chest tighten.

WHITNEY

Whitney Gilford couldn't get to the airport fast enough. The news had broken about her split with her co-star, Zane Blanchard, and she'd be surrounded by screaming paparazzi wanting to know what happened. They adored Zane and were already calling her difficult, disloyal, and spoiled. As confused as she was about her reaction to the breakup after her agent went ahead and broke the news in social media without warning, she knew for certain she'd screwed up by being caught in such a mess. New Hampshire had been a refuge in the past. She prayed it would serve as one now.

Tears formed in her eyes as the Uber driver she'd called made his way through the traffic heading to LAX for her red-eye flight to Boston. GG had always told her to be strong, to ignore the hurtful things others said about her. But now the entire world seemed to be against her with rumors flying about how difficult she was, how Zane had told everyone he couldn't stand her, and other such tales. And it hurt. But then the public didn't know the details, and she had no intention of filling them in.

Perhaps it was time to have a normal life away from Hollywood. She'd loved her career and appreciated all she'd been given in a job most others envied. But something was happening to her and those around her; something she didn't like. What she needed was to get away and think. From there, time would tell if she was right. Lately GG had been more on her mind. She couldn't wait to relax and do nothing but breathe in the fresh New Hampshire air.

CHAPTER ONE
DANI

The Lakes Region of New Hampshire was a special place for families and fishing, with a natural beauty to the area that was unique. Sitting in east-central New Hampshire, south of the White Mountains and about 100 miles or so north of Boston, the Lakes Region was a wooded wonderland with more than 200 lakes of all sizes, including the granddaddy of them all, Lake Winnipesaukee.

Just thinking of the state she loved, random thoughts gathered in Dani's mind. She recalled the purple finch was the state bird and one GG loved to feed with sunflower and thistle seeds at the inn. The Lilac was the state flower. Any late spring or early summer visit always included smelling the purple blooms filling the air with their distinct perfume. Dani had tried to capture their beauty in paintings. But like most things in nature, their colors could never be reproduced to equal what Mother Nature had done herself.

As Dani drew closer to Lilac Lake, one of the smaller lakes in this region, she opened the driver's side window and inhaled the scent of evergreens and the elusive aroma of lake water. The stone walls bordering the country roads and visible even within nearby forests were reminders of rural New England life in the 19th century. A huge granite rock appeared jutting out of the water at the southern edge of the lake, and her pulse sprinted. She was almost there. She and her sisters had spent hours sunning and climbing on the smooth surface in years past. Even now, whenever she visited, Dani liked to climb on top of it and sprawl out in the sun. Many visits had included lying there creating cloud pictures in the usually clear blue sky above.

The Lilac Lake Inn had been in the family forever. It had started as a summer camp, an escape for previous family members. Then, when GG was a young, widowed mother, she'd moved to the camp and enlarged it by adding two guestroom wings, making it a small inn open to families from May to Labor Day. With its success, GG extended the time it was open, adding early spring weeks to the summer family season and remaining open in the fall for the benefit of hunters and the "leaf-peepers" who came to see the beautiful fall colors that filled the hills and woods with paintbox colors. Dani didn't know which season she liked best. Not that she visited too often anymore.

She pulled up to the main white-clapboard building of the inn and got out of the car. Sighing happily, she breathed in the clean air and was retrieving her suitcase from the backseat when a young, blond-haired man walked toward her with purpose.

"Are you one of the Gilford women?" he asked, walking across the soft pine needles beneath his feet.

She studied his craggy face, gazed into his dark-green eyes the color of the pine trees, and nodded. "I am. Why?"

"Your grandmother asked me to tell you to go into town to the Lilac Lake B&B. I assume you know where that is."

"Yes, but why the change in plans?"

He gave her a friendly smile. "Because the inn has been sold, and I'm going to be the contractor for its renovation. I'm here just looking it over for the new owners."

"Really? What construction firm are you with?" asked Dani, feeling a little sick at the thought of new owners at the inn.

The man laughed. "I'm not with a big firm. My brother and I own Collister Construction here at Lilac Lake." He held out his hand. "I'm Brad Collister, by the way."

She gave his hand a firm squeeze even as she felt herself drawn into his gaze, making her feel unsteady for a moment. "Dani Gilford, one of Genie Wittner's granddaughters."

"A pleasure to meet you. I expect we'll be seeing a lot of one another," he answered. He tipped his Red Sox baseball cap and walked away, leaving her to wonder if the sale was why GG had needed to see her.

She got back into the car and returned to town and onto Main Street, where a two-story, colonial house painted a soft purple was known as the Lilac Lake B&B. Owned and run by a couple in their sixties, the B&B had been in operation for almost twenty years and was still a nice place to stay. With only ten available rooms, Dani assumed she and GG would have two of the downstairs rooms because, at eighty-two, GG didn't have the agility she used to have.

Dani grabbed her suitcase and headed indoors. She'd taken just a few steps when the sound of a car approaching made her stop and turn.

An Uber driver stopped the car and waited while a woman got out and retrieved two large suitcases from the back. It took Dani a moment to realize the woman behind the large sunglasses and wearing a LA Dodgers baseball cap low on her brow was Whitney.

"Whitney, what are you doing here?" Dani asked rushing forward to embrace her.

"Hiding out. I took a red-eye flight to leave L.A. as fast as I could. When I finally got here, I tried to get into the inn, but some hot-looking guy said it had been sold."

She tipped the Uber driver and gave Dani a hug. "Why are you here?"

"GG asked me to come spend the weekend with her," Dani said. "Come on. She must be inside."

"Is she all right?" Whitney asked, grabbing the handle of one of her suitcases, while Dani helped her with the other while also carrying her own.

They were met at the door by Cynthia Anders, a heavy-set, pleasant-faced woman. "Ah, two more have arrived. Hello, it's been a while. Whitney, poor dear, I heard the news on the internet. You and Zane Blanchard breaking up? Such a shame."

Dani turned to her sister. "Really?"

Whitney let out a groan. "That's only part of it." She noticed Cynthia leaning forward for more news and clamped her mouth shut.

"Is GG here?" Dani asked Cynthia.

"No, but Taylor is. Now that all three of you are here, I have some instructions for you. Come in and get settled, and then I'll give them to you."

"What's going on?" Dani asked. She didn't like not knowing the details.

"All in time," said Cynthia in a soothing manner. "As I said, get settled in your rooms, have some refreshments, and then you can be on your way. Dani, you're in Room 4, and, Whitney, you're next door in Room 5."

Dani carried her suitcase up the stairs and into a room that contained a four-poster king bed, a small bathroom, and sliding doors onto a balcony that overlooked the backyard and garden below. She hung up the skirt and sweater she'd brought for dinner and left the rest of her clothes folded in the suitcase. Lilac Lake was a lovely resort town, but the vibe was casual.

A knock sounded on her door. She opened it to find her younger sister, Taylor, smiling at her.

"Hi, Dani. I'm so glad to see you. Cynthia mentioned you'd arrived." Taylor gave Dani a hug that she was quick to return.

"When did you arrive?" Dani asked. "I didn't realize that all three of us were going to be here, or I might've tried to arrange to drive up with you. Do you know anything about GG's instructions?"

Taylor shook her head. "No, and I'm curious too. I sometimes come and visit GG to discuss my business. I thought her request was related to that."

Whitney joined them. Her red-rimmed eyes and lackluster appearance spoke of her recent troubles. Dani's heart went out to her.

"Is there anything I can do to help you?" Dani asked her.

"Dig a deep grave and drop me into it," Whitney replied, attempting gallows humor. "I've really messed up. Zane and I were once a real loving couple, but then it became just part of an act for the series. But now it's all fallen apart."

"Do you want to tell us about it?" Taylor asked, putting an arm around Whitney.

"Thanks, but I can't talk about it right now. Wait a minute. I know why *I'm* here. Why are the two of you in Lilac Lake?"

"Didn't you get a call from GG?" Dani asked.

Whitney shrugged. "I don't know. I turned off my phone." She shuddered dramatically. "All those nasty paparazzi and the rumors surrounding the split were too much for me to deal with."

Okay," said Dani. "Here's the deal or as much as I know. GG asked me to come to Lilac Lake this weekend. She was specific about it being this particular one."

"And GG called me to meet her here—something we do from time to time to discuss the book business," added Taylor. "But I don't understand why she didn't tell us she'd sold the inn. What's going on with that?"

"Let's find out," said Dani. "I don't even know where she's staying."

The three of them trouped downstairs to the front hallway, where Cynthia met them. "Ready for the next instructions?"

Trying not to stare at Whitney who'd put on sunglasses and donned her baseball cap again, Cynthia handed Dani a note.

Dani glanced at it and read aloud: *My darling granddaughters, please join me for tea at The Woodlands dining room. Cynthia will let me know when I should be ready. All my love. GG.*

"What's GG doing at The Woodlands? That's the new assisted living place," said Taylor. "She's not ready for something like that."

"She's eighty-two," Cynthia reminded them.

Dani looked at her sisters through blurry eyes. "We'd better go see her. I'll drive."

CHAPTER TWO
DANI

Dani slid behind the wheel of her SUV and waited for the other two to get in. She was surprised when Whitney told Taylor to sit up front in her usual place, then realized Whitney was going to hide in the backseat.

"GG doesn't usually keep things from us," said Dani. "I hope this doesn't have anything to do with the recent scandal in Boston."

"What scandal?" asked Whitney, sitting up.

"Tell us later," said Taylor. "I don't want you to put it out to the universe if that's not the reason."

Dani rolled her eyes. Taylor had always had too much imagination. "Okay, we'll wait to see what GG has to say."

She pulled up in front of an attractive, gray-shingled one-story building with sparkling white trim embraced by woodland trees. The town had been grateful when it was announced The Woodlands had chosen to build their facility nearby. Additional taxable property would help maintain the reputation of Lilac Lake as being one of the prettiest towns in the state. In return for some financial breaks, the company that owned the assisted-living facility had used local companies to build it and had made it as attractive as promised.

Dani and her sisters filed into the reception area and then followed the signs to the dining room. At the doorway, Dani stopped and stared at the woman she loved with all her heart.

Tiny but still active, GG looked up at them, and her lips

curved, allowing the mark of years on her face to soften. Dani studied those light-blue eyes, the same as hers. But they showed no sorrow, simply happiness at seeing them.

GG waved them over to the square wooden table where she was sitting. Fresh flowers sat in a vase in the middle of the table, and green floral placemats and matching napkins sat in front of all four chairs.

Dani waited while Taylor kissed GG hello, followed by Whitney, who did her best not to cry. Then it was Dani's turn to hug GG, which she did before kissing her cheek.

"It's so wonderful to see my three girls. Sit down, all of you, so we can talk," said GG beaming at them.

Once everyone was settled, GG spoke. "Before we relax with tea and treats, I need to tell you something. By now, you know I've sold the inn. Even though it's been in our family for three generations, I was forced to do so after learning that my financial advisor had me invest in a fraudulent scheme of his. I lost most everything except what I received from the sale of the inn." GG's sigh was painful to hear.

Dani observed the tears forming in GG's eyes and fisted her hands. "That's awful. We can't let that bastard get away with it."

GG help up her hand to stop her. "What's done is done. The authorities will try to collect the money, but it's going to be a long process, and I couldn't wait that long. Here's the deal I made with the new owners represented by a nice, ambitious young man. I sold the inn and most of the acreage to them. But I've kept three acres and the caretaker's cottage for the three of you. As long as one or all of you stay there for a period of six months or more each year, that property will continue to be yours. If you don't stay at the cottage, the new owners will receive it as part of the package for a fee and put it to use as they wanted. But, my darling granddaughters, we must keep a promise to my father and his father before him to retain ownership of as much of the property as we can. I did my best to hold onto more, but I couldn't afford to maintain and run the inn, and I needed a place to live. This was the best solution I could come up with so I wouldn't be a burden to anyone."

The silence around the table was deafening as Dani and her sisters tried to absorb the news of all that had happened.

"Do you mean we have to live at the caretaker's cottage?" said Taylor. "It's haunted."

"I know that's what people have said about it, but those rumors started with kids who shouldn't have been there in the first place. It's run-down and now in need of renovation, but that's something I've considered. A bank account has been set up to help fund those changes. It's not a huge amount but should handle most of what you need."

"So, we'd each have to take part in it?" asked Whitney frowning.

"Not necessarily. I figure Dani could get the project started, and as time passes, you each add your own input."

"What if we don't want to stay in the house? I ... I've seen a ghost there. I swear it," said Taylor, her voice shaking.

"A ghost living there is just a rumor kids started years ago. How you manage your part of the arrangement will be up to the three of you," said GG. "I've done what I could to honor my heritage. Now it will be up to you to continue to do so."

Dani's mind was racing. "Who will we get to help us with the renovations?"

"A local construction company, the same one who built this facility, has a team of talented men who can be a help to you."

Dani felt a frown forming. "Are you talking about Collister Construction?"

GG's face brightened. "Exactly. Two young men, Brad and Aaron Collister, own it. They owe me a favor for helping to get the contract for The Woodlands for them. They'll be happy to assist you."

"And any architectural changes?" Dani asked, already aware of the answer.

"I hope you can take care of them. Your talent is underrated at your firm. I'd like to see you use that skill on this project."

"This may be the godsend I was looking for," said Whitney. She took hold of GG's hand. "I've made a mess of things."

"I saw something about it on one of those entertainment news shows. We can talk about that later. No one is going to ruin your career over breaking up with your costar." GG's strong words brought a look of relief to Whitney's face. Dani was glad to see it.

GG turned to Taylor. "I thought this whole project might become the subject of one of your books. Nothing like a fresh start to get a romance going for all of you."

"Romance?" said Dani. "The last thing I need is a relationship. I'm barely over Jeremy, and he and I broke up eighteen months ago. I have no interest in starting anything new. I'm tired of men thinking they can order me around." Jeremy, new to the architectural firm, had worked with Dani on a project and changed from someone easy to get along with to an insecure man who wanted to control her.

"We'll see," GG said, smiling sweetly.

"What else needs to be done?" asked Whitney.

"I have just a few days to get all the family things out of the inn," said GG. "The furnishings are part of the sale, but personal items need to be retrieved. I was hoping the three of you could tackle that. I've had empty boxes delivered to the inn for your use."

Dani looked at her sisters and nodded. "I can do that."

"If any of us need to stay here in town to work on the project, can we stay at the inn?" said Taylor.

"You'll have to ask the owners. If that doesn't work, Cynthia said that with enough notice you can stay at the B&B at my expense," said GG. "I'm trying to make it as easy for you as possible."

"Oh, GG, how hard this must be for you," sighed Whitney.

"I've had a full life with lots of friends and the three of you. How many other people would be able to live up to their name and be able to grant wishes to others? Now I'm giving you the opportunity to give your lives a fresh start. That's my gift for you. A fresh start."

"I certainly need one," groused Whitney.

Dani knew how unhappy she'd been at work and decided GG was right. A fresh start is what she needed.

Taylor's face lit with affection as she gazed at GG.

A waitress walked over to their table. "Are we ready for tea now?"

GG smiled at her. "I believe we are."

Several other people filled tables near them as three o'clock approached.

GG said quietly, "There's no need to discuss our business here. Dani, you report back to me after the three of you have toured the cottage and have worked on the removal of family items at the inn. If you have any doubt about something being a personal item, just call or text me. I've taken all my things out of the inn, but I need to be sure I have anything that should stay in the family. I've already talked to your mother, and she has no interest in any of it."

Dani was quiet as their order was placed, but her thoughts turned to her mother. Laura Gilford was a beloved woman in Atlanta's social circles but a distracted and somewhat cold mother in private. While her mom's first marriage to an alcoholic had been a disaster ending in his death while driving intoxicated, her mother had carried on, raising Whitney and

Dani, and then had found true love with Taylor's father, Gavin. He was a renegade in his wealthy family who'd refused to go into the family business and had, instead, become a social worker in the court system. It was a perfect match.

"Lemon or milk?" asked the waitress, tearing into Dani's thoughts.

"Lemon, please," Dani answered, focusing once more on the topic of the caretaker's cottage.

"Remember, Whitney, you and Dani told me the cottage was haunted and then left me inside alone one day," said Taylor. "I don't think I'll ever be able to stay there."

Dani reached over and squeezed Taylor's hand. "That was a mean, big-sister joke. I'm sorry. We were fooling you at the time, not really thinking about what it might do to you."

"We kids at the lake used to try to scare each other all the time," said Whitney. "I thought you knew it was just us teasing you."

"This time we'll be right there with you," said Dani. "We'll take a quick look around. That's all."

Taylor gave her a worried look. "Okay."

"Make sure there's no further teasing there," said GG. "It will become a home away from home for you all, I hope. A place to relax and feel safe from everyday life."

They finished sipping tea and eating the small sandwiches that came with it. Dani could see that GG was getting tired and got to her feet. "Thank you, GG, for thinking of us and making sure we'd be able to fix up the cottage. I, for one, promise to try to fulfill your request."

GG's eyes glistened. "Thank you, Dani. I love the three of you so much." She handed Dani a key. "This is to the cottage."

Dani gave GG a kiss and embraced her, suddenly aware of how fragile she'd become. She waited to one side as Whitney and Taylor said their own farewells to GG, and then they headed for the door.

At the entrance, Dani stopped and turned.

GG waved and blew her a kiss.

Feeling better about her grandmother's situation, Dani went to her car determined to do as GG had asked.

In the car, the mood was solemn.

"What an awful thing to have happened to GG. How can someone just take your money?" said Whitney.

"It happens," said Dani, "when you trust someone to do the right thing and they, instead, defy morality and do something like GG's financial advisor did to her and others. I know of a few others in Boston who got stung by his fake deal. It's ugly when you take money away from older people who've saved it for their retirement."

"I remember seeing something about it on the news," said Taylor. "But it's been overtaken by other, worse events. Knowing GG, I'm sure she figured out she'd better take care of things in her own way."

"She sure is smart," said Whitney. "The inn for all we love it needs a lot of cash to maintain it."

"And she was wise to get settled at The Woodlands and make it a done deal so Mom couldn't try to force her to move to the South where she wouldn't know anyone," said Taylor.

"It was a lovely gesture for her to make sure we'd have a place at the lake," said Dani. "The cottage and the three acres that go with it are valuable. More importantly, the inn holds precious memories for all of us. Even you, Taylor, though I'm sorry we made you afraid of the cottage."

"Yeah? You're the one who's going to spend the most time there fixing up the place," said Taylor arching an eyebrow.

Dani laughed. "I think I'll be all right. The ghost should be gone by now. They don't stick around forever. Besides we have a duty to keep it in the family."

"Ghosts can't leave until they've resolved issues here on earth," said Taylor, looking serious.

"Well, this one has had plenty of time to resolve them," said Dani. She wasn't going to get caught up in nonsense like ghosts.

"Didn't Mrs. Maynard die alone one winter's evening?" said Whitney. "She froze to death is what I remember."

"Yeah, and no one knows how long she'd been lying there in the snow outside the cottage. They said her body was frozen solid," said Dani.

"Right," said Whitney. "Now I remember. It's so sad when you think about it."

"It gives me the shivers," said Taylor.

Dani pulled the car through the gates of the inn and took a hard right turn toward the cottage.

A chain with a metal sign attached that said "Keep Out" blocked the dirt driveway.

"I'll take care of it," said Taylor. She got out of the car and unhooked the chain from one of the wooden posts that stood beside the road.

Taylor hurried back to the car, and Dani continued down the dirt driveway. It seemed strange to think of all the changes that were coming to the family property.

She pulled up in front of a one-car, white clapboard garage beside a two-story house with a high peaked roof and a sweeping front porch. The two run-down structures sat atop an incline above the lake. White paint was peeling from the clapboards of both buildings. The landscaping that had once softened the edges of the house had long since become overgrown.

Dani glanced at the others with surprise. "It's in worse shape than I thought. I wonder what the inside is like."

"Why didn't GG keep it up?" asked Taylor.

"Probably she couldn't afford to," said Dani. "With all the land associated with the inn, taxes must be enormous. Maybe it was a matter of keeping the inn looking as beautiful as possible and letting this unused building go untouched."

"Or maybe, she didn't want to disturb Mrs. Maynard's ghost," teased Whitney.

"Okay," said Dani. "Let's do it. I've got the key. Who's following me?" She gave a stern look at her sisters. "It's not fair of either of you to let me go in there alone. C'mon, it's all the Gilford Girls or none, and we have to do this for GG."

Groaning together, Whitney and Taylor climbed out of the car and followed Dani.

In front of the house, Taylor said, "Look! There's our sunning rock. How many hours did we spend on it each summer?

"Too many to count," said Whitney smiling.

Dani stared at the scene in front of them. A breeze was rippling the surface of the lake sending shimmers of light across it. Mallard ducks were swimming in the water nearby, while others had settled on the soft ground just beyond the water's edge, preening or resting. The green-headed males and the soft-brown-feathered females were among Dani's favorites. Farther up the lake, a couple was paddling a canoe. A sense of peace filled her.

"Feels nice to be back, huh?" she said, and led her sisters to the house.

A warning sign was posted on the door announcing the house was private property and trespassers would be prosecuted.

Dani pushed the key into the lock with difficulty and turned it.

The door suddenly sprang open, and all three jumped

away.

"Okay, it's open. Now look around and make mental notes of what needs to be fixed," said Dani. She drew a pad of paper and pen from her purse and entered the living room to the right off the hallway.

A stone fireplace sat on the outside wall and was flanked by bookcases. Two windows on the front facing wall gave a pretty view of the lake. A couch looked as if mice had made nests there. Dani made a note to get rid of it as soon as she could.

Across the hall, a dining room still held a long wooden table and eight matching chairs. Though they were dusty and dirty, Dani noted the quality of the oak and decided they would be worth keeping. Like the living room, this room needed to be repainted, and the popcorn ceiling would need to be removed.

"EEK!" came a cry from the kitchen beyond the dining room.

Dani took off toward it and couldn't help laughing when she saw Whitney standing on an old wooden chair sitting near the stove.

"It's not funny. There's a whole family of mice living here. Help me!"

"Just jump down and stamp your feet so they run away," said Dani. She didn't like the thought of mice either.

After a glance around the kitchen, Dani marked the room as a total loss. The appliances were dated like something from the fifties or sixties. The floor, the cabinets, everything would need to be replaced.

Upstairs they found three bedrooms that shared a good-sized bathroom, and a larger bedroom with a private bath. The bathrooms, especially, would need total renovation.

"Okay, now it's time to check the attic," said Dani. "With those large windows facing the water, it's got to be more than ordinary. In fact, it could end up being a favorite spot."

Taylor shook her head. "I'm sorry, but no matter what you say, I can't go up there."

Dani turned to Whitney. "You ready?"

"Do I have to?" said Whitney.

"Yes, you do," said Dani. She wouldn't admit it, but she was scared too. She thought she'd seen a shadow or something in one of the bedrooms but when she looked again it was gone.

"Okay, I'll come with you, but you have to go first," said Whitney.

A door at the end of the upstairs hallway opened to wooden stairs to the attic.

Dani climbed them step by step, telling herself not to worry, that Mrs. Maynard's ghost was just an old campfire tale.

At the top of the stairs, Dani stood a moment. Light from the front windows seeped into the dimness, allowing her to see the space, giving her an idea of what a beautiful room it could become. She felt Whitney behind her and turned to talk to her and realized Whitney was already heading down the stairs.

Dani swallowed hard and said softly, "No one is going to hurt you."

Then she followed Whitney as fast as she could.

"Are you all right?" Whitney asked catching her in her arms. "You look as if you've seen a ghost."

At Whitney's teasing words, Dani managed to give her a weak smile. "I'm fine," she said, but she couldn't get out of the house fast enough.

CHAPTER THREE
WHITNEY

Back at the B&B, Whitney went to her room, eager to have some time alone. She had a lot to think about. Tossing her sunglasses, hat, and jean jacket on the bed, she went to the upholstered chair next to the window overlooking the back garden and sat down.

Outside, several of the tulips had opened to give the world a last glimpse of their beauty. Rose bushes were beginning to bloom, along with peonies and other spring flowers. Lilac bushes were still in bloom though their showtime was almost over. Still, Whitney loved the varieties of their colors and the sweet perfume they produced.

She was grateful for the ability to hide out at Lilac Lake, but she knew her stay couldn't last forever. She couldn't let the other cast members on the show down. The situation would have to be dealt with, but in its own time.

The shock of finding Zane high on coke and in bed with two women was something Whitney couldn't forget. It told her how far Zane had fallen from the young man she'd once loved to the druggie he was today. She decided she was tired of Hollywood, the games people played, the infighting, the lack of people she wanted to befriend. She and Zane had been thrown together because of the show, had been young enough, eager enough to go along with the gimmick of publicly being together, but then had fallen in love for real. But now, with drugs more important to Zane than anything else, she'd had enough. Worse, she was questioning everything about her life choices.

When Whitney told Zane it was over, he'd screamed at her, told her she was a baby who couldn't handle real life, that she'd been brought up in a glass bubble, and that she had no idea what most people were really like beneath their fake surfaces. He told her that if she ruined his career, he'd ruin hers. His words had crushed her. Whitney had thought he understood she would never risk her reputation and career by getting into the drug scene or have kinky threesomes with women he'd admitted were prostitutes.

A long sigh escaped her. Her world, the one she'd loved, had become tainted.

A knock sounded on her door, and Dani peered inside her room.

"Taylor and I decided to go to the inn tomorrow to search for personal and family items. It's getting to be dinnertime, and we thought it best to wait until we all had a fresh start to the day."

"I think that's wise," Whitney said, relieved she wouldn't have to deal with that today. They'd already had a lot to handle with GG's surprise announcement.

"Are you all right?" Dani asked her.

Whitney sighed again and her eyes filled with tears. People told her she made everything so dramatic, but this time her situation was real. She'd just realized her life was one staged event after another. It wasn't real, and that wasn't what she wanted.

"I've decided to leave Hollywood. It's eating me alive with lies, rumors, and innuendoes, to say nothing of the drugs and competition. Now, there's a rumor I'm pregnant with Zane's baby. As if." At one time she might've welcomed such news, but Zane wasn't the man she'd fallen in love with. He'd become a stranger she detested.

"How can you leave? What about the show?" Dani asked, her eyes wide.

"I'll have to go back to California to wrap up this season. Then, I want to come back here for the summer. After that, I'll decide."

"Okay, big sister, until you head back to California, let's not have you make any big announcements about being here. We don't want to turn Lilac Lake into a circus with the gossip rags."

Whitney stood and gave her a solemn look. "You're right. If Lilac Lake is going to be a place for me to hide, I can't draw attention to it."

"What about the rumors that you're pregnant with Zane's baby?" Dani asked, practical as always.

"I could wait a few months, and it would soon be obvious it isn't true, or I might get a dog and tell everyone this is the only baby everyone should be talking about," she answered. "I've been thinking about getting a puppy lately, and this would be the perfect time to do it."

"Hm-m-m, you could probably get away with something like that. Where are you going to find a dog?"

"Here in town," said Whitney. "Maybe there's an animal rescue facility nearby."

"Okay. We'll try to take care of that. I've always wanted a dog, but with my schedule it wouldn't be fair to have one. I've been thinking of asking for extended time off from my firm to help with the renovation. Having a dog on the property will be reassuring. Maybe I'll look for one, too."

A knock sounded on the door and Taylor poked her head inside the room. "How about dinner?"

"C'mon in," said Whitney. "I'm almost ready."

A short while later, the three of them headed out.

###

As Whitney walked with her sisters down Main Street of Lilac Lake, she fell in love all over again with the quaint New England town. With its pretty storefronts, decorative streetlamps, and postcard-worthy churches' white steeples reaching for the sky, the town had become one of the best-known resort communities in the state.

Most of the shops were closing for the day, but Jake's Bar and the three upscale restaurants in town were scenes of busy activities. Residents and vacationers from nearby areas came to Lilac Lake for good food and unique shopping.

They decided to go to Fins, a popular seafood restaurant owned by people they'd known while growing up. Jack and Susan Hendrickson were a well-matched couple who'd made a success of their restaurant with his excellent cooking and her easy-going social manner putting customers at ease even when things were tense in the kitchen. Their daughter, Melissa, was Whitney's age, but Whitney figured it was a form of jealousy that kept them from being real friends.

They walked into the restaurant. The pale-blue painted walls above dark wainscoting suited the restaurant's nautical theme. The matching blue-linen tablecloths continued the theme with imitation pink coral and candle centerpieces.

Susan hurried over to greet them. "I'm so happy to see the three of you. I heard you might be coming for a visit. Genie was in for dinner last week with a friend. Sorry to see the inn being sold, but when times are tough you must do whatever it takes to survive."

Dani and Taylor nodded but didn't comment.

Whitney spoke up. "Hi, Susan. We didn't call for reservations. But we're wondering if we could have a table."

"Sure thing. We're busy, but you're early enough that we can do that for you. Melissa is here working in the kitchen. I'm sure she'll want to say hello."

"Okay," Whitney said pleasantly.

Susan led them to a table by a front window. "Will this be all right?"

"Could we be seated somewhere else?" Whitney said. "I'd rather not be seen."

"Oh, of course, poor dear," Susan cooed. "With all that fuss about you and Zane and the split-up." She shot Whitney a look of sympathy.

Whitney forced a smile even though she wanted to run out of the restaurant. If people in Lilac Lake were aware of all her problems, she could easily imagine how much worse the gossip would be in LA.

Susan gave them a table in the back and then said, "I'll let Melissa know you're here."

A waitress came over to them, and after greeting them, she handed them menus and then poured bottled water into their crystal goblets. "May I get you something to drink? We have some wine specials by the glass tonight."

"I'll have a glass of chardonnay," said Taylor.

"And some of your finest pinot noir for me," Dani said.

"Perrier with a lime," said Whitney, as pleasantly as she could. Until she was off the show, she had to watch her weight.

"The price of being a star," quipped Dani.

Whitney knew Dani was trying to put her at ease and gave her a grateful look.

She perused the menu hoping to find something suitable. She chose broiled scrod and a simple green salad.

Dani chose the shrimp scampi, and Taylor chose a shellfish stew not caring about calorie counts. Whitney wondered if the day would ever come when she could eat like that.

"Hey, cheer up," said Dani nudging her with an elbow. "Here comes Melissa."

An auburn-haired young woman wearing a white chef's

coat walked toward them. "Welcome to Fins," she said. "I hope you're trying a little bit of everything. I've joined my father in the kitchen, and we've been updating the menu."

"It's nice to see you," said Taylor. "Congratulations on getting your culinary degree. Your mother told me about it last time I was here."

"Thanks. It was worth it. We're doing well," said Melissa. She focused on Whitney. "I'm sorry to hear about your troubles. Must be hard to lose a guy like Zane Blanchard."

Whitney put on a brave face and nodded. If everyone knew the truth, they'd be surprised. But she wasn't about to ruin Zane's career, even after he'd threatened to ruin hers.

Dani once more came to her rescue. "So, Melissa, how about you? What's your love life like here? Many chances to find someone?"

A smile spread across Melissa's face. "Aaron and Brad Collister are both available. And Nick Woodruff is divorced and is now chief of police. Several of the old crowd have summer homes here. So quite a few of the original gang are around. And I hear one of the new owners of the inn is Ross Roberts. He's smokin' hot."

"Ross Roberts, the ex-baseball star?" said Taylor. "GG never mentioned his name."

"He's part of the trio who now own it. A silent partner, I guess," said Melissa. "I've only seen him from a distance, but all I can say is 'wow'. Crystal at the cafe told me he was very nice when he came in for coffee."

"How's Crystal?" Whitney asked, genuinely interested. Crystal Owens was a couple of years older than Whitney. During summers growing up, they'd bonded over fashion and movies and all things theatrical. Whitney had even heard that Crystal had taken a few minor parts in summer theater productions at the Ogunquit Playhouse on the coast of Maine, not too far away.

"She's fine," said Melissa. "She and Nick couldn't make their marriage last, but they're friends. She says they married too young and simply grew apart." She looked around at the restaurant filling up and said, "I've got to go, but I hope to see you around. Thanks for coming in."

After she left, Taylor turned to her. "Melissa's changed a lot. She seems much more mellow."

Whitney gave her a thoughtful nod. "We all have changed. Maybe she and I can get past some of her old nasty tricks when we were growing up. She used to tell terrible lies about me."

"I remember," said Dani. "I think being away, living and working in New York for a while made Melissa realize how little she knew about a bigger life."

"Living in New York without a lot of resources will humble most anyone," said Taylor. "I know."

"That was then. Now, you're a famous author," teased Dani.

Taylor laughed. "I'm a hardworking wordsmith. That's all."

"A very successful one," Whitney said, giving her a wink. She was proud of both of her sisters for their accomplishments. Taylor had an impressive following, and Dani was well respected in the world of architectural design. Dani grumbled about the struggle to compete with male counterparts, but she'd done well.

Their dinner came, and they dove into the hot, aromatic food. Whitney concentrated on her plainer meal while inhaling the aroma of garlic and butter and spices from the other two entrees.

Nick Woodruff walked into the restaurant as they were finishing, looked around, and came over to their table.

Whitney observed him. Wearing dark blue pants and a light-blue shirt that couldn't hide his athletic build, he was a woman's dream of a hero. She noticed a few gray streaks in the dark hair at his temples and how the shirt matched the color of his eyes.

"Evening, ladies." His smile crinkled the corners of those intriguing eyes. "It's great to have the Gilford girls back in town." He faced Whitney. "I want you to know if any reporters or others become a problem for you, I'm here to help. I understand how difficult publicity can be for you and other famous people drawn to our town."

"Thank you, Nick," said Whitney, hoping he hadn't noticed the way she'd stared at him. "How are you? It's been a while."

"I'm okay, thanks. Crystal and I split a few years ago, but we're still friends, which is important considering we both live and work here. Aside from that, I still play soccer with the guys and keep busy with my job." He studied her. "Sorry to hear you're going through a tough time."

"Thanks," she murmured as he turned to Dani and Taylor.

"I see you from time-to-time, Taylor, when you come visit your grandmother. Dani, I haven't seen you in a while."

"That's about to change," said Dani. "I'm going to be working on renovating the caretaker's house on the inn's property. I think I'll be staying here for most of the summer."

"Glad to hear it," Nick said. "I look forward to seeing you around."

He bobbed his head and left them.

"Wow," said Dani. "Does that guy just get hotter and hotter?"

"Definitely does," Whitney said. She remembered what he'd been like in high school. Even then, he'd been a magnet for girls. After working with actors in Hollywood, she thought he seemed much nicer, more real.

CHAPTER FOUR
TAYLOR

As she and her sisters walked back to the B&B, Taylor was quietly placing Nick in one of her books. People asked her all the time where she got her ideas for her books, and she always told them stories were all around them. This evening had proved it to her again. Small towns had a way of providing all kinds of information, and Lilac Lake was no exception. Maybe by spending the summer here, she'd get her groove back.

Ahead of her, Whitney and Dani were talking. Resentment flashed inside her and quickly disappeared. Her two older sisters were nearer in age and had been close siblings for five years before she was born. That age difference had always been a problem. It was something she'd fought against, but it couldn't be helped.

As if Dani had heard her thoughts, she turned and held out a hand to her. "C'mon, little sis. Join us."

The three of them managed to walk back to the B&B side by side on the wide sidewalk.

Inside the house, standing in the hallway, Whitney gave them an apologetic look. "I don't know about the two of you, but I'm going to bed. I'm exhausted. I hardly slept last night on my flight."

"No problem," said Dani. "After breakfast tomorrow, we'll head to the inn to go through it searching for personal items as GG asked."

"Okay, I'll be ready. 'Night, you two. Love you both," said

Whitney giving them hugs.

After Whitney left, Dani faced her. "What about you, Taylor? Are you ready for bed or do you want to watch a movie together?"

"Let's do a movie. Come to my room. I'll make some popcorn for us to have a bit later."

"Okay. I'm going to get in my jammies, then I'll join you." Dani grinned. "I've missed movie nights with my sisters."

"Me, too," Taylor said. "With each of us busy doing our own thing, it hasn't happened often enough."

Taylor went into the kitchen and used the microwave to make popcorn. She thought about the months ahead. GG was a generous person, but she wondered if the gift of the cottage and the commitment that came with it were doable over the long term with the three of them spread across the country. She suspected each of them might have a reason to want to spend some time in Lilac Lake this summer and hoped it would continue, honoring GG's thought of the cottage as a future haven for them.

CHAPTER FIVE
DANI

D ani awoke with a sense of excitement. She'd lain in bed last night thinking of the opportunity GG had given her by having her work on the renovation of the cottage. With the permission of her sisters, she was going to draw up plans to make it a beautiful home by enhancing the interior with open space. It was the kind of project she'd been looking for. After asking for personal time off to work on it, she would decide what she wanted to do about her future.

The nagging feeling that they might have to deal with a ghost who may or may not reside there was something she wasn't going to think about. She knew Taylor believed in ghosts, but even though she'd had that spooky incident in the attic, Dani wasn't convinced they existed.

She went to the window and lifted the shade, smiling when she saw the bright blue sky and yellow glow of a sunny morning. It was a promising omen.

Dani took a shower and got dressed, eager for one of the B&B's famous breakfasts.

When she arrived in the dining room, Taylor was already sitting there talking to an older couple. Dani went to the sideboard and poured herself a cup of coffee.

She wrapped her fingers around the thick mug and carried it to the table, savoring the hot steam that rose from it and tickled her nose.

Taylor introduced her to the couple sitting with her and then said, "No sign of our sister?"

Dani shook her head. "I thought I'd give her a little more time before waking her." She and Taylor had discussed not using Whitney's name in front of strangers.

Cynthia joined them in the dining room. "This morning, we're serving omelets with homemade muffins and fresh fruit. Let me get your orders for the omelets. In the meantime, please help yourselves to the juices, coffee, and tea on the sideboard."

Dani ordered a tomato, onion, and bacon omelet and took another sip of her coffee. Usually, her breakfast consisted of coffee and a piece of toast. This big breakfast would serve her well as they pored through items at the inn. Maybe she could put old family pictures on display in the renovated cottage. She'd see.

As they were being served their omelets, Whitney appeared. "Hope I'm not too late. I'm hungry."

Cynthia glanced at her. "Would you like an omelet? We're serving them with fruit and muffins."

"Thank you. I'd love some fruit and a small omelet," Whitney replied as she poured herself a cup of coffee.

The woman eating with them stared at Whitney. "You look a lot like that television star in the show about young people in show business."

Whitney shook her head. "I get that a lot. I'm just visiting my grandmother."

"Oh. Just thought I'd mention it," said the woman, digging into her omelet again.

They finished their meal in silence and then Dani rose. "C'mon, sisters. We'd better get going. It'll be a busy day."

She poured coffee into a disposable cup, called "Thank you" into the kitchen, and headed upstairs to her room to get ready to leave.

Her sisters showed up at her door, and they headed

downstairs dressed alike in jeans, light-weight sweaters, and comfortable shoes. Whitney changed her LA baseball cap for one with the inn's logo on it, making her less noticeable.

Dani drove the fifteen-minute trip to the inn and pulled into the driveway. As promised, a silver truck with the name Collister Construction painted on the doors sat in the driveway. She parked beside it and climbed out as a dark-haired man approached them.

"I assume you're Genie Wittner's granddaughters. I'm Aaron Collister." His smile brightened his classic features. "I was told you're to be allowed to go through items inside the inn and remove those that are personal, family items."

"Yes," said Dani. "GG told us she'd had packing boxes delivered here."

"They're inside by the front desk area," he said and studied each of them with brown eyes so deep in color they almost appeared black. He gave no sign of recognizing Whitney.

Dani glanced at her, and they both breathed a sigh of relief.

Inside the inn, Dani studied the lobby area. Even though the Oriental rug was worn, and the couches and chairs could use freshening, the huge stone fireplace lent a welcoming feel to the area. It was meant to be a place to relax whether it was a cold fall day or a hot one in summer. A huge television sat on one wall, and two bookcases lining the wall on either side of the fireplace were filled with books, games, and other items to keep people of all ages occupied.

Wooden beams crossed the room below a cathedral ceiling and met wooden paneling on the walls. All this attractive space needed was a big dog lying in front of a burning fire.

Dani turned to Whitney. "Remember, we want to go to the animal shelter today. There's one in Pine Ridge, not far from here."

"Animal shelter? What are you two up to?" said Taylor.

Dani told her about their plans.

"Great idea," Taylor said. "That way, Dani, you'll have help chasing away Mrs. Maynard's ghost."

"Ghost? Did I hear you say ghost?" said Aaron, carrying a stack of folded empty boxes to them.

Taylor shrugged. "It's a story that's been associated with the caretaker's cottage where we're going to live."

"Really? I know all about the three of you taking over that house," said Aaron. "In the past, I've looked at it, hoping I could buy it. The house has good bones."

"I've been assigned to oversee the renovation of the house. I'm an architect and have some suggestions about making it something special. I was told that you and your brother would be willing to have your crew work on it."

Aaron studied her. "As a matter of fact, Ms. Wittner told us about her plans, and we agreed to help." He shuffled his feet. "I looked you up, Danielle. Your work is impressive. I thought if this project went well, we could work together on others."

"That might be interesting." Dani was flattered but disappointed that any projects coming from them would be too small for her plans to leave the firm with a big bang.

"Let's get started on this task for GG," said Whitney, "so we have time to get to the animal shelter this afternoon."

"Are you looking for a dog?" asked Aaron. "I've got one you might be interested in. He's a little over a year-old, the last in a litter. I own his mother."

"Why hasn't the dog been adopted?" said Dani, giving him a suspicious look.

"He's blind in one eye. No hunter wants that."

"What kind of dog is he?" asked Whitney.

"A black lab. His mother is a beauty, and so is he, except for the eye problem. But I won't let him go to just anyone. He gets to decide for himself who he wants to live with."

"I'd love to see him," said Dani. "I want a dog to stay at the cottage with me. It's a perfect place for him to roam."

Aaron's face lit with a smile. "I'll bring him by. This just might work."

"Do you have any small dogs?" Whitney said. "I need a very small dog."

Aaron shook his head. "No, but I'll ask around. Or go see Crystal at the café. She'll know."

"Well, let's get started here or we'll never get done," said Taylor. She picked up one of the boxes. "Where should we begin?"

"I suggest here in the lobby area, move to the offices, and then the storage rooms," said Dani.

"Okay, let's do it," said Taylor. "I'll work on the bookshelves."

"I'll help you," Whitney said.

"I'm going to check the front desk area and take a look at the paintings," said Dani. "GG said to ask her if we had any questions, so, if necessary, I'll call about any of the paintings I think she or we might want."

In the small office behind the front desk, Dani made note of a couple photographs of family members. She studied a round-bellied man with a mustache, who reminded her of pictures of President Theodore Roosevelt. She knew from stories GG told her that her great-grandfather, Charles Wittner, was an enthusiastic outdoorsman who'd loved to come to New Hampshire from New York to hunt and fish.

The other photograph in the office was one of GG when she was a young woman. Dressed in pants and a wool plaid shirt, she stood in front of the inn smiling at the camera. She'd been a strikingly pretty woman.

Dani looked through the drawers of a desk and saw the usual pens, paper clips, and other office supplies, then noticed a key attached to a soiled pink ribbon in the back of the drawer. She lifted it out and studied it. The key was old-fashioned and looked like it could be used to open a trunk or lockbox. Dani tucked it into her jeans pocket and took down the photographs from the wall and brought them to where Whitney and Taylor were working.

"What do you have?" said Taylor rising from where she'd been kneeling.

Dani showed them the photographs. "I'm thinking we could use these in the cottage, sort of a tribute to the family history at the inn."

"I love that," said Whitney. Her eyes filled. "That is important to me, maybe now more than ever."

"Group hug," said Taylor.

Dani loved that they were so close, and joined in. "It'll all work out, Whitney."

"I hope so," Whitney said. She took a deep breath and stepped back. "Let's get this job done. There are so many things to look at that it'll take us forever."

"I've saved a few books for my own collection," said Taylor. "That shouldn't matter to the new owners."

"I wouldn't think so," said Dani. "I'll go through the hallways to check the walls for paintings or photographs important to us."

She left the lobby area and entered one of the wings. There was no reason to check guestrooms, but she thought personal items might have been mounted in the hallways or in the dining room. She remembered a few from past years.

She stopped in front of a painting of a lovely young woman and realized it was a portrait of her mother as a young girl. As she was trying to take it off the wall, the man she'd met yesterday, Brad Collister, suddenly appeared from one of the guestrooms.

"What are you doing?" he asked.

"I'm trying to get this portrait of my mother off the wall," she said. "Can you help me?"

He took a screwdriver out of his toolbelt. "I'll get it for you. Best to let me know about any others because I don't want you to damage either the picture or the wall."

"Okay. I understand." She stood aside as he fussed with the mounting bracket behind the painting and minutes later, handed it to her.

"Beautiful woman," he said. "Should we look for other items together? We can set this here and come back for it when we are through with this wing."

"Okay. I don't believe there will be many." She liked that he was so helpful and hoped that would continue when they worked together on the cottage.

"So, Dani, I understand that my brother Aaron spoke with you about helping you with the cottage. I think we can make that house beautiful. We tried to buy it from your grandmother a year ago, but she said she was saving it for her granddaughters."

"We didn't know about that until now, but the more I think about the cottage being ours, the more I like it."

They moved down the hallway and stopped in front of a framed photograph of the three of them as young girls sunbathing on the granite rock. "That one," said Dani. "Can you get it down for me?"

"Sure," said Brad. He took a few minutes, removed it, and set it down on the carpet. "Do any others catch your interest?"

Dani shook her head. "No. Not in this wing. I know the upstairs hallways are alike with commercial decorations."

"Okay then, let's get these two back to the lobby and we'll take a look at the other wing."

He picked up the photograph and followed her down the

hallway to pick up her mother's portrait.

They entered the lobby area, set them down near the desk, and made their way to the other wing. Each wing had three floors of twenty guestrooms, making a total of 120.

"Are the new owners planning to expand the inn?" Dani asked.

"Yes, but in a different way. I'm not at liberty to tell you of all their plans."

"Oh, I see. I won't put you on the spot by asking you more questions, but I hope I'll be able to speak to the new owners."

"One of them was here recently. The other two will be around in the next week or so. You should be able to meet them then."

"Okay," Dani said, but she had every intention of looking up information online about the sale of the inn as well as sitting down with GG with questions about it.

In the other wing, Dani found two photographs of family members and a portrait of GG that she'd never paid much attention to. She carried it over to the window. Now, seeing it in brighter light, she treasured it.

As they were carrying the framed items back to the lobby, Dani heard a dog barking. She gave Brad a questioning look.

He laughed. "That must be Pirate, Aaron's dog. He's been looking for a new home for him. He said you might be interested. But if the dog and you don't share a mutual understanding of one another, Aaron won't give him to you. He's turned down a few other offers." Brad shook his head. "It might seem crazy, but my brother is right. This has to be a mutual match."

They entered the lobby to see Aaron holding onto the leash of a black lab who was wiggling with happiness at the attention Whitney and Taylor were giving him.

"Hi, Pirate," Dani called to him.

The dog stopped and stared at her, then when Aaron let go of the leash, Pirate dashed over to her and sat down staring up at her.

"Hello," Dani whispered, stroking the top of his silky head, caressing his fur with her fingers.

He lay down and turned on his back for a belly rub.

Dani obliged and bent over to ruffle fur. She could see now that one eye was an odd gray color and the other eye, a brown one that missed nothing. He was staring at her as if sizing her up.

"Well," she said. "Do I pass your inspection?"

She stood, and he scrambled to his feet and stood before her wagging his tail.

She patted him and then rubbed his ears. When Dani looked, she could swear he was smiling at her. She giggled. "You're adorable."

The dog rose on his hind legs and placed his front paws on her shoulders, not in a rough way, but almost like a hug.

"I think Pirate has finally picked his new person," said Aaron, looking on with satisfaction. "What do you say, Dani? Do you think you can take on the work of a young dog? He's very smart and eager to please, but he's still not full-grown."

She and Pirate stared at one another and then she nodded. "I love him already."

"That was easy," said Whitney. "Now I need a dog for me."

"Ask Crystal," said Brad.

"That's what I told her," Aaron said.

Taylor laughed. "That settles it then. We'll go to the café for lunch."

"Let's work a little longer, then go," said Dani. "We're not done here."

"Deal," Whitney agreed. "We have GG's quarters, the offices, and storeroom to get through."

CHAPTER SIX
TAYLOR

Taylor helped Dani place the pictures and paintings in a box to go to GG's storage room at The Woodlands. They'd decided to take advantage of that space until they could put any items placed there to use. She'd chosen a few special books for her collection—books she'd either loved as a child or read as an adult. If she'd had the room in her apartment, she would've been tempted to take more. She always loved adding new books to those she had.

Pirate now seemed to understand he belonged to Dani and stayed by her side while they worked. Their examination of the offices garnered a few more photographs but nothing of any real excitement, and by the time they'd gone through them, they were all ready for lunch.

"What are we going to do about Pirate?" Whitney asked.

"He's coming with us," said Dani, as if it wasn't even a choice. Taylor exchanged looks of dismay with Whitney but said nothing.

Later, when Dani opened the back of her SUV and Pirate jumped up inside, Taylor realized the situation wasn't as bad as she thought—until Pirate placed his head over the back of the seat beside her and panted in her face.

Dani found a parking spot near the Lilac Café where Crystal worked.

"What are we going to do about Pirate?" Whitney asked as she climbed out of the car.

"We can eat on the patio," said Dani. "Dogs are allowed

there. When I was getting Pirate's bowl and his favorite toy from him, Aaron told me Pirate was not only housebroken, but he was trained to eat in a dining facility with him."

"Okay," said Taylor. "Let's go. I'm hungry."

"Can't wait to see what specials Crystal has," said Dani. "It's been a while since I've been here, and she always does something special for each season."

"The last time I was here, she had a fiddlehead fern soup that was to die for," Taylor said, wishing she was a creative cook.

"Just something pretty simple for me," said Whitney, patting her flat stomach.

"I'll get us a seat on the patio," said Dani, holding onto Pirate's leash as he sniffed the ground.

"I'll sit with you," said Whitney.

Taylor went inside to tell Crystal they were there.

Crystal looked up from serving someone at the counter and grinned. Of medium height and build, and with purple hair that almost matched her eyes, Crystal Owens was like a bright sunbeam in any gray room.

"My sisters and I are sitting outside," said Taylor, "and we need to talk to you about getting a small dog."

"No problem. Aaron Collister already told me. I'll send someone right out to wait on you, and before you leave, I'll come talk to you."

Taylor gave her a wave and headed outdoors pleased they'd chosen to sit outside. It was a beautiful day with a bright blue sky above them and the sweet smell of lilacs floating in the air. As part of the conversion of the town to an upscale resort area, citizens had planted a variety of lilac bushes everywhere they could. It made the arrival of late spring and early summer air seem like a potpourri of floral perfumes.

Taylor sat down with her sisters and gazed around the

town. Across the street, the white-clapboard town hall looked as if it could be a church with its two wide black doors welcoming people inside. But unlike its twin, the Congregational church down the block, it lacked a steeple. The red brick building hosting the police station sat between the two as if it couldn't decide whether to guard against sinners or keep the town quiet.

She noticed a tall, lanky, red-haired man coming out of town hall and took a moment to study him. He had a roll of paper that looked like design plans in his hands.

"Who is that?" said Dani. "What a hottie."

A waitress approached their table, stopped, and looked at where Dani was staring.

"Oh, that's Quinn McPherson. One of the new owners of the Lilac Lake Inn. He came in for coffee yesterday and I agree, he's one hot guy."

Taylor stopped staring and took a sip of water from the glass the waitress handed her. The sale of the inn was turning into an interesting event for the whole town

CHAPTER SEVEN
WHITNEY

Whitney was sitting eating her soup when she felt a shadow over her and looked up. Nick was standing there in uniform holding a black and tan, short-haired dog.

"Heard you wanted a small dog. This is Mindy, a miniature dachshund. Her owner was killed in a crash a couple months ago. I've been taking care of her, but I already have two dogs and this little gal needs some female company. She's a good dog. How about it, Whitney?" He held out the dog wagging her tail. Whitney didn't hesitate, simply gathered the dog in her arms and held her close.

Mindy licked Whitney's cheeks and then curled up in Whitney's lap.

Crystal came outside and joined them. "Oh thanks, Nick. You've brought Mindy here." She grinned. "I see that Mindy already loves you, Whitney."

"She's adorable. How old is she?" she asked Nick.

"She's two years old, beyond the puppy stage. The vet has all her records. She's smart and likes to be in charge. My two big retrievers follow her around and if they get too frisky with her, she lets them know they're out of line. It's funny to see."

Mindy was sniffing the cracker beside Whitney's soup bowl.

"Another thing," said Nick. "Mindy will eat anything she's given. A real garbage hound."

"She's adorable," said Dani, holding onto Pirate who

desperately wanted to get close to the smaller dog.

When Pirate finally got closer, Mindy just glared at him, and he backed away, much to Whitney's delight. She needed this feisty dog not only as an excuse for the rumors of her pregnancy, but as a worthy companion.

"If you're interested, I'll give you the proper paperwork, Mindy's favorite toys, and her special blanket," said Nick.

"Oh, I'm interested," said Whitney, wishing her work schedule had allowed time for a dog as Mindy once more wiggled happily in her lap.

Nick tipped his hat at her and said, "Okay, then. I'll catch up with you later."

Whitney looked up at him. "Thanks for thinking of me. You, too, Crystal. I'd forgotten what it's like to be in a small town where everyone steps in to help you."

"Maybe you can spend some time here, participate in a few summer stock theaters with me," said Crystal.

Nick left and Crystal let out a sigh. "Nick and I had so many reasons to break up."

"Who are you dating now?" Whitney asked, stroking Mindy's smooth fur.

"I'm playing the field. It's so much better that way," said Crystal, giving her a wink.

Whitney chuckled. It would take the right kind of man to settle down with Crystal. She was like a butterfly unwilling to land anywhere for too long. She'd always been that way.

Crystal left them to greet other customers, and Whitney looked at her sisters and grinned. "Who'd have thought we'd end up with two dogs. How about you, Taylor? Are you looking for one too?"

Taylor shook her head. "Not as long as I live in the city."

Dani reached over and patted Mindy's head. "She sure is cute. And so happy. She can't stop wagging her tail."

Whitney cupped the dog's face in her hand and kissed her forehead. "You're a sweetie, Mindy. From now on, it'll be me and you."

Mindy's brown eyes stared at her and then she let out a yip of approval, making them all laugh.

Back at the inn, they entered GG's private quarters. As she'd mentioned, it had been pretty well cleaned out, but they each took a section of the room, checking the walls, drawers, and closets for anything GG or they might want.

In the closet in the living area, Dani found a small metal box in the corner of the top shelf.

From the stepstool where she was standing, Dani handed it down to Whitney. "I think I may have a key to the box. I found it in the office behind the front desk."

Whitney set the box down on the floor, and her sisters watched while she tried the key. It slid into the lock awkwardly but after jiggling it a bit, the key turned.

Inside, they found GG's marriage license to William Duncan and two photographs of their wedding day, and three of GG, William, and a baby daughter, who they knew was their mother. A deed to the property was there, an insurance policy for a million dollars, and some other legal and financial papers that included information on stocks and bonds. At the very bottom of the papers stacked inside was a large white envelope with a metal clasp with GG's name on it.

Whitney looked at her sisters and opened it. Inside was a birth certificate for a baby boy named Isaac Thomas. The mother was listed as Lyn Thomas. No father was mentioned. A death certificate for the same infant was attached to it.

"Isaac Thomas? I wonder who that is," said Dani.

"Let's take this box to GG after we finish going through the storage area," said Taylor. "There's an interesting story there. GG must have a lot of them."

"There's a lot of history between these walls," said Whitney, unable to hide a shiver. She might not believe in ghosts, but she didn't like prying into the pasts of people.

"GG will tell us what she wants us to know," said Dani. "But like Taylor says, there must be a lot of hidden stories behind GG. She's always been such an independent woman."

They headed into the storage area trailed by the two dogs who'd spent a lot of time sniffing and playing together. Dani found some tennis balls in the storage closet and tossed two to the dogs who made a mad scramble to get them.

"Come look at this," Whitney called to her. She held up a purple T-shirt with the Lilac Lake Inn Logo on the front. "There's a whole box of them."

"Perfect to wear around here," said Dani. "GG must have ordered them for something special. We can ask her about them."

"Other than that," said Taylor, "I don't see anything of any personal nature."

"I'm ready to call it quits and go back to the B&B," said Dani. "I've got to make sure that Pirate can stay in the room with me overnight."

"Me, too, with Mindy," said Whitney. "The B&B advertises it as a place that will accept pets, but I don't want to do anything to jeopardize staying there. It's such a convenient place to be, within walking distance of the activity in the center of town."

"First, let's drop off the items to GG," said Taylor. "To complete the task that she gave us."

"The dogs can stay in the car with me," said Dani. "I'll leave the windows open and park in the shade. It's cool enough that it shouldn't be a problem."

"No, you go ahead. I'll stay with the dogs," said Whitney. "I'm not feeling well. Just tired."

Dani glanced at Taylor and then faced her with a look of concern. "Okay, we'll hurry."

Whitney watched them go, grateful for some time alone. She'd tried hard to keep her spirits up, but they'd begun to droop.

CHAPTER EIGHT
DANI

Dani and Taylor added the metal box and one T-shirt to the box filled with the framed pictures and paintings they'd taken from the inn.

Together, they carried the heavy box inside and to GG's apartment.

After they tapped on her door, they stepped inside.

GG watched them from the couch where she was sitting with a handsome white-haired man. A woman who looked about GG's age sat in a chair nearby.

"Hello, my darlings. Come meet my new friends. Dailey Howell is an old classmate of mine and Betsy Norris has recently moved to the area to be closer to her son."

Dani couldn't help smiling. No matter where GG went, she quickly made friends. It was no wonder she was a natural hostess at the inn. People were naturally drawn to her, and GG loved it. Even now, she was acting as a hostess.

Dani and Taylor kissed her cheek, shook hands with GG's friends, and explained they'd brought items for her to look at.

"Thank you," said GG. "Please put the box in the corner over there and I'll take a look at it later."

Dani inched the heavy box into the corner, gave GG a wave, and left, relieved GG hadn't asked about the contents in front of her friends.

At the B&B, Dani and Whitney talked to Cynthia about having the dogs in their rooms, and after careful consideration, Cynthia agreed they could stay in the rooms with them so long as Dani and Whitney agreed to pay for any damages.

Dani took Pirate to her room. She placed his bed in the corner of the room and got out his dog dish, and realized she'd need to go to the pet store in town for food and treats.

"C'mon, Pirate. We need to go shopping."

He looked up at her and wagged his tail, allowing her to snap his leash onto his collar.

She knocked on Whitney's door, smiling when Mindy stood at Whitney's side as if to guard the woman who stood several feet above her.

"I'm getting dog food for Pirate. Want me to pick up some for Mindy?"

"Thanks. That would be marvelous."

They turned as Nick appeared dressed in jeans and a black V-neck sweater that emphasized his ripped body. He held up a large paper bag. "I've got Mindy's paperwork, food, treats, toys, and her favorite blanket here for you, Whitney." He handed her the bag. "I don't know what plans you have for dinner, but if you'd like, I thought we could eat together, catch up with one another. A new restaurant called Fresh, with farm-to-table menus, has opened outside town. It might be a little more private than one here."

Dani couldn't help smiling when color flushed Whitney's cheeks. Whitney had always thought Nick was a nice guy.

"That sounds lovely," said Whitney. She looked down at Mindy. "What'll I do about her?"

"Bring her with us. The restaurant has a beautiful deck that will be a perfect place for a dog. It's sort of a new thing, accommodating travelers with pets."

Dani said goodbye to them, took Pirate downstairs, and loaded him into her car. She liked having him around if she was going to be spending time working at the cottage.

After she finished purchasing food and treats for Pirate at an upscale local grocery store, Dani decided to see if GG was available to talk. She didn't want her grandmother to think she was snooping into private matters and yet, she was curious about the unexpected birth certificate for a baby boy named Isaac

She punched in GG's cell number and GG picked up right away.

"Hi, Dani," said GG. "I had time to glance at the things you took from the inn. I see you girls were busy."

"I thought those framed photos and portraits could be used in the cottage after it's renovated. The metal box is something we thought you should have. We didn't mean to pry, but we went through the papers there. We found a birth certificate and a death certificate for Isaac Thomas."

"I saw that you'd opened the envelope. I had no idea about its content. I was keeping it safely sealed for someone who'd asked for help," said GG. "I'm sure there's a sad story behind it, but I have no details and it's too late to ask now. By the way, Crystal came to The Woodlands to deliver dessert, and she told me both you and Whitney now own dogs."

"What? Is nothing a secret in Lilac Lake?"

"They're few and far between," said GG. "Best to keep on your toes around here."

"Oh, dear. Whitney is going out to dinner with Nick. I suppose everyone will make a big deal out of it," said Dani. "And none of us wants any publicity about her being here."

"Some could spread the word, but then it'll give way to other news. Along with the beneficial part of living here are the parts you wish would disappear. But it makes life interesting."

"Tomorrow, may I come see you? I want to talk to you after I've written down more suggestions about renovating the cottage. I'm going to ask Brad or Aaron to walk through the house with me."

"It's fantastic that they'll work with you. I trust them not only to do an excellent job for you but to be totally honest. They will also enable you to use builders' discounts for materials and all. We've talked about it."

"It seems you've had this planned for some time," said Dani.

"I had some thoughts about it earlier but didn't think it would happen so soon or so fast. The three new buyers were organized and looking for a deal, and that made things easy."

"Speaking of the three owners, we know about Ross Roberts and Quinn McPherson. Who's the other man?"

"It's not a man but a woman, Rachael McPherson. She and Quinn are siblings. Both wealthy."

"The plot thickens. What is their experience in the hospitality industry?"

"Rachael and Quinn each attended Cornell University in the Hotel program there. Their father has been a consultant to the industry for some time and has a reputation for being honest. I was impressed with his children's forthrightness too."

"At some point, it'll be wise to set up a meeting for the six of us," said Dani. "But it can wait until Whitney, Taylor, and I make some personal decisions of our own."

"That's reasonable," said GG. "Gotta go. We're having a little birthday party for one of the residents. A piano player is providing the music."

Dani clicked off the call feeling sad. So many changes were taking place it was hard to keep up.

A warm wet tongue swiped her cheek.

She startled and then let out a laugh. "Hey, Pirate, should we go back to the B&B and get you some supper?"

His loud bark of approval made it clear he was hungry.

Dani unloaded the food and took Pirate up to her room. He watched eagerly as she opened a bag of food that had been recommended to her and filled Pirate's bowl.

He was eating quickly when Taylor knocked on her door. "Want to order some pizza? We can eat it in the dining room and avoid going out. I don't know about you, but I'm ready for some quiet time."

"Me, too," said Dani. Taylor was one of the rare people who was content to stay home most of the time. But then she had her books and fictional characters to keep her company. "Pizza sounds delicious. I want to make sure Pirate is comfortable and knows the rules here. He's a smart dog, but he's not used to me and my routines."

At the sound of his name, Pirate looked up at her and wagged his tail. She leaned over and patted him, which made his tail go even faster.

Taylor put in an order for pizza to be delivered, and then the two of them led Pirate downstairs to the dining room. The B&B offered wine to guests in the early evening, and they helped themselves to glasses of red wine. No one else was around so they sat in the living room.

"How are you coming with your latest book?" Dani asked Taylor. "It seems to me you're always writing a new one."

Taylor chuckled. "It seems that way to me too. But that's the business. This new one is going to be interesting because it takes place in Mexico. So, I've had to do a lot of research." She made a face. "But I can't seem to do more than that. Like many authors, I'm stuck wondering if I have it in me to write another successful book."

"Oh, hon, of course you can do another one," Dani said.

"I'm hoping spending time in Lilac Lake will help open the floodgates, so to speak," said Taylor. "I think it's wonderful that you're willing to work on the renovation of the cottage. But I still don't like the thought of the cottage being haunted."

Dani noted the earnest expression on Taylor's face and felt her heart swell with love for her little sister. "Thanks. That's sweet of you, but, really, I'll be fine." Even as she said the words, she remembered the eerie sensation she'd had of a presence behind her in the attic. "Besides, if it makes you feel any better, I'll ask one of the Collister men to go with us as we go through it tomorrow."

"They both seem charming. And their work at The Woodlands is beautifully done," said Taylor. "I'm so glad GG already had them lined up to help you."

Dani texted both men and asked if one of them could accompany her on an initial walkthrough of the property.

A few minutes later, Brad responded, telling her that he would meet her and her sisters at the house at nine o'clock in the morning.

Satisfied things were in order, Dani sipped her wine as she waited for the pizza to arrive.

And when Pirate nudged her hand for attention, she gave it to him, glad that he'd help protect them.

CHAPTER NINE
DANI

Dani, her sisters, and the two dogs were waiting at the house when Brad pulled up to it in his red truck. As he got out, Dani wasn't the only one studying him. He was worth looking at with his broad shoulders, trim waist, and cute butt.

He brushed back his blond hair from his forehead and smiled, lighting his dark green eyes. "Guess we're ready to see what we can do for this tattered lady. Once she's dressed up, she'll be a very beautiful house."

He approached them holding a clipboard. "I like to take as many notes as I can before any construction takes place. First, I want to know how each of you intend to use this house."

Whitney spoke up. "I want to be able to use it as a hideaway from Hollywood, and step back from my job."

"You're thinking of creature comforts? Or a more simple, rustic setting?" he asked her.

"Definitely creature comforts," said Whitney smiling.

"I want to be able to use it as a place to write," Taylor said. "I'd like a lot of light, windows, and a comfortable office."

"And you?" Brad asked Dani. "You're the architect. What do you say?"

"I want to open up the house, making it easy to meet anyone's demand for a special retreat. None of us had any idea this was a plan of GG's. We want to honor her wishes, but we all have busy lives and want to be comfortable here."

"So, you're going to share the space, but not necessarily do it together at the same time?"

"At this point, I'd say yes," said Dani. She waited for a response from her sisters and they each nodded. Dani held up her own clipboard. "Actually, I've made notes on what I'd like to be able to do to the space, but I need some input from you."

"Okay, we can spend some time inside going over them," said Brad.

As they moved forward, Taylor said, "You know the house is haunted."

Brad turned to her. "That's an old rumor. I'm not afraid. Are you?"

"I'm not going to be spending any time there alone until I'm sure the ghost has gone," said Taylor.

"If I see any signs of a ghost, I'll let you know," Brad said with some amusement. "I'll even go into the house first." As Taylor rolled her eyes, he held up a set of keys. "Your grandmother already gave me these."

"Okay," said Dani. "Let's do it. I want input from everyone on my ideas. The dogs should be alright outside."

Brad led them to the door, fiddled with the lock, and opened the door.

A cold breeze met Dani's face. She shivered but didn't dare look at Taylor. Weren't ghosts often felt by drafty cold spots? But it could be only the cool morning air escaping.

Inside, Dani announced that she wanted to open the space as much as possible by taking down what existing walls they could. She and Brad studied the walls downstairs to determine if they were load-bearing and then Brad marked the ones they could get rid of with a big red X on the walls.

"Maybe we could add a kitchen nook with lots of windows," said Taylor.

"Could a downstairs bathroom be added near the kitchen?" Whitney asked.

"I've already thought of that," answered Dani. "I plan on drawing schematics, and I'll try to make that work. An open floor plan will help. Luckily, we're able to get rid of a lot of the walls downstairs. We'll have to keep what supporting posts are necessary, but they can be made attractive."

While Taylor and Whitney made their own inspections, Dani and Brad stood in the kitchen.

"I'm thinking of removing the little window that opens up to the living room and tearing down that wall," said Dani. "I want the kitchen as open as the rest of the floor. People gather in kitchens."

"Yes," said Brad. "But all the exterior walls, which is where appliances are situated, will naturally have to remain. We could put in a center island with a sink and dishwasher. That should clear up some wall space and give you a breakfast bar area, too."

Dani turned to him. "Looks like you've already thought of a few things yourself."

He grinned back at her. "Aaron and I wanted to buy this place. We were thinking of doing several of the things you've already mentioned. The bones of the house are good. That's what matters."

"Even if it's haunted?" teased Dani.

He laughed and pretended to look scared.

One of the open cupboard doors in the kitchen suddenly slammed shut, and they stared at one another with surprise.

"We need more respect for the lady of the house," said Brad, and Dani laughed with him.

"So, the kitchen is a complete gut," said Brad. "I agree. We'll get our demolition crew in to take care of the walls and the kitchen. After they've done their work, we'll see about space for a small downstairs bathroom."

"Okay," she said. "Let's take a look at the second floor. I

think the attic could be a bedroom if we can plumb in a bathroom. Otherwise, it can be a retreat or an office."

Taylor and Whitney approached them.

"We trust you, Dani," said Whitney. "You take all the time you want here with Brad. Taylor and I are going to walk over to the inn to see what's happening there."

"Okay. See you later," she said, pleased to have this time with Brad. So far, they've agreed on most things, but she wanted to be thorough. Plans had to be practical too.

Upstairs, both she and Brad agreed the two small bedrooms could be made into one and tied in with the third one with the bathroom between them serving as a Jack and Jill arrangement. The largest bedroom with an ensuite bathroom of its own was fine, though both bathrooms would need total renovation.

"Now, let's check out the attic," said Dani. "The two front windows and the height of the roof make it a desirable space." She led him to the door that led to stairs to the attic and paused.

"Guess you want me to go first?" said Brad, giving her a teasing look.

"If you don't mind," she said, grateful for the suggestion.

He opened the door and stumbled back against her. "Sorry. Guess I tripped."

Dani thought she'd seen something, a movement of some kind, and then it was gone. She shivered.

Upstairs, they were able to get a look around, even take measurements of the height they had to work with.

"It's a nice workable space," said Brad.

They went downstairs and out to the front porch. "You might want to strengthen the railings and redo some of the boards. Otherwise, this is a perfect spot for relaxing," said Brad.

Dani grinned and showed him a sketch of the porch with a hammock strung at the far end. "Perfect for a summer day, don't you think?"

"Perfect for me," he said, winking at her.

Dani liked how easy Brad was to work with, how fast his mind worked, how in tune they were with one another.

"All set for now?" Brad asked her.

"Yes. I'm going back to Boston to ask for a leave of absence and work on these plans. We need to be able to go for permits and work on building cost estimates to present to GG."

"Aaron and I are here to help you while we're working on the inn. We owe your grandmother. She lent us the money to start the business when no one else would and helped us get the contract for The Woodlands. We've paid her money back, with interest," he said with a note of pride.

"That's a lot of work," said Dani. "No wonder she trusts you."

"We've been lucky by getting some interesting projects statewide, and we have loyal subcontractors willing to pitch in, giving us reliable support."

Dani had been working with enough builders and contractors to know that kind of support didn't just happen, that it was a matter of respect for owners of the company. She was pleased she was working with them.

She called for Pirate, and when he didn't come, she figured he was with Mindy and her sisters.

"Thanks for spending so much time with me," Dani told Brad.

He gave her a quick bow. "My pleasure any time. I think we're going to be great partners on this project. We'd better exchange phone numbers in case any questions come up."

Dani handed him her phone. He put in his information, and she did the same for him.

"I'll call you later to see when you're going to be ready to start. In the meantime, Aaron has some connections on the town board and can help you with building permits."

After he drove away in his truck, Dani got into her car and headed to the inn. As she pulled up to it, Pirate and Mindy both barked and wagged their tails.

Taylor and Whitney rose from the front steps where they'd been sitting and walked over to her.

"We're ready to go," said Whitney. "Let's have lunch, and then while you talk over plans with GG, I'm going to take a nap. I'm still trying to catch up after that awful time in LA with the news of my breaking up with Zane and the horrible rumors about me that followed before the trip here."

"I'll go with you to talk to GG about the renovations, if you wish," said Taylor.

"It won't be necessary, but you're always welcome," Dani said.

"Okay, then I'm going to do a little work after lunch. If I don't get my thoughts down pretty fast, they get lost. So far, I haven't made much progress on this new book."

"No problem. How did the dogs do?"

Whitney chuckled. "My little Mindy is the boss. She may be small, but she has Pirate under control like any strong female."

The three of them laughed together.

Dani sat with her sisters on the deck at Crystal's café where the dogs were welcome. Her mind was still whirling with ideas for the house. She was hopeful they could use some of them to convert the simple house into something unique and beautiful.

She was eating her Caesar salad with grilled chicken when Aaron walked onto the deck and over to the table. "May I?" he asked, pointing to the empty chair. He laughed when Pirate rose and rushed over to him, wiggling like crazy.

"Sure, have a seat," said Whitney.

Aaron sat down and turned to Dani. "I understand you had a successful meeting with Brad. He was very impressed with your suggestions. After you do some drawings, I'd love to see them."

"Not a problem. On Sunday, I'm traveling back to Boston to wrap up a few things at work, and then I'm moving to Lilac Lake for the summer. If I don't get the leave of absence I want, I plan on quitting my job. I was thinking of doing something a bit different anyway."

"While you're here in town, we might be able to use you for a project or two. Even help us with the inn. Are you interested?"

Dani's heart pounded. She pulled herself up straight. "I'd love to do that. Thanks. I'll let you know how it goes in Boston." This sign of respect from both men was something unusual for her.

"How's it going with Pirate?" He rubbed the dog's head. "He's a good dog. Real low key."

"I love him already," said Dani, and realized it was true. When he wagged his tail and gave her a doggy smile upon seeing her, he touched her heart.

Aaron left them and went inside.

"You're really going to move here?" Whitney said.

Dani nodded. Something told her it was the right thing to do.

CHAPTER TEN
WHITNEY

Whitney sat in her room trying to build up her nerve to make the call she knew she should. Taking a deep breath, she phoned her agent and waited for Barbara Griffith to pick up. An older woman who'd worked in Hollywood for some time, Barbara was as tough as nails. She'd seen and heard it all.

"Yes?" said Barbara.

Whitney took another deep breath. "Hi, Barbara. Guess you've made sure that everyone knows Zane and I have broken up. I'll let you handle any requests for more information. But as we talked about earlier, we agreed to say only that it was time to move on. He was a big help to me starting out, and I'll always be grateful for that. I don't want to ruin his reputation."

"He's doing a good job of that on his own," quipped Barbara. "Now the word is you're pregnant with his baby. That true?"

"No, you know better than that," said Whitney. "The reports of a pregnancy have been exaggerated as usual, but I have in fact added a new addition to my family. I've adopted a little dachshund named Mindy. Tell the reporters that's the only talk of family."

"Hm-m-m. Okay. Then what?"

"I'll go back and finish filming this season; we're almost done. Then, I'd like some time off. Can you work on that? If there are any issues about doing that, I want out of the show.

I'm done with all the crap of trying to cover up a real problem. I can't believe Zane can't see what he's doing to himself."

"How much time off are you talking about?" Barbara asked tensely.

"Several months. Some family issues have come up, and I want to be able to help my sisters." Whitney realized it was true. If the cottage was going to be transformed into a lovely home away from Hollywood, she wanted to have some input.

"Let me see what I can do. You're a hard worker, Whitney, or I wouldn't proceed with your request. But you do an excellent job, and the viewers love you. But I'm warning you, if you leave the show before they're ready to let you go, you'll be burning a lot of bridges."

"I know," Whitney replied. "But I have to get away, have time to reconsider my life."

"Okay, this is serious. I'll talk to the producers and find out when they're scheduling the filming of the next season, or if there is even going to be one. There's always a chance the network might not renew the show. It's been four years. You never know. At any rate, we'll go from there."

"Thank you, Barbara. I appreciate your help."

"You're welcome, sweetie. Good luck! I hope you can get your personal life squared away."

"I do too," said Whitney as Barbara ended the call.

CHAPTER ELEVEN
DANI

Dani headed to The Woodlands eager to talk to GG. Since meeting with Brad, she'd made a list of the things that needed to be done at the house. Once she got GG's approval, she and Brad would put together a budget for the project. GG hadn't mentioned how much money she'd designated for the renovation. If they ran out of her money, Dani supposed she and her sisters could add some of their own. As she pulled up to The Woodlands' main building, she studied the lines of it. It was a one-story building with gray clapboard siding and sparkling white trim. Windows lined the front of the sprawling building giving those inside a look out at the woods and colorful landscaping, accommodating the needs of the people who lived there without looking like an institution.

She parked, picked up her briefcase, went up to the front entrance, and took another moment to look at the construction. No doubt about it, Collister Construction had done a commendable job. Even the basics were done well as if care had been taken. The trim around the door had no unsightly gaps or nail holes. The soffit under the roof overhang was properly vented, and the gutters mounted on the fascia looked solid. The paint work was carefully done; none of the stain of the front doors showed on the creamy paint of the trim. She'd worked in the field long enough to know quality work when she saw it.

Inside, she greeted the receptionist, and walked back to

GG's room.

She knocked and opened the door. GG was sitting on the patio, reading.

"Morning!" Dani called to her, but GG didn't react, and when she stepped outside, GG was startled to see her.

"I called to you, but you didn't hear me," said Dani.

"My hearing is going like the rest of me," GG said, giving her an apologetic look.

Dani kissed her on the cheek. "I'm here to talk about the renovation of the cottage. Is this a good time?"

GG smiled at her, appearing much younger. "It's always a perfect time to talk with you."

Dani pulled up a chair next to GG's, sat, and opened the briefcase. "First of all, I want to thank you for your generous gift. Whitney, Taylor, and I have talked about the importance of the time we've spent with you at the inn. If I'm being totally honest, it was an escape for me to be able to come here each summer, away from the pressures placed on me at home."

GG took hold of Dani's hand. "I know that, dear. And for me, summer visits with my granddaughters were the highlights of any year. To be able to spend time with you, watch you grow into beautiful, capable women is truly a gift. That's why I wanted to give you and your sisters the same opportunity one day. It also enables me to fulfill a promise to my father to keep as much of our land as possible."

"Well, we're the lucky ones who get to benefit from that," said Dani. "Now let's talk about the cottage. It has a lot of potential. We couldn't ask for a better location, a more beautiful outlook."

"I've always thought so," said GG, "but after the death of Addie Maynard, I could never bring myself to stay there. I've always wondered if I could've prevented her dying. But I was away for the winter and thought she was well provided for."

"Do you think she haunts the house? Taylor is convinced her ghost is there."

"I don't know what to believe," GG said honestly. "You know how small-town people tend to make up stories about things like this. Still, logic says there are no ghosts."

"But you didn't stay in that house," said Dani.

"No, I came to realize I couldn't run the inn efficiently unless I moved there and was available to my guests. They liked the reassurance that I was there if they needed anything. That's certainly one reason I used to do so well. Now, the inn needs upgrading and a younger, more energetic group to run it. Like you, they want to make changes. I think they should. Similar to the house, the inn has good bones and can be made more energy efficient and modern unless they decide to tear it down."

"You've talked to them about the changes?" Dani asked.

GG's eyes twinkled as she nodded. "Oh, yes. One of the conditions of the sale was my general approval of what they planned. They have the money to make it a first-class resort and have every intention of making it tasteful."

"That's important," said Dani, relieved. Even though the house and acreage GG was giving them was not a part of the inn, they'd be close neighbors.

"What have you got for me? Some ideas of your own?" GG asked leaning forward with anticipation.

Dani took out the list she'd created. "We intend to make the first floor an open space with nooks and crannies to suit the work of the three of us. For Taylor, it means a pleasant writing space in the kitchen. Whitney wants a quiet space to read scripts or do other work."

"And you?" GG asked.

Dani clasped her hands. "I've decided to either take time off from work or resign. There might even be a possibility of working with Collister Construction. I'll go back to Boston, talk to my boss, and figure it out from there. I'm tired of not getting the recognition I deserve."

GG's blue eyes studied her. "Bravo. I think it's wise to continue to grow in your work. If this opportunity gives it to you, that makes me very happy indeed."

"Thanks," said Dani. "I've needed something to get me started on something new."

They went over the list, going from room to room in the house.

"What about the attic?" GG asked.

"Both Brad and I think it could be transformed into a marvelous space to work and play. The northern exposure provides outstanding lighting for me to use while drafting architectural plans. And the outlook could be useful for Taylor as she writes."

"But?"

"But I want to be sure there's no ghost before we complete that room. We'll do the attic last."

"So, you believe in ghosts?" GG asked, her eyebrows raised in surprise.

"Like you, I don't believe it makes sense logically. But I find myself lulled into thinking I've seen or felt things that aren't there. It's my imagination getting the best of me."

"I'd hate to think the cottage was haunted." GG checked her watch. "Time to go for tea. Would you care to join me?"

"Maybe another time," said Dani. "I'm meeting Brad for an early dinner so we can talk about moving forward with a cost analysis."

"When you get that done, I'll tell you about the funds I've set aside," said GG. "Walk me to the Tea Room, and I'll send you on your way."

Dani waited while GG freshened up and picked up her

phone.

Then they walked together to the Tea Room, where several residents called out to GG to join them.

Leaving GG among friends made it easier for Dani to go.

That evening, Dani took a shower and put on a pair of black slacks and a blue sweater that brought out the blue in her eyes. She told herself it was a business meeting, but she knew she was lying to herself. She was intrigued by Brad and his brother, Aaron. Unlike the men on the staff at her firm, they didn't act as if they knew better than she about construction and creating a design for something new. They were humble and polite.

She fed Pirate his meal and then turned him over to Whitney who planned to order in Chinese food for dinner. Now that they had the opportunity to make Lilac Lake their special home, Whitney didn't want anyone else to know about it. She'd told Dani and Taylor that she'd leave Monday morning and head back to California but would stay only as long as filming required her to be there.

Dani had arranged to meet Brad at Jake's Bar and Grill, a favorite place for people to hang out. She walked toward it with excitement. Situated in the middle of town on Main Street, it was typical of many bars. Inside, dark paneling covered the walls, several televisions were placed in strategic places showing sports games, and a fireplace along one wall helped to provide heat in the winter. She knew from past experience that in the fall, both Saturday and Sunday football games drew people from all around. And though a lot of fun rivalry took place among the fans of various teams, the Patriots' football fans outnumbered any others.

It took a moment for Dani's eyes to adjust to the dimness after being outdoors in the sun.

"Over here," said Brad, rising to his feet.

Dani made her way through the crowd to him.

He stood back while she slid onto the bench in the booth. Dani gazed at the couple opposite her. The man had a pleasant face, brown hair showing a few strands of gray at the temples, and a friendly smile. Next to him sat a woman about her own age with frosted brown hair and brown eyes.

"I thought you should meet Garth Beckman and his wife, Bethany," said Brad. "Garth's family owns Beckman Lumber. We work exclusively with them. He'll help us determine what lumber and other supplies we need."

"Fabulous," Dani said, pleased.

"I run the gift shop at the company," said Bethany. "I'll be able to help you with some things you might want for the interior."

"Thanks. We've only just begun work on the project, but that's nice to know," said Dani.

"What'll you have to drink?" Brad asked her.

She glanced at the beers in front of the men and the coke in front of Bethany. "I'd like a glass of red wine, pinot noir."

Brad signaled the waitress, and she came right over. "Yes, Brad?"

"How about a glass of pinot noir for my ... guest?"

The pretty young waitress studied Dani and then said, "For you, Brad, anything."

Dani noticed Bethany roll her eyes and held in a laugh.

Bethany winked at her and this time, Dani did chuckle as Bethany said to Brad, "Honestly, you're such a chick magnet."

Brad blinked and his ears turned red. "I'm not up for dating."

Bethany grew serious. "I'm just teasing you. You know Garth and I love you."

He nodded but didn't say anything, just took a sip of his beer.

Dani gave Bethany a quizzical look.

"Brad's wife died two years ago from cancer, and every female around thinks it's time Brad started dating again."

Dani turned to him. "I'm sorry for your loss."

The waitress returned, ending the conversation.

After she'd been served, Dani lifted her glass. "Here's to new friends."

Bethany raised her glass. "I can't have alcohol with a baby coming, but I'm happy to toast you, Dani. I'm glad we could meet. We, like everyone in town, love your grandmother. Are you planning on spending much time in Lilac Lake?"

"I want to move here as soon as possible to work on the cottage and am hoping to find enough business opportunities to enable me to stay more permanently."

"She works at a big firm in Boston," Brad explained. "If we have the chance to keep her here, it'll be lucky for all of us. Housing in the area is booming."

Pleased by the welcome and Brad's kind words, Dani settled back in her seat. This kind of opportunity didn't come along every day, and she grew even more resolved to make it work.

They chatted for a while longer, and then the waitress returned to take their dinner orders. Both men ordered the bar special—burgers with bacon, cheese, and a spicy chipotle sauce. Bethany opted for a veggie omelet, and Dani went with a turkey club sandwich.

As they chatted, Dani learned that Garth and Brad had gone to high school together and then to the University of New Hampshire. Noting the premature gray in Garth's hair, she realized that while Brad didn't have any gray mixed in with his blond hair, he might be older than she'd first thought. The thought of his grieving from the death of a wife sent a rush of sympathy through her. Life was unpredictable. Sitting here in

Lilac Lake with these new friends was proof of it.

CHAPTER TWELVE
TAYLOR

Taylor didn't mind staying at the house with Whitney and the dogs. Even though they were sisters, Taylor had always been a fan. In some ways, the show, *The Hopefuls*, seemed like a true story about Whitney's journey. Taylor knew how difficult breaking into show business was and couldn't help comparing it to the publishing industry.

Other more successful authors told her: "Write what you love, write from your heart." And she'd stuck to it, gathering more and more readers along the way. She was pleased by her success, but it was a lonely occupation with more and more pressure to produce. And now she had to get past her writer's block. She hoped after the transformation of the cottage took place, she could stay in New Hampshire and continue writing there. Only one thing would stop her, and that was the ghost issue. She'd have to be sure the ghost was gone before she could live there.

"What do you think, Taylor?" Whitney asked her. "Do you think Mindy will stay inside this carrier for the entire trip to California?" Cynthia had agreed to lend the airline-approved carrier to Whitney, and they'd been teaching Mindy to settle down inside it on her favorite blanket.

"Even though it hasn't been long, she's already bonded to you. I think that as long as she can see you and hear you, she'll do all right."

"I have to be able to make it work," said Whitney, "or else I can't use her to end the rumors about me. After they see how cute Mindy is, reporters and others may buy my story about leaving LA suddenly to reflect on my breakup and getting a dog from a friend. Who doesn't love a post-breakup pet? I won't say more than that, or else they'll begin digging into the story."

"It's awful to be in the spotlight," said Taylor. "Even though some people, a relative few, really, know my pen name, Taylor Castle, they don't care much about me personally. They just want another book."

"Thanks. I know I sometimes treated you like a pesky little sister, but I love you. I really do."

Taylor filled with warmth and a touch of sadness too. Everyone thought she loved her work creating her characters. She did, but she was beginning to find it way too lonely.

CHAPTER THIRTEEN
DANI

After dinner, Dani shook hands with Garth and Bethany. "Thanks so much for taking time to meet me. I look forward to working with you."

"I want you to keep your promise to come see me at the store. There are lots of cute things you might like for later," said Bethany, caressing her stomach. She and Garth had talked about their excitement that Bethany was pregnant. In the quiet that had followed, Dani had noted a sadness in Brad's eyes and suspected he was missing his wife.

After Garth and Bethany left, Brad turned to her. "May I walk you back to the B&B?"

"I'd love it," said Dani. After spending some time together, she'd felt an invisible tug, a connection to Brad and wanted to get to know him better.

They walked slowly, enjoying the summer evening.

"I'm sorry about your wife," said Dani. "Cancer is such a horrible disease. And she was much too young to die."

"Tell that to the big guy in the sky," grumbled Brad. "There wasn't a damn thing anyone could do to save her. We all tried."

Dani remained quiet as they moved ahead. When they reached the front door of the B&B, Brad said, "Thanks."

"For what?" she asked.

"For not going on and on about my wife and how lonely I must be. So many people think that's what I want to hear, but I don't. What's done is done. I'm doing the best I can. That's all anyone needs to know. Don't get me wrong, I'm grateful for the people in town who rallied around us, but I need to do things my own way, in my own time."

Dani grinned. "Now you're sounding like me talking to my mother. She can't understand why I won't settle down. I will when I'm ready."

"I get it," said Brad studying her thoughtfully. "It was nice having dinner with you. I know we'll be able to work well together. 'Night."

They stood for a moment staring at one another and then Brad turned and walked away.

Dani entered the house. Her thoughts about Brad were shredded when Pirate bolted down the stairs to greet her.

Taylor followed Pirate down the stairs. "How did it go with Brad?"

"Fine. He introduced me to Garth and Bethany Beckman. Garth's family owns the lumber yard, and he's going to work with us on costing the project. He'll also give us deals on the lumber and supplies we need. His wife, Bethany, is a sweetheart who's just found out she's pregnant."

"Who's pregnant?" asked Whitney joining them.

Dani told her sisters about Bethany and the shop she ran at the lumber yard. "She says we all need to look at the beautiful things she has."

"What fun," said Taylor. "I'll try to do that in the week ahead. With Whitney leaving for California and you leaving for Boston, I've decided to stay here until you get back. That way, if anyone has questions for us, I'll be here."

"Thanks," said Dani. "I'm not sure how long it's going to take for me to get things in order so I can spend the summer here."

They went into the dining room. While Dani helped herself to a cup of hot coffee, Whitney and Taylor took a seat at one of the tables there. Dani joined them, needing to get a better idea about who was going to be present during the renovation.

"How long are you going to be in California?" she asked Whitney.

Whitney shook her head and sighed. "I have to finish filming for this season. And then it's a wait-and-see game to find out if we've been picked up. The show is on the bubble. That gives me a little time before making a final decision on whether I stay or not."

"Okay, if any big decisions need to be made, we can talk over the phone. But you've already agreed to the general changes to the design. Right?"

"Yes. Thank you for making sure we're all happy with it."

Dani gave her a quick hug. "If it's okay with the two of you, I'm returning to Boston tomorrow."

"In that case, can I get a ride with you? I'm scheduled for a late flight to California. I couldn't get an earlier flight because of Mindy," said Whitney.

"Where is she?" Dani asked.

"Upstairs in my bed," said Whitney. "She loves to sleep right next to my pillow."

"Thankfully, Pirate is too big for that," said Dani, and noticed the sly smiles on her sisters' faces. "What?"

"I don't think he's going to be happy sleeping on the floor," said Taylor. "He was sleeping next to Mindy before you came home."

"We'll work it out, won't we, Pirate?" Dani said, rubbing his ears. He was another reason to plan on staying in Lilac Lake for the summer. It was his home.

The next morning, Dani rose early and took Pirate for a run. Jogging along the sidewalks in town, she admired her surroundings and liked the idea of making it her home for a few months.

When she returned to the B&B, Whitney and Taylor were in the dining room.

"I'm packed so I'll be ready anytime you are," said Whitney. "I can't wait to get home and get my work done. Only then will I be able to return. That thought alone will keep me going."

"I'll get ready as fast as I can," said Dani. "Even though I'm not expected in the office until tomorrow, I thought I'd go in today and tell them what I have in mind."

She grabbed a cup of coffee to take to her room and called Pirate to follow her. Cynthia had promised to save a room for her return.

After sharing a tearful goodbye with Whitney at Logan Airport with promises to talk often, Dani drove to the condo she owned in the old Leather District of the city. It was a perfect location for her because she could walk to work from there.

She parked her car behind the building and led Pirate by leash to the elevator. He gave her a quizzical look when the door opened, but he stepped inside with her. On the third floor, she unlocked her apartment and urged him inside. He gazed around and then, nose to ground, he made a thorough inspection of the place.

Amused by him, she gazed at the condo with fresh eyes. She was lucky to have found it. A two-bedroom with a small office, a bath and a half, and a modern kitchen with a small laundry area was a real find. Still, if the opportunity was worth it, she'd be willing to sell it.

Before she left, she made sure Pirate had his favorite toys and a bowl of water. "I'll be back soon. You be a good boy," she said, patting him on the head.

As she walked to her office, she compared it to her early morning run. She loved Boston; it was one of her favorite cities. But now, the buildings seemed cold and unwelcoming.

She reached her office building and took the elevator to the tenth floor, which gave a lovely view of the city and the harbor.

The receptionist, a sweet older woman, waved at her. "They're meeting in the smaller conference room."

"Oh, thanks," said Dani, wondering why she hadn't received notice of the meeting.

When she walked into the room, conversation stopped.

"What are you doing here?" asked Frank Crespo, her nemesis at the office, worse than Jeremy had ever acted. "I thought you were away."

"I came back early," she said, gazing at the people around the room. "What am I missing?"

"We're bidding on a new project in Providence, Rhode Island," said Frank. "I'm in charge of it."

"I see," Dani said, understanding now why she hadn't got notice of the meeting. Frank was going to do his best to keep her out of it. "I'll leave you to it."

She took a seat in her office and stared out the window at the scene below, deep in thought. Once again Frank was trying to keep her out of the best projects, and others allowed him to do so without objection. Being the only female architect in the office had always had its challenges, but she was tired of the discrimination. It was all done very subtly, of course, until a blatant action like this occurred. Again, with silent compliance.

She'd confided to GG about the situation before. She wondered if this was another reason her grandmother had made this move so quickly—to protect her granddaughters. It was a huge opportunity for all of them to make changes in their lives.

Taking a deep breath, she began to type her resignation. She wasn't going to simply ask for a leave of absence, she was leaving the firm. She had excellent rapport with new and existing clients and a solid history with new construction and rebuilds. If she chose to go with another firm in the future, she could. But for now, a simpler, better life awaited her in Lilac Lake.

As she finished typing, Herb Watkins, the managing partner of the firm knocked on her door.

She waved him inside and rose to meet him.

"I know you're upset," he began.

Dani held up her hand to stop him. "I'd come into the office to talk to you about my future plans." She handed him her resignation. "I'm doing a family project for my grandmother in Lilac Lake. After some consideration, I've decided to make it a clean break. While I've learned a lot here and am grateful for that, it's time for me to go out on my own."

Her boss studied her. "I understand. While we'll miss you, it's important for you to be happy. When will you leave?"

"I'd like to make it as soon as possible. I'm not attached to any projects at the moment," she replied unable to keep a bitter edge from entering her voice.

"All right. Let's say, the end of the week. That will give us time to make sure everything is in order. You signed a non-comp agreement, but if you're working on a personal project that won't be a problem."

Cold fury ran through Dani. "I don't expect it to be. You are aware of issues here in the office, I'm sure. Today's meeting is typical."

They stared at one another and then her boss looked away. "Like I said, I don't anticipate any problems with your leaving. You're talented, Dani, and I truly wish you well."

Dani was both angry and hurt as she watched him go. He didn't even try to convince her to stay. Then her anger was replaced by a sense of freedom, and she raised her fist in the air. On to a new life!

The week flew by in a flurry of activity. She cleaned out her office and her computer of personal items and went through her commissions for the firm, making sure they had what they needed. One evening, her three best friends took her out for martinis and a dinner at Grill 23, one of their favorite bars. She spent as much time as she could with Pirate, walking him morning, noon, and night.

At last, it was Friday, her final day at the office. Individuals had come up to her during the week to say how sorry they were about her departure, but it wasn't until that afternoon that the whole office came together to bid her farewell at a lunch that they'd had catered.

When her boss stepped forward and handed her an envelope with two airline tickets to Paris, Dani couldn't hide the tears that threatened her vision. She'd talked often about wanting to see some of the beautiful architecture in Europe. For all the frustration of working at the firm, there'd been some good times too.

Still, as she left the office for the last time, she knew she was doing the right thing.

CHAPTER FOURTEEN
DANI

Dani went through her closet taking only casual things with her. She'd need jeans, denim work shirts, tank tops, hiking boots, and other items she could work in comfortably. She'd also need some dressier items to wear in the evenings. She gleefully left her Boston work clothes, mostly suits, skirts, and conservative outfits, behind and packed eagerly for what she thought of as her new life. She wouldn't do anything about her condo for the time being. Maybe she'd rent it out later. Or even sell it.

Pirate stayed right at her side giving her a woeful look from time to time.

She rubbed his ears. "Don't worry, Pirate, you're coming with me."

As she was packing, her cell rang. *Her mother.*

"Hi, Mom. How are you?" she asked, waiting for the message of doom that was sure to come.

"I'm fine, but I'm worried about you. I talked to your grandmother, and she told me you were moving to Lilac Lake for the summer. What about your job? Your firm is a prestigious one, and I doubt you'll be able to find a better offer elsewhere."

Dani drew a deep breath and let it out slowly. "I was very unhappy at the firm because no matter how I tried, I was never going to be one of the "boys." I've resigned, and over the course of the summer, I'll decide what I want to do next."

"Oh, Dani, I thought you were doing so well. Maybe it's

time to come home to Atlanta and settle here. You know I'd love that."

"Yes, I do," Dani said politely while knowing moving to Atlanta would never be an option for her. Not if she wanted to maintain her mental health. "I'm really excited about the opportunity to oversee the renovation of the caretaker's cottage at the inn. GG has given it to Whitney, Taylor, and me to keep it in the family. It's going to be beautiful."

"But who are you going to be able to meet in the country?"

"You forget that Lilac Lake has become an upscale resort town. Besides, I don't want to worry about meeting anyone." She thought of Brad.

"And I hear you and Whitney each have a dog. Have you both gone crazy?" her mother said. "Poor Whitney must have enough on her mind without worrying about a dog. And you? Where will you keep a dog in Lilac Lake if the house isn't livable?"

"Cynthia Anders at the B&B has given me permission to have Pirate in my room. He's well-behaved."

"Pirate? Oh, my, I can't keep up with you girls," said her mother. "I don't understand why you don't live closer. I suppose your father and I will have to make a trip to New Hampshire this summer."

"That would be fun, Mom," said Dani. She loved her mother; she just didn't need any guidance from her. "Maybe you can stay at the inn. I understand the three new owners are going to spruce it up, expand it, and give it back some of its early glory."

"That will be a sight to see," said her mother. "Okay, darling, we'll talk later. Love you."

"Love you too," Dani said, quickly clicking off the call before her mother thought of something more to say.

It took several trips to load her SUV, but she was glad she'd put in some of her sports equipment. This summer wasn't going to be all work and no play.

As she drove back to Lilac Lake, Dani had the comforting sensation that she was going home. That feeling grew when Taylor ran out of the B&B to greet her. They embraced and then Taylor helped her carry her luggage inside while Pirate pranced around them as if he understood he'd come home too.

After everything had been loaded into her room, Taylor said, "C'mon, let's go see GG. She and I have been waiting all week to see you, and she wants you to give her the details of your resignation. It was a brave thing to do."

"Not so brave, just smart," said Dani, frustrated again by the fact that she was never going to be given a fair chance to make a name for herself in that firm.

Dani drove to The Woodlands with Taylor and the dog, pleased that the facility allowed dogs inside for others to enjoy if they were suitable as a pet.

Pirate strolled beside her into the building and then left her side to go to an outstretched hand, where he received pats on the head. Delighted, Dani stayed with him while he greeted other residents and then led him to GG's room.

At the sight of them, GG beamed. "Oh, my girls. And Pirate too. How delightful to see you. Come sit and let's talk." She patted a place beside her on the couch and indicated the chair next to it. Taylor sat next to GG as Dani lowered herself into the chair. Pirate lay at GG's feet.

"Now, Dani, you must tell me about your resignation at the firm," said GG, a gleam entering her eyes. Dani knew GG had always felt Dani was underrated at her job.

Dani gave GG and Taylor the details and then leaned back. "I'm pleased with my decision. I want to oversee the cottage renovation and then maybe join forces with Collister

Construction."

"Brad and Aaron came to see me while you were gone. They're eager to work with you on this project and told me they may be asking for your help with the renovation of the inn. While the owners have had plans drawn up, they want your input on tweaking them."

"I'd love to do that. I imagine they want me on board with that job because I'm available to come on site."

"Yes, something like that," said GG, giving her a grin that evaporated years from her. "Brad told me he had dinner with you and introduced you to Garth and Bethany Beckman. Such a lovely couple. Brad's always been one of my favorites. A tragedy about his wife dying so young, but I think he's ready to move forward."

Dani shook her head at GG's mischievous grin. "I agree, he's very nice. However, many available females in town seem to be interested in him. At least the waitress at Jake's is."

"You mean Deanna. She's desperate to find someone. I've seen her in action before," said Taylor. "While you've been gone, I'd often get a salad at Jake's and bring it back to the B&B. It makes it convenient while I'm starting to work on my next book."

"As long as I'm going to stay awhile, I thought I'd look into renting an apartment," said Dani. "It'll be easier with Pirate and give us women more privacy."

"I'll help you look," said Taylor, tucking a strand of dark hair behind her ear. "I've decided to spend the summer here, too, with just a couple of trips back to New York. In fact, as soon as we find a place, I'll head back to the city to pack."

GG clasped her hands together. "It makes me so happy to see you girls here and to know you'll maintain the family land. Promises in families can be difficult to keep, but life seems so worthwhile if they're honored."

Pirate stirred, and Dani got to her feet and gave GG a hug. "Why do I have the feeling you've planned this for some time?"

GG chuckled. "I truly haven't, but I love how it's all going to work out."

Dani and Taylor exchanged dubious looks, then Taylor rose. "Any suggestions for apartments, GG?"

"No, but I'm sure that Melanie Perkins at Lake Realty can help you. She knows everyone in the area and will have the latest news." GG winked. "That's a warning. Be careful what you say around her."

Dani laughed. "We won't mention Whitney. That can be a surprise for later."

Dani and Taylor left The Woodlands and decided to go directly to Lake Realty. There, an older woman acted as a receptionist in the small office and asked them to wait while she let Melanie know they were there.

She emerged a few moments later followed by a middle-aged woman who obviously dyed her hair a bright orange offset by strong dark eyebrows above silver-gray eyes. The combination was shocking at first, but Melanie's smile was genuine.

"Hi, I'm Melanie Perkins. When I heard your names, I knew you must be Genie's granddaughters. And the family resemblance is there. Is it true? You're going to be spending time here while the caretaker's cottage is renovated?"

Dani bit back laughter at how Melanie already knew their plans and reminded herself to be careful with her words. "Yes, that's true. I'm Dani Gilford and this is my sister, Taylor." She patted Pirate's head." And this is Pirate."

"Oh, yes. Aaron's dog. I heard about that," said Melanie.

"We're interested in renting a place for the summer, possibly beyond. Can you help us?"

"You've come to the right place," Melanie said brightly.

"I've lived here all my life, so I know everyone, and they trust me to do an excellent job for them. Let's go into my office and talk. We'll look through what might be available."

Dani and Taylor followed her into her office and took seats in the two chairs in front of her desk.

Melanie sat in the big leather chair behind the desk and took out a paper and pen. "What are you interested in? Something small? An apartment? Or, perhaps, a house, something bigger for the dog."

Dani glanced at her sister and back to Melanie. "We're open to anything, but a place that would be suitable for a dog would be best."

Melanie stared off into space and then clicked her fingers. "I'm not supposed to tell anyone about it, but a friend of mine is going to spend some time with her daughter's family in Colorado this summer and is thinking of moving there. She might be willing to let you rent her house with the thought of putting it on the market sometime in the early Fall. Would that be of interest? It's a lovely house right outside of downtown."

"What would it cost?" Taylor asked.

Melanie gave her a thoughtful look. "The fact that you would be house sitters, in a way, could mean a reasonable rent. Here's her address. Drive by and look at it and see if it's something you'd consider, then let me know right away. I'm sure we can work something out to make you all happy."

"Thanks so much," said Dani, accepting the slip of paper with the address. "We'll go there right now and call you. It could be a perfect short-term solution."

"We appreciate your help," said Taylor rising.

They left the office and drove to a quiet little neighborhood outside of town. At the end of the cul-de-sac of eight houses, a gray clapboard Cape Cod caught their attention.

"Is this it?" asked Dani.

"Yes, that's the one. It's cute, don't you think?" responded Taylor. "And look! The backyard is fenced."

Dani glanced at her sister. "If we split the cost, we should be able to manage, unless Melanie was wrong about a reasonable price. I'm keeping my condo until I know what I'll be doing long-term."

"I'm all for it," said Taylor, looking out the window as a large red truck with the name Collister Construction pulled up into the driveway next door.

Dani stared at the blond-haired man getting out of the truck. He gave them a quizzical look and then walked over to them, wearing jeans and a T-shirt that showed off his body.

"What are you two doing? Casing the neighborhood?" he asked, settling his gaze on Dani.

"Sort of," said Dani, smiling at Brad. "We might be renting a house here. Do you live there?" She pointed to the sparkling white Cape Cod with dark-green shutters and the white picket fence that lined the front yard.

"Yes, that's mine." Brad glanced around. "Which neighbor of mine has their house up for a rental?"

Dani hesitated and then replied, "We're not supposed to mention it, but the address we were given is for the house next to yours."

"Oh, Marjorie. She told me she might spend the summer in Colorado." He chuckled. "Sweet lady. She keeps me supplied with cookies."

"Please don't say anything to her about our visit. Melanie Perkins is helping us find a place to rent for the summer, and she thinks she can make a deal with the owner."

Brad raised a finger to his lips. "I promise I won't tell a soul." He gave them a wave and walked away.

Dani and Taylor stared at him departing and then before

Dani could stop herself, she murmured, "That's some cute butt."

"His entire body is hot," said Taylor. "What's going on between the two of you? He couldn't take his eyes off you."

"We're just friends who'll be working together this summer and maybe beyond. I'm taking it one day at a time. For once in my life, I'm not going to plan everything ahead of time. I'll simply let things unfold."

"I know what you mean," said Taylor. "That's why I've decided to spend the summer here, letting the story in my head unfold to perhaps begin an entire series."

Dani turned to her. "That's exciting. You haven't done a series before. This slower pace is a way to let creative juices flow."

"I'm hoping so. It's also an interesting way to meet more people. I'm so used to working alone in my office that I don't get out enough. I have a feeling that won't happen here. I've already met some pleasant people in town."

"Yes, me too," said Dani, thrilled by the thought of renting the house next door to Brad. She'd felt a connection to him from the beginning and though she knew he wasn't ready to move on in his life, she hoped they could at least be friends.

CHAPTER FIFTEEN
WHITNEY

Whitney stepped off the plane in California feeling as nervous as she had auditioning for the show. This time, the stakes were even higher. The games she'd been playing with her co-star, Zane Blanchard, were over. They'd been friends, then lovers, then caught up in the lie of pretending they were still dating. Now, everyone knew they'd broken up. More than that, she was tired of the life she'd built in Hollywood.

Holding onto Mindy's airline carrier and talking softly to her dog to keep her calm, Whitney joined the crowd headed to the baggage claim area. She hoped her agent had followed through in arranging for a limo and driver to meet her. She still hadn't worked through what to say to reporters asking her about the breakup.

It was all Zane's fault. She'd thought they had a deal to keep to a clean life as their viewers thought. But after seeing him drugged and fooling around with not one, but two women, she'd lost all respect for him. And then, when he got so angry with her about it, she knew the breakup was the right thing to do. She might be considered naïve, but no one was going to drag her or her family into an ugly situation that would undoubtedly become worse.

In the baggage claim area, she saw a driver holding up a card that read "W. G. pickup." Grateful her name hadn't been shown, she hurried over to him and handed him the carrier so she could lift Mindy out of it.

Mindy gazed up at her sleepily from the medicine the vet had recommended and then licked Whitney's face just as a photographer snapped a picture.

Whitney, for once, was grateful for the attention, making it easier to have viewers think all that talk of babies was really talk of puppies.

She gave a description of her luggage to the driver and waited with him while he got them off the baggage belt.

Stroking Mindy, Whitney followed the driver to the black Town Car waiting at the curb. After he opened the back door for her, she slid into the backseat and let out a sigh of relief. She was well-known, but not as big a television star as some.

After being dropped off at her condo in Redondo Beach, Whitney changed into comfortable clothes and led Mindy outside. While dogs weren't allowed on the beach, there was plenty to see as they strolled along the sidewalks. For Mindy, it was a whole new world to explore, and Whitney patiently waited for Mindy to stop and sniff every few feet.

Her cell phone rang. *Zane.*

Her pulse sped up. The last time they'd been together he'd screamed at her, called her a baby, told her he'd get even with her for ending their little game. If he thought she'd forgotten, he was mistaken.

"Hello, Zane, how are you?" she asked in what she hoped was a neutral tone.

"We need to talk. Can I come over?" Zane asked in that low musical voice everyone loved.

She held back a sigh. "I just got in from the East Coast, but I'm free for a short while."

"See you soon," he said and ended the call.

Back at her condo, Whitney hurried about, straightening things. She was enough of her mother's child to do so, not that

Zane would notice. He wasn't the tidiest person she knew.

She checked the refrigerator. She'd been gone only a few days so she still had chilled flavored water and some fresh fruit inside that could serve as a snack.

She filled Mindy's bowl with water and fixed her blanket in a corner of the kitchen. She knew that a doggie bed was useless for Mindy. The dog had made it clear she would be sleeping in Whitney's bed at night. It was fine with Whitney. She loved cuddling her.

The doorbell rang, setting off Mindy, filling the air with her barks.

Whitney dragged her fingers through her long hair and drew a deep breath, telling herself to be strong.

She opened the door and faced Zane Blanchard, television star. In a pair of jeans and a black T-shirt he looked as swoon worthy as he did on screen. A few inches taller than she, he was a solidly built man with chestnut-brown hair, ruggedly handsome features, and hazel eyes that changed color with his mood.

"I had to see you before we go back on the set. You took off in a hurry, and I wanted to make sure you were all right. I know you were shocked when you burst in on me."

"Your addictions have become worse," Whitney said quietly, uneasy with his fake concern. "We had an agreement that as long as you remained someone that I'd really want to date, we'd fake it for the ratings and additional publicity to catch the viewers' attention. Now, that time has come. We're just another Hollywood romance gone wrong."

"You've got to be kidding me," snapped Zane.

At his angry tone, Mindy growled at him.

"What's that?" Zane asked, trying to focus on the dog.

"That's my dog, Mindy."

"She's why you had to leave town in such a hurry?" Zane

asked frowning at her.

"I left to get away from the media circus surrounding our "breakup". As it turns out, my sisters and I have inherited a house on a lake in New Hampshire. We're going to renovate it, and I'm planning to return there as soon as possible."

"You're leaving? What about the show?" asked Zane.

Whitney studied him. He was a handsome man with a true talent for acting, but he had no idea of what real people were like—their hopes and dreams, their decency. He had success with other talented actors, but he was already losing that position to the lifestyle that was drowning him. By being firm with him, she hoped to make him see what was happening.

"C'mon in," Whitney said. "Let's talk for a minute."

He followed her inside to the kitchen.

Mindy stayed at Whitney's heels making no attempt to make friends with Zane. That told Whitney a lot.

"How about some flavored water?" she asked him, trying to be helpful.

"No booze?" Zane said.

"No," Whitney said firmly. "That's part of the problem. You've gone way beyond just booze. That's not who I am. I'm done with it."

"So, you're just going to let me take a bad rap?" Zane said, eying her incredulously.

Whitney held up her hand to stop him. "Don't even go there. If you want sincere help, I'll always be there for you ..."

He cut her off. "You bitch! You're ruining my career. Once you broke up with me, I became the bad guy. People are saying I'm abusive even though I've never put a rough hand on you. A movie dried up because of the split. Now there's a chance the show won't go on for another season."

"*I'm* not doing that to you. *You* are," said Whitney doing her best to remain calm and not let his anger unnerve her. "I thought we could talk things over, get help for you, maybe even go back to being real friends ..." She went to her front door and opened it. "This is useless. You'd better leave."

Grumbling to himself, Zane stood beside the open door and snarled, "You're not going to get away with dumping me. I'll get you for this, Whitney. You think you're so high and mighty, but you're not. I'll make sure our viewers know all about how you led me on because you needed me to help you with the show."

"I don't know what you intend to say. Just tell the truth," Whitney warned him, feeling sick. She had nothing to hide, but that wouldn't count with this new Zane. All her hard work through the years could be discounted by his lies—lies that people fed on.

CHAPTER SIXTEEN
DANI

After they signed a contract with Marjorie Hight, the owner of the house next to Brad's, Dani and Taylor moved into it, delighted by the way she'd decorated it, how clean it was. Before allowing them to rent it, Marjorie had given them a thorough tour of the house and instructed them on how to maintain it to her standards.

Marjorie met Pirate and seeing how well-behaved he was, she was open to having him stay at the house. That alone was worth a lot, giving Dani a sense of ease that he had a nice, safe place to stay when he couldn't be with her.

Though small, the house had three bedrooms, two baths, a huge, fenced-in back yard, and an updated kitchen. The one rule Marjorie was strict about was not smoking in the house. Because of her allergy to tobacco, she'd never permitted it and wouldn't do it now, especially with the idea of selling the house in the future.

The decision as to who got what bedroom was an easy one. Dani readily agreed that Taylor should get the master bedroom where she could set up her office and have a private space for writing.

Dani happily took one of the other smaller bedrooms. Though Marjorie had left things behind, she'd tried to give them as much space as possible.

Once they were moved into the house, Dani walked Pirate through it, letting him sniff and get used to it. Then she took him outside to the back yard, which held a large maple tree. A small patio extended from the house and looked out over the roomy lawn. She sat and watched as Pirate made the rounds, stopping and sniffing at several spots.

She heard her name being called and looked up to find Brad waving at her. She got up and walked over to the wooden fence between them.

"Hi, I see you've moved in," said Brad. "While you're staying there, let me know if you need help with anything about the house. I told Marjorie I'd check in with you and your sisters."

"Thanks," said Dani. "I'm pretty handy myself, but I'll let you know if something comes up." She felt a smile spread across her face. As part of her training and education, she'd spent a couple of summers on a construction crew. "And if you need help with anything, just let me know. I'm also handy in the kitchen when necessary." Laughter burst out of her. "I'm sorry I made such a sexist remark. No doubt, you're a better cook than I am."

"Someday, we'll put it to the test. I'm ordering pizza in tonight. Do you and Taylor want to join me?"

"Thanks. I'd like that. I think Taylor has plans, but I'll check with her. Why don't you bring the pizza over and I'll make a salad to go with it."

"Okay. Any special kind of pizza for you?"

"I like it all," said Dani. "Taylor too."

"Give me thirty minutes to get cleaned up and pick up the pizza. See you then."

"Deal," said Dani, watching him walk away and then turning to Pirate. "Inside, boy. We're going to have company."

From the kitchen, Dani called to Taylor, who appeared wearing a fresh pair of jeans and a new sweater.

"Where are you going?" Dani asked.

"I have a date with Aaron," Taylor said, beaming at her.

"Oh, well, I was going to tell you that Brad is bringing over pizza, and I'm going to make a salad. Thought you might want to join us."

"You're sweet, sister dear. I know how excited you are about being with Brad and would do nothing to stand in your way. I'll make sure Aaron and I leave you two alone."

"And ditto for me—leaving you and Aaron alone," said Dani.

They grinned at one another and then Taylor said, "I think I hear Aaron's truck now. See you later."

Taylor left and Dani watched as Aaron got out of his truck and helped Taylor into the passenger seat.

She quickly fed Pirate his dinner and hurried into the bathroom to freshen up. A little dab of sexy perfume might be just the touch she needed because time for a shower was out of the question.

A few minutes later, Dani answered the front door knock to see Brad standing there, his hair still wet from a shower, holding two pizza boxes.

She opened the door, waved him inside, and told Pirate to stand down before leading Brad into the kitchen.

"Is Taylor going to join us?" said Brad looking around after setting the pizza boxes on the counter.

"No, she left earlier with Aaron. They had plans for the evening."

Brad grinned. "No wonder Aaron didn't want to do anything with me tonight. Just as well. I'm glad to have time with you. I like that I'm able to really talk to you. It's nice that neither one of us is looking for anything more than getting to know one another better. It makes it a lot easier to spend time together."

Dani forced an agreeable nod. She had to remember that

was all Brad was ready for. And, she reminded herself, she couldn't let anything like dating interfere with the renovation of the cottage and possible employment afterwards. Still, she understood how lonely Brad was and wanted to help him.

While Dani tossed a salad, Brad sipped on the beer she'd offered and watched her.

"Patti used to do that," he commented and then stood and looked out the sliding glass door to the back yard. When he turned around, he said, "Sorry, I shouldn't have mentioned her."

"Why not?" Dani said, puzzled. "I assume Patti was your wife."

He sighed and nodded. "The two women I've dated don't like me to talk about her."

Anger flared inside Dani. She knew it was healing for him to be able to talk about his deceased wife. "With me, you can talk all you want about Patti. She was your wife and you obviously loved her. I want you to feel comfortable talking about whatever is on your mind."

He blinked with surprise and then a slow smile spread across his face. "Thanks. I still miss her. I know it's time for me to start thinking of dating seriously; it's been a lonely time. But I can't just pretend she never existed."

"Of course not," Dani said more gently. "I lost a friend in college. She was a drunk driver, and I still think of her often. A death doesn't erase someone; it places them in your heart."

Brad approached her and studied her with those dark-green eyes of his, giving her a glimpse of the man inside.

"I like you, Dani, and I'm happy we can talk this way."

"I'm glad we can speak openly too. And I think we can have some fun renovating the cottage." She wasn't ready to think beyond that.

They walked back to the kitchen counter. Dani served up

salad while Brad opened the boxes of pizza, and they each helped themselves to one slice of each kind.

Dani sat at the small kitchen table, and Brad joined her. From there she could look out the glass door and see Pirate wandering in the yard. For a moment, her insides squeezed with delight at the thought of sharing this time with a man she admired. She chewed slowly, thinking.

"Penny for your thoughts," Brad said.

She gazed at him. "I think I'm going to like living here. It seems so peaceful compared to my life in Boston."

"Life here is at a slower pace, but it suits me. There's nothing like an evening canoe trip across the lake and back, or hunting in the woods in the fall, or skiing up north in the winter."

"You're a real outdoorsman," commented Dani.

"Mother Nature settles your soul," Brad answered.

Dani gazed at the smile that lingered on his face and felt a shiver travel down her back. She was already falling for him. But she knew enough not to let her feelings show. He wasn't ready for more than friendship.

After they finished eating and Dani had put the dishes in the dishwasher, Brad said, "Want to take Pirate on a walk through the neighborhood? It's been a while since I've had a dog, and it will feel good to do it."

"Sure. It's a beautiful evening out. But tell me, why don't you have a dog?"

"My dog died last year. He was fourteen, which is old for a lab. I just haven't wanted to start with a new puppy. Someday, I will. Not yet."

"Pirate is the first dog I've owned, and I'm still getting used to the routine of owning one. It's like having a child."

"Oh, yes. And puppies are like newborns." Brad paused. "Or so I've heard. My sister Amy has a new baby. He's awfully cute, but he's a lot of work, too."

"Are you interested in having children of your own?" Dani asked, holding her breath while waiting for an answer. She definitely wanted children.

"With the right woman, I'd love children. Maybe three or four," said Brad, and Dani let her breath out.

She called Pirate, hooked him up to his leash, and she and Brad left the house with him.

As they walked, they continued talking about their lives—everything from their favorite school topics as kids to their favorite desserts. They were comfortable together and thought alike about a lot of things.

By the time they returned to the house, Dani was even more smitten. But once again, she kept those feelings to herself.

"Thanks for dinner," said Brad, standing in front of the house. "I'd better go. I have an early morning staff meeting, and then we're going to begin tearing down sections of the inn."

"Not the original main building, I hope. Some of the finish work inside is very special."

Brad shrugged. "Aaron and I have indicated we want to keep as much of that as possible, but the plans call for a complete teardown. We'll see. The new owners are willing to be flexible. That's why we're meeting with them. Do you want to be present? We can say we've hired you for extra input."

"That would be fantastic. The main building has a lot of integrity, history, and character, and I'd hate to simply throw it away. I know it's not my project, and I have an emotional attachment to it, but I have enough knowledge to make sense of it all."

"Well, then, why don't you join us at the inn at seven-thirty tomorrow morning? I'll explain to Aaron ahead of time."

Dani clasped her hands. "Thank you! I'd appreciate it so much. Since knowing the inn was sold, I've thought a lot about it—how it was used, what people liked about it, and other things about the inn that I hoped wouldn't be lost with new owners."

"I bet you have," he said kindly. "I've looked up your business information online. Pretty impressive."

Dani made a face. "My old job was not nearly as fulfilling as I thought it was going to be. I like to be hands-on with any project and didn't get the chance to do it often enough."

"Maybe that will change," said Brad. His gaze rested on her for a moment before he turned and walked away.

The next morning, Dani turned off her alarm and jumped out of bed, eager to get ready to join Brad and the others at their meeting at the inn. Last night, Brad had sent her the plans for the inn. She hoped to be able to make a strong case for keeping some of the handcrafted woodwork and other details of the main building, even if it was decided the main building would be torn down. Better yet, she wanted the new owners to see her as part of the renovation team. That would help her secure future work in the area.

She dressed in black slacks, a crisp white shirt, and low black shoes before driving over to the inn. She pulled her car up in front of the inn and climbed out.

Brad and Aaron met her on the porch.

"Glad you're here," said Aaron. "Brad told me you wanted to have a voice as both a family member and an architect on our team."

Dani beamed at him. "Thanks for having me. Retention of some of the original, finer details of wooden trim and other examples of architectural design or historical interest should be considered in any renovation."

"Aaron and I agree," said Brad, "which is why you're here. Let's go inside. The owners are waiting."

Dani accompanied Brad and Aaron inside to the small conference room off the lobby.

As they entered it, Ross Roberts and Quinn McPherson stood.

Ross Roberts, with his sandy hair, blue eyes, and boyish grin, was as appealing in person as he had been on television playing baseball for the New York Yankees.

Dani's gaze settled on Quinn McPherson. He was just as tall and lanky as she'd seen from across the street, and he had burnt-orange hair offset by light-brown eyes, a freckled nose, and pleasant features.

Rachael McPherson, sitting between the two men, sat erect studying her with gray eyes. Her straight auburn hair was pulled back in a severe bun exposing her classic features short of being beautiful but nevertheless striking. Dani had read that Rachael's real love was horses and from time to time she liked to hunt in Virginia, where her parents owned a luxurious farm.

Of the three owners, Dani knew instinctively that Rachael would be the most difficult to please by the way she was looking dismissively at her.

Aaron made the introductions, and after shaking hands, Dani took a seat between Aaron and Brad.

"We're here to discuss the plans we've had drawn up," Quinn began. "I understand there are some details you wish to discuss."

"Yes," said Aaron. "I know you intend to make the Lilac Lake Inn something new, something spectacular. But I'm hoping we can convince you to keep some of the simple woodland features and feel to the property. The inn, like the town, has always had a classic New England style that complements its surroundings. It would be a shame to see that completely discarded."

"So, you want us to redraw all our plans?" said Rachael sounding incredulous.

Aaron turned to her, and Dani picked up the conversation from there. "The new wings as proposed with skylights, patios and balconies, and large windows are going to be beautiful, if a bit impractical, but losing the main building and its classic New England style could be problematic. For instance, the wide front porch with its rocking chairs served guests well for relaxing. It was sometimes used for receptions, family gatherings and even small weddings. Most of all, it served as a welcoming entrance to guests. Without it, the property is a bit sterile in our opinion," said Dani.

"You're saying the building should suit the setting more," said Quinn, giving her a thoughtful look.

"Yes, the setting is very important to any building. In this instance, you're in a wooded, lakeside spot where people come to hike, swim, hunt, and relax, expecting an upscale but natural-looking destination."

"I saw that you won an award for a design of a contemporary building in downtown Boston. What makes you qualified to add any comments to our hotel project?" asked Rachael giving her a superior frown. "My brother and I earned our degrees in hotel management at Cornell and have been part of that business for almost ten years."

"Not that I'm playing a game with you," said Dani coolly, "but my professional career as an architect with Watkins Dailey Architects LLC in Boston has given me opportunities for renovation projects like this in other areas of New England. Also, my sisters and I have been coming here for over twenty-five years, helping with the inn in the summers. I don't claim to be an expert, but I know what guests liked about the inn in its prime."

"Hold on," said Ross. "What exactly are you suggesting?"

"We're suggesting that you keep the look of the original lobby with its carved wooden trim, big fireplace, and cozy nooks and crannies," said Brad. "Given that the weather a good part of the year has a chill to it, cozy places to sit and read, or play games, or simply relax inside should be part of the main building. As the plans show now, all those are scheduled to be demolished and replaced with new construction to give the inn a clean and contemporary look."

"As Dani has said, the guestroom wings can handle that change. The main building and lobby can't without destroying the character and ambience of the inn," said Aaron.

"I like it," said Ross. "When in Rome do what the Romans do..."

"And when in Lilac Lake territory, do what the natives do and want," said Quinn grinning.

"I believe it's important," said Dani. "It doesn't change the basic plan to upgrade the resort, just adds a little more interest to the interior that shouldn't increase the cost."

"Just what is your position with Collister Construction?" asked Rachael.

Dani turned to Aaron.

He smiled at her and said to the group, "Dani is going to be on our team helping to determine how best to approach any project. When questions come up, she'll be able to provide perspective on most of those that relate to design."

"With her on board, we won't have to delay work on a project waiting for input from others or have to slow progress on our work to figure out if something can or should be done," added Brad.

Dani worked hard to hide her feelings, but gratitude filled her at their responses that gave her more credit than any men had done before them.

"I like the concept," said Ross.

Rachael studied her. "Let's see how it goes. It's a tough business for a woman, but I admire your commitment to it." She turned to Ross. "It's terrible when a career like yours is cut short, but I love that you've found another so quickly. It's an agreeable working partnership."

"So far, it has been." He gave Dani a teasing look. "Guess you're not a fan. The Red Sox and Yankees have always been rivals."

"I'm not going to lie," said Dani with an impish grin. "I've used the term 'Damn Yankees' before."

Ross laughed. "I think we're going to get along just fine."

The men joined in the laughter that followed, but Dani noticed Rachael was quietly assessing Brad.

CHAPTER SEVENTEEN
DANI

Dani left the meeting feeling good about herself and her new connection to Collister Construction. Aaron and Brad had supported her, making her feel a genuine part of their team.

She went back to her empty house to change. Taylor had left for New York to pick up more clothes and personal items and to shut down her condo for the summer. So far, she hadn't heard anything from Whitney as to when or even if she would return to New Hampshire. She understood the stress her sister was under and didn't want to push it.

Pirate greeted her with a wagging tail and a whimper of welcome. She couldn't help smiling. After living alone, it was touching to be greeted like that.

Dani went to her room and changed into jeans, a T-shirt, and work boots. She was going to meet Brad at the cottage to discuss in detail what materials they would need to begin construction before going to meet with Garth to cost it out.

She put Pirate in her car and took off.

As she pulled up to the cottage, Dani saw Brad's red truck in the driveway and let out a sigh of relief. She wouldn't want to admit it to her sisters, but she was glad Brad would be with her to do a more in-depth analysis of the interior. She told herself she didn't believe in ghosts, but she'd felt something inside that had made her uncomfortable.

She picked up her leather notebook, got out of her car, and walked to the house. Pirate kept pace with her as far as the front porch, stopped, and then took off. Dani watched him race away and spied a rabbit hopping frantically in front of him. She prayed the rabbit would be safe and stepped inside.

"Hello?" she called. "Where are you?"

"In the kitchen," came Brad's reply.

He was leaning against a counter writing on a clipboard when she entered the room. She approached him, felt something behind her, tripped, and fell forward.

Brad moved quickly and held onto her while she struggled to get her balance.

"I didn't know you were so anxious to see me," he teased, steadying her on her feet.

She felt her cheeks grow hot. "I swear I don't know what happened. Just got clumsy, I guess. Thanks for catching me."

His gaze rested on her. "Anytime."

"I've taken measurements of the cabinet space on the walls, including inside the pantry after taking down the wall. We'll need a list of what you want in the way of cabinets and drawers."

"We'll use all the space we can in the island for drawers and cabinets. It will be large enough to provide plenty of storage even with the sink and dishwasher there," said Dani.

"We'll mark the outside walls reserved for the new stove and ovens and storage and counter space around them," said Brad. He stopped and smiled at her. "I like what you're doing to rearrange the space."

"Thanks. It's not going to be large, but it will efficiently take care of everything," said Dani. Her eyes widened at a shadow drifting across the room. She blinked again and it was gone.

"What's wrong?" Brad asked her.

"Nothing," Dani said. She glanced outside and saw big puffy clouds playing hide and seek with the sun, spreading shadows around, and told herself to stop being so fanciful.

After they worked in the kitchen area, which included a new dining/writing nook, pantry, laundry/mudroom, and a small powder room, they moved on to the living room and dining room, measuring for wood baseboard and crown molding.

They determined that they needed to replace all windows with double-glazed sashes.

"As you know, that alone will be expensive, but well worth it in this climate," said Brad.

They measured the windows and made a note to research replacement styles that would be compatible with the fundamental building design and character. Going over the list so far, Dani was sure the improvements would require her and her sisters to put in some money of their own. She hoped Taylor and Whitney would be willing to do so.

By the time they finished with the downstairs, it was too late to see well on the second floor. "Guess we'd better come back tomorrow. I'm busy in the early morning, but I can meet you here by eleven," said Brad after checking his phone.

"Fine. I'm glad we're taking our time with this part of it," she said. "Every renovation project I've ever worked on has cost more money than planned, and I want to be as close to the right number as possible."

"Yeah, me, too," said Brad.

"Speaking of renovations," said Dani, "it looks like you've done a beautiful job on your house. It's really cute."

"It's helpful to be handy," said Brad. "One of the first things I did when I got enough money to buy the house was to begin to renovate it one room at a time. It sometimes drove Patti crazy, but it's been well worth it."

"That's what I hope for this house," said Dani. She zipped up her leather folder and waved. "I'll see you tomorrow."

"I'll walk out with you," said Brad.

As they headed to the front door together, Brad stumbled forward, and Dani caught his arm.

He shook his head. "These floors are dangerous. Can't wait until they're redone."

"They're going to be so handsome sanded, stained, and refinished," she replied.

Outside, Pirate was stretched out on the grass asleep, but he jumped up when they stepped onto the porch. He waited until they were heading for the cars and pranced around them, eager for attention.

Laughing, Dani hugged him. "Such a love," she murmured, and looked up to find Brad's gaze on her.

That evening, rather than sitting home alone, Dani decided to go to Jake's for a salad and company. It was the kind of establishment where anyone dining alone would be comfortable.

The bar was crowded when she showed up. She grabbed a seat at the bar not recognizing the person beside her until she settled her purse on a hook below the counter of the bar and glanced up.

"Hi, Quinn," she said. "Nice to see you again."

"Thanks. Dani, right?"

"Right." She smiled. "I'm with the brothers from Collister Construction."

The bartender, a young woman she didn't know, took her order, and turned to Quinn. "Now that your date is here, do you want another IPA?"

He and Dani blinked in surprise at one another and then Quinn said, "My date should be here in a minute. But in the meantime, let me buy a drink for my friend, Dani."

It was the bartender's turn to blink with surprise. "Oh, sorry ..."

"Not a problem," said Quinn smoothly.

"When she arrives, I'll gladly move to another seat," Dani said to him.

"No worries. Liam is in contention to manage the inn when it's completed, and I wanted him to get a feel for the area. Sort of like what we were talking about this morning."

"Oh, that'll be useful," said Dani with understanding.

The bartender delivered Dani's red wine and Quinn's beer, and then Dani said, "Setting does make a big difference. I'm glad to see you're open to the new suggestions we proposed."

"Makes all the sense in the world." Quinn turned as a tall, handsome man approached. With light-brown hair naturally frosted by the sun and sparkling topaz eyes in a fine-featured face, he filled the area with his presence.

Quinn stood and clapped the man on the back. "Glad you could make it. Meet Dani Gilford, the granddaughter of the woman who sold us the inn. She's working with Collister Construction as an architectural consultant. Dani, this is Liam Richards."

Dani shook Liam's hands and got to her feet. "I'll find another place," she said, glancing around.

"No, no," said Liam. "I'm fine standing. The couple on the other side of Quinn is close to leaving. He's looking over the check."

Quinn lifted his arm for service and the bartender came right over. "Another IPA?"

"Yes, and one for my friend."

The bartender flashed a smile at Liam and said, "I'll be right back with it."

"Do you live here?" Liam asked her.

Dani chuckled. "Yes and no. I've moved here for the summer and hope to stay beyond that time. But I still have a condo in Boston."

"I just finished managing a property in Florida, and I'm anxious to try living in New England. It's a whole different feel, but I like it."

"This is a beautiful area," said Dani. "My sisters and I spent summers here growing up. Like you, I'm eager to try living here."

Liam looked at Quinn with affection. "We're going to see how it works out."

"We want to be able to use this time together to plan for the future," Quinn explained. "We're keeping the place in Florida but summers there are hot, so being up north is a pleasant break."

The couple next to Quinn got up, and he quickly grabbed a stool for Liam as Brad walked over to them. Quinn took control of the other free barstool.

"Hi. Have a seat," said Quinn. He moved down the row of bar stools, giving Brad the empty seat next to Dani, and then introduced him to Liam.

"What's everyone having?" Brad said. Quinn held up his glass.

The bartender came over, and Brad ordered an IPA before turning to Dani. "Long time, no see."

She laughed. "Taylor is away, so instead of eating alone, I'm here for dinner."

"Yeah, eating alone is the pits," he said. He turned to Quinn. "Thanks for being so open this morning. The new inn is going to be beautiful. We can't wait to get started on it."

"As soon as all the approvals and permitting are in place, we'll begin," said Quinn. "And Liam, here, is going to manage it, I hope."

"Yeah? What other hotels and inns have you managed?" Brad asked politely.

"I've just come from a boutique property in Miami Beach,"

said Liam, "but I'm excited about possibly running the inn."

"I'm sure they're happy to have you on board," said Brad. He turned to Dani. "Do you want to order dinner here and take it to my house?"

Dani's pulse raced but she calmly said, "I'd like that."

A short while later, Dani sat in Brad's kitchen eating her salad opposite him at the kitchen table. She was delighted to be able to see what Brad had done to the interior of the house. The exterior was in excellent condition, and she was pleased to see the same amount of care had been taken with the upgrades to the kitchen. A wall containing a pass-through to the living room had been torn down, opening the kitchen up, making much of the first floor an open space. What once may have been a small dining room was being used for a den with a large television mounted on the wall along with bookcases holding books and musical and gaming equipment. Seeing how different Brad's house was compared to Margaret's, she realized how naturally Brad used space. For some reason, that was important to her.

"So, you like what I've done with the house?" Brad said.

"Yes. That makes me excited to work on the caretaker's cottage," said Dani. "I'm looking forward to our inspection of the second floor tomorrow."

"I like getting everything down in writing. Renovation work always comes with a few surprises. I'm sure we'll find a few there."

"As long as it's not Mrs. Maynard's ghost, I can deal with it," said Dani.

Brad laughed. "That's nothing but an old wives' tale. I just meant surprises like termites."

"Oh, my god! Have you seen any signs of them?" said Dani.

He shook his head. "Not yet, but I'll keep looking for them

and anything else that could be trouble."

"It's too bad the house has stayed empty for so long. It's like entering a time capsule of the '50s."

"As much as I don't like the décor of the place, I admire the workmanship back then. That's what makes the cottage so special."

"Are you working on other projects with older homes?" Dani asked him.

"No. As a matter of fact, Aaron and I are partners with others in a development that's underway at the other end of the lake. It's all new housing, but the difference between our houses and some others is the quality of finishes we're putting in throughout."

"Oh, I like that," said Dani. "I'd love to take a look."

"I'd like that, too. The first couple of houses have been well received, but people have already suggested a few changes in the plans. That's where I think you could make a big difference for us."

Excitement rolled through Dani. "Making someone's dreams come true is thrilling. If I can be of any help, I'd love to be a part of that."

"No wonder your grandmother wanted you on the renovation team for the cottage. She's very proud of you, you know."

"Thanks," said Dani. She wasn't famous like her sisters, but she took pride in her work.

After they finished their meal, Dani rose to clean up.

Brad stopped her. "I can get that later. Come on outside. I want to show you something."

He led her out to the sizeable back yard enclosed by a white picket fence like the one in front of the house. "I'm thinking of putting in a small gazebo in the southeast corner. A place to relax, maybe with a hammock, maybe even with screening so there would be no problems with black flies and other critters. What do you think?"

Dani stared at the empty space, gazed around it, closed her eyes, and imagined the transformation. "I'd go with something simpler. Maybe even put in an outdoor kitchen. Or add a screened-in porch to the back of the house. It would give a sense of increased space and be much more convenient."

They stood together and studied the back of the house.

"We could tie in the roof lines quite easily," Brad said. "I guess I was thinking of a gazebo because Patti always wanted one."

"It's a decision you'll have to make. But if you're open to other ideas, I'd go even further, and instead of doing a screened-in porch in the back, with the back of the house having a southern exposure, I'd add a sunroom that could be opened up for warm months and heated during the cold ones. I've seen pictures of some I love."

"I really like that. New Hampshire is cool or cold a lot of the year," said Brad. "And a sunroom would make the house even more livable."

"How many bedrooms do you have upstairs?" Dani asked.

"A master and two smaller ones," Brad answered. "It's a comfortable house and a super location so close to town."

"I agree," said Dani. "I can walk to town from here."

"Thanks for your input. It's something I can work on in the fall. Maybe start it, and once it's closed in, finish the interior during the winter when not too much is going on." Brad turned to her. "I'm happy we're working together on the cottage. You and I think a lot alike."

"I'm happy about it too." She couldn't stop a sigh from escaping. "I'm used to working with someone in my office who'd try to find a way to rip apart what I suggested. It's lovely to be heard."

Brad chuckled. "If I didn't agree with you, I'd let you know, but there's no need to be mean about it."

Dani felt her lips curve. Leaving the office might be the best decision she'd made in a long time.

They headed indoors.

"Thanks for sharing a meal with me," said Brad. "It was a pleasant change."

"I enjoyed it too. I'd better go check on Pirate. I'm leaving him alone in the house for short periods of time until I'm sure he's used to it. When Taylor returns, it'll be easier because she'll be spending so much time at the house writing."

"Let's see...an architect, an author, and a television star. No wonder Ms. Wittner is so proud of you."

"She's pretty impressive herself," said Dani, pleased.

Brad walked her to the door. "Okay. I'll see you tomorrow morning at the cottage around eleven."

"Yes." Dani could feel herself being drawn into his dark-green eyes.

They continued to stare at one another and then Brad turned and opened the door.

CHAPTER EIGHTEEN
DANI

The next morning, just before eleven o'clock, Dani loaded Pirate into her car and took off for the cottage. She could've gone earlier but decided to wait for Brad so she wouldn't be at the house by herself.

As she pulled into the driveway, she saw Brad's truck parked in front of the garage, and she let out a puff of relief. She knew she'd have to get used to being alone at the cottage, but if there was such a thing as a ghost, she wanted to give it time to get used to new activity and leave.

Dani parked the car, grabbed her notebook, let the dog out, and walked around the house to the front porch.

The door was open.

She walked inside and hearing a noise upstairs, called out to Brad. "I'm here."

Brad walked out of the kitchen. "Hello, there."

The way his gaze settled on her sent a shiver of awareness through her. Maybe she hadn't imagined his attraction to her.

"I was looking at the initial sketches for the kitchen. After talking last night, I wanted to check to see why we couldn't add a screened-in porch or sunroom off the kitchen here."

"I thought of that, too. That's something we can add on to our plans after we establish how much the initial project will cost. I have no idea how much my grandmother has set aside for this renovation. My sisters and I may add something to the amount, but again, we have no information on what might be needed."

"Let's take a look upstairs and maybe we'll have a better idea," said Brad.

Dani followed him up to the second floor.

"Let's start here," said Brad, heading to one of the smaller bedrooms.

She entered the room behind him. It was a clean space with a window facing the lake and one facing the side yard. The only other feature was a small closet they would need to enlarge, leaving enough room for a king bed, bedside tables, and a bureau. She stood at the front window a moment, looking out at the lake.

Brad fell against her back.

She whipped around and propped him up. "What???"

"Sorry. I wasn't looking where I was going and didn't see you there."

They stood face to face, staring at one another. Sexual tension filled the room.

Brad wrapped his arms around her and kissed her. It was tentative at first, then grew deeper.

Dani melted in his arms, forgetting everything but how perfect it felt to be like this with him. When she opened her eyes, she saw little sparkles in the air, blinked, and they were gone, leaving her filled with the magic of their kiss.

"I don't know why I'm so clumsy here at the house," Brad said. His lips curved. "But I'm glad that happened."

Dani's smile rose out of her in a burst of happiness. "Me, too. The kiss, not the fall, I mean," and they both laughed, easing the sexual tension for a moment before he leaned forward to kiss her again.

She eagerly met his lips, loving the feel of them, the taste of him.

When they pulled apart, Brad captured her face with his strong hands. His fingers were rough from his work, but his touch was gentle. "I really like you, Dani, but I don't want to rush into anything."

"Me either," said Dani, lying to herself. She was ready for more than a kiss. "I understand you haven't done much dating."

"I've been waiting for the right woman," Brad said, stepping away from her. "But let's not have regrets."

Dani nodded her agreement, but she didn't want to think about something so special being wrong.

They went back to work taking measurements of the rooms on the second floor, making notes on each room, and finished in time for a late lunch.

"Do you want to grab a bite to eat in town?" she asked Brad.

He shook his head. "Sorry, I can't. I'm meeting Melissa Hendrickson for lunch at Fins. It was arranged a while ago."

"Oh, okay. I'll order takeout from the café and go home to start drawing up schematics for this project. In the next day or two, I'll visit your development at the end of the lake. What are you calling it?"

"The Meadows. You'll see why. The land was part of a large farm at one time."

"Lovely," said Dani. She waited for Brad to get his things and then locked up the cottage still thinking of his kisses.

"Pirate!" she called, and he came bounding out of the woods, his tongue lolling back as he ran to her.

Brad walked her to her car and then went to his truck. She waved to him, loaded Pirate in the car, and drove away filled with dreamy thoughts. Then she scolded herself. As much as she liked the thought of being with Brad, she needed to be cautious. He was still thinking of building a gazebo because it was something his wife had wanted. She didn't resent that fact, but she knew it was a warning to go slow.

###

She parked at the café and went inside to pick up her food.

She saw Rachael seated by the window and waved before going to the counter to place and pay for her fish sandwich to go.

Rachael walked up to her. "Hi, Dani. Just a quick question. Is Brad available? I'd like to ask him out, but I thought he might be dating someone. I figured you'd know, as you're working together. I'll be spending some time here this summer, and Brad seems like a great guy. He sure is cute."

"Oh, yes," said Dani, wondering what she should say. It wasn't up to her to decide if Brad was free. They'd only kissed once. Well, twice. Actually three times.

"Your sandwich is ready," said Crystal, catching Dani's attention.

She turned back to Rachael. "I think that's a question you'd better ask him." Dani took the bag Crystal was holding out to her and left, too confused by her feelings to want to stay and talk to Rachael.

Back at her house, Dani was unsettled. The thought of attractive, wealthy Rachael dating Brad made her insides squeeze with apprehension.

She let Pirate out to the back yard, checked his water dish, and then sat at the kitchen bar to eat her sandwich. Her cell rang. *Whitney.*

Dani eagerly clicked onto the call, glad for the diversion. "Hi, how are you?"

"I'm hanging in there," said Whitney with a sigh. "Some of my best acting is being done as I complete the show with Zane. Just a few weeks and I might be able to return to Lilac Lake."

"Have you been able to talk to the people out there?" Dani asked her.

"I've spoken to my agent and then to Zane. But that didn't

go well."

"How are the episodes of the show coming along?" Dani asked her, alarmed by the pain in Whitney's voice.

"Fine. I think the cast has learned to play off one another in a more natural style," said Whitney, sounding more upbeat. "What's going on there?"

"Brad and I have gone through the cottage taking measurements and making notes for each room. I'm just about to begin drawing schematics. Then we'll get the cost numbers and go from there. It's a long process, but it's worth it to be careful."

"Seems as if you have everything under control," said Whitney. "I'm not surprised."

"Well, there is one thing I have no control over." Dani stopped and then blurted, "I'm falling for Brad in a big way."

"As soon as I met him and saw the two of you together talking about the family pictures you were taking from the inn, I thought that might happen. Maybe not quite so soon."

"That's it. I've agreed we can't move quickly, and now Rachael McPherson is interested in dating him. She even asked me if he was available."

"What did you tell her?"

"I said that's something she'd have to ask him," said Dani. "Was that a stupid thing to do?"

"If he was really interested in you, it shouldn't be a problem. Everything is so brand new, it wouldn't hurt for him to date her and see for himself how wonderful you are," said Whitney. "But I feel your pain."

"Thanks, I think." Dani drew a deep breath. "He hasn't dated much since his wife died two years ago. Maybe I'm just a test to see if he's ready to see other women."

"That doesn't sound like the man GG thinks the world of," said Whitney. "And he seemed straightforward when talking about the house."

"You're right," said Dani. "I need just to let things play out. But you know how I've fallen too quickly for a guy in the past and how that turned out. That's what scares me."

"Speaking of scaring, any sign of Mrs. Maynard?"

Dani laughed. "I'm not certain. But I don't like the idea of being there alone until after we get a work crew in. They'll chase any ghost away."

Whitney laughed. "Thanks for making me feel better. I've got to go."

They ended the call and Dani sat back. She loved that she could talk to her sisters about anything.

Dani looked around the kitchen and decided to set up her "office" on the kitchen table and move it by the sliding glass door, so she'd have plenty of daylight to help her see. Drawing plans was slow, careful work, but it brought her satisfaction to create details of a room, a house, or a building. She'd loved drawing and coloring from a young age, but this was an entirely different discipline. And when moments of creativity appeared, she embraced them.

After setting up her drafting table, Dani set to work. These first schematic drawings would simply show the room layouts with their dimensions. Later, more details would be added to show plumbing, electrical and other requirements. For now, she wanted to see how the spacing worked and inter-room traffic would flow.

Her thoughts flew to Brad. She liked that he was creative too. She lifted her fingers to her lips, remembering his kisses, from sweet and tender to hot and passionate.

CHAPTER NINETEEN
TAYLOR

Taylor grabbed a cup of coffee and a bagel from a neighborhood coffee shop in New York City and carried them back to her condo. Her neighborhood offered several convenient places for meals from morning to night, and easy access to the subway system meant that she could conveniently meet with her editor and her agent. Still, Lilac Lake had something she'd been missing—a quiet contentment that crept into her bones when she looked out the window at woods and flowers instead of high-rise buildings, heard the sound of birds chirping and calling to one another instead of horns honking and auto alarms going off, or smelled the indefinable aroma of the lake and surrounding evergreens instead of automobile and diesel exhaust.

It was time for a change. After publishing ten books she needed a break from the worry that was stalking her. This worry was nothing new; it happened every time she started a new book—the fear that this book wouldn't be as well received as the last one. She'd talked to other authors and knew they suffered from the same insecurity as she.

Lilac Lake was full of new possibilities. She'd had a fun time going out with Aaron Collister. Though she wasn't certain yet how she felt about him being more than a friend, she'd experienced feelings she could use in a book. And if that's what it took to get her motivated, she'd happily see him again.

More than that, in Lilac Lake she felt as if she belonged.

People knew her from the time she had been a child spending summers there. And with her sisters and GG around, she had the family she wanted. Not that she didn't love her own parents. They were kind and loving, but they'd never really understood why she immersed herself in a world of her own creation instead of living in the real world. Taylor knew her writing was a form of escapism, but it was what she needed to overcome the shyness that had plagued her for as long as she could remember.

Her cell rang. *Her mother.*

"Hi, Mom. How are you? Is it hot in Atlanta?" she asked in her usual opening.

"Hi, darling. Yes, it's hot. So hot in fact that we're going to Jekyll Island earlier than normal for our annual stay. How are you doing?"

"Fine," Taylor replied. "I'm packing to go to Lilac Lake for the summer. Dani and I are renting a house. She's already moved in. I'll head there in a day or two."

"I talked to GG this morning and she's thrilled you girls will be there for the entire summer. I think it makes her feel young to have you around. I'm glad."

"I've always loved it there, and it'll be helpful to get away from the city for a while," said Taylor avoiding any mention of the problem she was having with her latest book. "Enjoy Jekyll and give Daddy a hug and a kiss for me and one for you too."

"And back to you, darling," said her mother before ending the call.

Taylor was relieved her mother didn't want to talk for long. She had a way of discovering Taylor's innermost thoughts, and right now, Taylor's mind was spinning with promise about more than books.

CHAPTER TWENTY
DANI

Dani was working on her drawings, caught up in the moment with dimensions and other measurements of rooms in the house, making notes on what changes might work when Pirate barked and raced to the front door.

Dani checked the time and was shocked to see it was past five. She got up and went to the door.

Brad was standing there. He smiled when he saw her. "Hi. May I come in?"

"Sure," she replied, opening the door for him. "I was working in the kitchen on some of the initial plans for the cottage."

"That's why I'm here. I got to thinking about the additional room suggestions you gave me for my house, and I'm wondering if I could hire you to draw up plans for it. The more I think about it, your suggestion makes all the sense in the world. I can get a foundation poured from the guys who are doing the work at The Meadows, and Garth will work with me on lumber and other building supplies."

"You've really thought this through," said Dani, impressed.

He grinned. "Once I make up my mind about something, I'm set."

Dani laughed. "I guess so." She led him into the kitchen and took out her sketch pad. "Let's begin with the arrangement of space."

They tossed ideas back and forth, and an hour later, they both agreed the basic plan they'd drawn up was perfect. The sunroom with an outdoor kitchen opened through French doors to a fire pit with seating around it on a patio of brick pavers. Skylights in the ceiling that could be opened for ventilation would supplement the screened windows overlooking the back yard. It was an ambitious decision but would completely change the living style at the house.

"It's late. Why don't I buy you dinner?" said Brad. "We could go to Fins. Melissa says she owes me a dinner for talking to her about possibly building a house at The Meadows. That's why I met her for lunch. Now, Rachael McPherson wants to meet with me. Something about the spa they're going to build."

Dani pressed her lips together, warning herself to say nothing. It was Brad's business who he met and why. The trouble was, he didn't seem to realize those two wanted more than information from him. Still, she couldn't and wouldn't say a word. Now that Brad was starting to get out more, he had a lot to discover on his own.

"Well, what do you say?" Brad said.

"Dinner at Fins sounds perfect. Their food is delicious."

"I'll give the restaurant a call and then we can go."

"Give me a few minutes to change," Dani said. She knew everyone in town would be staring at them, and she was vain enough to want to look her best.

He called the restaurant and turned to her. "Okay, I'll meet you back here in let's say fifteen minutes?"

She chuckled. "Okay." It normally would take her more than fifteen minutes to get properly showered, dressed, and polished for an evening out. Still, it was that naivete that made Brad so appealing.

After feeding Pirate, she raced up to the bathroom, washed her face, and hurried into the bedroom to change into a pair of black pants and a silver sweater that looked especially attractive with the silver earrings she was wearing.

She'd just finished putting mascara on when the doorbell rang. Smiling, she went to answer it, feeling as if she'd just won a marathon.

Brad looked her over and let out a long, slow whistle. "You clean up nice."

She laughed. If any of the men in the office had ever said that to her, she'd take offense, but coming from him it sounded cute.

The restaurant was starting to fill up when Dani walked through the doorway. Susan Hendrickson, acting as hostess, came over to them. "I've saved a lovely table for you, Brad. Melissa told me she had a productive meeting with you."

"Thanks," Brad said, indicating Dani should follow Susan to their table.

Dani sat in the chair Susan offered her.

Susan helped Brad into his seat and beamed at him. "It's so exciting that you and Melissa are working on her project together, building a lovely home for the future."

"Yes. It's going to be beautiful," Brad replied.

"I'm sure it will be," said Susan, lingering a moment as she continued to smile at him.

After she left, Brad said, "It's important that we have interest in the development from the locals, and Melissa and her mother will be busy spreading the word," Brad said.

"Yes, they will," agreed Dani.

They were looking over their menus when Rachael walked into the restaurant. Seeing them, she came right over.

"There you are, Brad. I've been trying to reach you. May I join you?"

Brad glanced at Dani. "You don't mind?"

"Not at all," she said, doing her best to hide her

disappointment. Had her meeting with her in the café given Rachael the wrong impression about her feelings for Brad? The thought of Rachael eating with them didn't seem to bother Brad at all.

Dani remained quiet as Rachael talked with Brad about the inn and other things, waiting in vain for an opportunity to join in. Rachael seemed determined to prevent her from doing so.

Rachael leaned closer to him. "I'm hoping now that I'm alone in Lilac Lake, we'll spend some time together. It's important to our project that we have a clear understanding of how we want the plans to unfold."

"Aaron and I are available to help anytime with you and your partners," said Brad pleasantly though he was frowning slightly.

Rachael's lips curved. "That's what I'm hoping. But it's really you I want to work with."

"Aaron and I maintain close contact, so he can help you as well as I can," said Brad crisply. "We'll do our best to keep you informed as we would any client."

Observing Rachael lean toward Brad with her hand on his arm, Dani's stomach clenched. How often had her mother called her a dreamer for thinking that wishes could come true by simply hoping they would. She'd thought she and Brad had something special between them, but she now realized it wasn't more than simple attraction. He'd been wounded by his wife's death, and she'd understood that he wasn't ready for anything serious. At least, not with her.

The meal seemed to last forever as Rachael dominated the conversation, facing Brad most of the time. He gave Dani a look of concern but was forced to answer Rachael's questions.

When at last the meal was at its end, Dani stood. "Thank you for dinner, Brad, but I need to get home. I forgot to enclose Pirate in the kitchen, and I can't leave him for too

"I'll drive you home," said Brad, jumping to his feet, a look of relief on his face.

"Thanks, but I think I'll walk. It's still early, and I need the exercise." She knew he was unhappy with her decision to leave but she'd had enough.

"Okay, if you're sure. See you later, neighbor," he said and turned to the waitress who'd approached him.

Dani made her way to the entrance, wishing she could run, not walk. At the doorway, she stopped and turned to see Brad and Rachael continuing their conversation.

Swallowing her emotions, she stepped outside and started along the sidewalk, relieved her house was within walking distance of the center of town. She couldn't spend another moment being an onlooker to the way Rachael had carried on with Brad. But then, she'd let her imagination carry her away, allowed herself to believe that apart from her old work environment she could begin a whole different life, maybe even find a man to love. She'd been in Lilac Lake only a short time, but it was long enough to warn her not to be foolish. Especially where a man was concerned.

When she walked into the house, Pirate greeted her with his tail between his legs. It took only a moment to find out why he was acting so guilty. The quilt from the top of her bed, something she'd had for a long time, lay in the middle of the living room, a corner shredded.

"Pirate! What have you done?"

He slithered toward her on his belly and gave her a woeful look.

Dani ignored him and walked over to the quilt. Holding it up for him to see, she shook a finger at him. "Bad Dog."

He studied her for a moment and then bounded over and

looked up at her with adoring eyes.

After the horrible evening she had, Dani couldn't help reaching out and rubbing his ears, no doubt confusing the dog. But his look of love was too soothing to ignore.

"C'mon, let's put you outside in the back."

Pirate followed her outside, and while he went about sniffing and doing his business, Dani drew deep breaths of the fresh air. Though she felt better, Dani reminded herself that the only thing she needed to concentrate on this summer was renovation of the cottage. She liked working with Brad, liked his manner, but even though she was attracted to him, that's as far as she could afford to let it go.

Back inside, she was checking out the damage to her quilt when the doorbell rang. She knew who it was before she answered it.

"Are you okay?" Brad asked her. "Is Pirate all right?"

"He's chewed my favorite quilt but otherwise things seem okay."

"Will you go to Jake's with Rachael and me? We're meeting Liam there. I'd really like you to join us."

"Thanks, but no. As a matter of fact, I had some new ideas at dinner and want to make notes on them. But have fun!"

He studied her. "Okay. See you later."

She watched him walk to his truck and then closed the door behind her. Tears blurred her vision. She blinked with determination and vowed to move forward with her new life without him in it as more than a friend. Even as disappointment raged inside her, she realized it was the right thing to do. He was just beginning to move beyond the past. He deserved to do it freely. Still, it hurt.

Taylor's arrival in Lilac Lake made Dani feel much better. She helped her sister carry in luggage and other belongings, pleased Taylor would fill the emptiness she'd felt being alone in the house.

They chatted happily as they lugged Taylor's things to the master bedroom upstairs, which was now serving as Taylor's office as well.

"After I get settled, let's go to the café for lunch," said Taylor setting her computer carefully on the desk. "I've been thinking about their spring salad and homemade biscuits the entire drive here."

Dani chuckled. "I'll wait for you downstairs and work on plans until you're ready."

Pirate followed her down the stairs.

"Time for you to go outside and play," said Dani. "I don't want you to get into Taylor's things. You have plenty of new chew toys and balls to play with."

As if he understood her, Pirate happily went outside. She realized she'd begun talking to him and laughed at herself.

Not long after, Taylor came downstairs. "Okay, I'm ready. Let's go. You drive. I'm tired of that."

"Deal," said Dani. It would do her good to get out of the house. It had been a couple of days since the disastrous dinner with Brad and Rachael at Fins.

It was another blue-sky day, warm but not hot, and a perfect time to sit out on the patio at the café. They grabbed a free table in the shade and sat.

"It's nice having you back here," Dani said to Taylor. "I'm glad we have this summer to spend time together. We've seen each other mostly at holidays and special events these last few years."

Taylor grinned. "Nothing like sharing a house together to get real. After thinking I did my best writing alone, I now understand that being around people helps keep my mind active on things other than my book. I think it'll make for better stories."

A shadow crossed their table.

Dani looked up to find Rachael approaching and stiffened.

"Dani. Just the person I hoped to see. I wanted to thank you for leaving me alone with Brad the other night. That was so sweet of you to give us the chance to get together. I've enjoyed his company so much these last few days."

"That's nice," Dani said, aware she was lying. But the last thing she wanted anyone to realize was how she'd thought that she and Brad might have a future together. Even now, thinking of it, a flush of heat colored her cheeks.

"Well, I'm off. Hope to see you around," Rachael said, looking gorgeous in a floral sundress and wearing a floppy straw hat that made her seem sophisticated.

After she left, Dani closed her eyes, drew in a deep breath, and let it out in a long sigh.

"What was that all about?" said Taylor, giving her a look of concern.

Dani lowered her voice and told Taylor the story of that horrible evening.

Taylor studied her. "I know you well enough to realize that the situation was awkward." She squinted her eyes and studied her. "You were falling for him."

Dani made a face and nodded. She held up a hand to stop Taylor from saying more.

"My bad," said Dani, wanting to leave it at that.

CHAPTER TWENTY-ONE
TAYLOR

Taylor observed the hurt and disappointment on Dani's face and decided to drop the topic of Brad. She knew Dani's story was a lesson for her, too. For someone who wrote a lot about romance, she didn't have that much experience. Oh, she'd had plenty of chances to date and she'd gone out with a few men, but never let it get serious. New York seemed to be full of men struggling to make it, always on the go, or men who had enough money to be bored but too settled in their lives to change. She was waiting for her special prince.

Taylor and Dani ordered their salads, biscuits, and iced tea and settled back in their chairs.

Nick walked out onto the patio in his sheriff's uniform. After looking around the crowded space and seeing them, he approached.

Smiling, he bobbed his head. "Mind if I join you two ladies? The other tables are filled."

Taylor smiled up at him. "Sure, have a seat. I'm resting and getting some of my favorite food after making the drive from New York."

"Are you here to stay for a while?" he asked her.

"For at least the summer," Taylor replied, reminding herself to breathe after his blue-eyes settled on her.

"That's great," Nick said and turned to Dani. "I heard you're renting Marjorie Hight's house. She called to tell me, so I could keep an eye on it."

Dani raised her right hand and gave him a playful grin. "I

promise Taylor and I will take care of it."

Nick laughed. "When is Whitney coming back?"

"Not for a while," Dani said. "She's filming the show."

"It'd sure be nice to have all you Gilford girls here," Nick said. "I remember what it was like being together when we were young."

Crystal came out with their order. "Hey, Nick. Heard you were going into Boston for a Red Sox game tonight. Have fun."

They studied each other for a moment, and then Crystal handed out Dani and Taylor's lunches, deftly holding onto the tray. "I'll bring you your sandwich," she said to Nick and left.

"It's amazing you and Crystal are still friends," Taylor said, unable to stop herself. She was curious to see how it worked, if she could put something like it in a book.

Nick shrugged. "We like each other a lot so long as we're not married to one another. You can't walk away from a marriage unless love has turned to hate or you realize it was never meant to be. Hate has no place in my life."

Taylor sighed, realizing she might have just met a true prince of a man.

CHAPTER TWENTY-TWO
DANI

The next morning as Dani drove to the cottage to meet Brad, nerves made her swallow hard. She'd made up her mind to shut down her growing feelings for him, knowing heartbreak was just ahead. He was a good man who wasn't ready for what she wanted. Her timing had always sucked.

Brad's truck was already in the driveway when she pulled up beside it and parked. She got out of her car, let Pirate out, and headed for the front door.

She stepped inside the house and called to him.

"Upstairs," he answered.

She went to the bottom of the steps and was about to climb them when Brad came tumbling down the stairway toward her.

Dani shrieked and held out her arms to try and stop his fall, but the force of his body knocked her off her feet. When she was able to sit up, she saw Brad crumpled beside her.

His eyes fluttered open, and he gazed at her in a daze. "Patti?"

"Brad, it's me, Dani. You've had a fall," she said cupping his face in her hands to check his eyes. "Are you hurt anywhere?"

She studied his body as he moved his legs and arms. All seemed fine.

"All right. Let's have you sit up. I think we should go to the emergency care center outside of town and have you examined."

"Okay," Brad said, surprising her with no pushback. "Something's weird. I swear I was pushed down the stairs."

Goosepimples, like giant ants, raced down Dani's back. She whipped around, studying their surroundings, praying she wouldn't see a ghost. Thoughts flew through her mind. *Would a female ghost, Mrs. Maynard, do something to hurt them? Not unless she was angry. But wait! Ghosts aren't real. They're part of someone's imagination. Right?* She looked down at Brad and her body turned cold. She had to get them out of there.

Dani managed to get Brad to his feet, and they walked a bit unsteadily to the door and out onto the porch. Pirate looked up at them from the lawn, waited for them to descend the stairs, and then bounded over to them. It occurred to Dani that Pirate had never entered the house. Did he sense something unusual inside?

Hurrying away as fast as she could, she led Brad to her car, and after getting both him and Pirate settled in it, she slid behind the wheel. On her way into town earlier, she'd noticed the emergency care center, so she knew exactly where to go.

She pulled up to the front of the building and parked.

"Okay, we're here," she said to Brad. "Let's go inside and have someone examine you. You've got a couple of bad bumps for them to inspect."

Brad shook his head. "No, I'm all right. Let's go home."

Dani turned to him. "I have to make sure you're all right. What happened is pretty scary in more ways than one."

She got out of the car, went around to his side, and opened the door.

Moving stiffly, Brad stepped onto the pavement and allowed her to take him inside.

Brad registered with the receptionist, then took a seat in the waiting room beside her.

When his name was called, Brad turned to her. "Maybe you'd better come with me. I don't remember anything about it."

"You told me you were pushed down the stairs. Is that true?" she said.

He shook his head. "How could that happen? No one was there. I tripped again. That's all it was."

"Okay," said Dani. She followed him into the examination room and stood aside while the doctor checked him over. "You've got a bit of a goose egg on your head, but your eyes look fine, your responses are normal. I see no need to worry, but I do suggest you rest for the remainder of the day. You're a big strong guy, but your body has gone through trauma." He looked at Dani and back to Brad. "Maybe your girlfriend can keep an eye on you."

Brad shook his head and started to speak.

Dani cut him off. "We're just neighbors."

Brad looked at her and away. "Just friends."

A stab of disappointment hurt Dani, but she shook it off and instead said goodbye to the doctor and helped Brad to the car. "The doctor said you could have some Tylenol when needed. Do you have some at your house?"

"I think so," said Brad. "Don't worry about it. I'll be fine."

On the way to his house, Brad called Aaron to tell him what happened. "I'm going to rest for a while and then I'll come to the site." He ended the call and turned to her. "Thanks for being there for me. Sometime later, I'll get my truck from the cottage. Aaron said he'd help me."

"Okay," Dani said. "I'll go back to work on plans at home. When you're ready we can meet at the house like we'd planned."

"Aaron said he'd meet you tomorrow morning to take care of it. Rachael and I have a meeting tomorrow." Brad gazed out the window, and she didn't say anything more until she pulled into his driveway.

"Are you going to be all right?" Dani asked him.

"Yes. Thanks. I appreciate your help." He climbed out of the car, gave her a wave, and went into his house.

Seeing that he was fine, Dani pulled away and drove next door. When she went inside, Taylor met her. "What's going on? I saw you pull into Brad's drive, then come here. Where's his truck?"

Dani let out a long sigh. "The strangest thing happened." She told Taylor about Brad's fall, the fact that he called out for Patti, and he'd told her someone had pushed him.

Taylor's eyes were as round as pies by the time Dani finished. "Oh, my god! Do you think it was Mrs. Maynard's ghost? Or even an evil spirit?"

"I don't believe in ghosts," said Dani, "but I've got some concerns. I've sensed something weird going on inside. I admit I was scared."

"Let's call Nick and have him check out the house for trespassers."

"Okay, then I'm going to ask GG what she knows about the old tales about Mrs. Maynard," said Dani, more upset than she wanted Taylor to know.

"You said Brad called out for Patti?" Taylor said.

"Yes. And he told the doctor we were just friends. It's important those feelings came out now because there's no way I want to get involved with Brad."

"I think that's smart of you," said Taylor giving her a quick hug. "No sense setting yourself up to get hurt." She stood by while Dani placed a call to the sheriff's office.

Once Nick came on the line, Dani started to explain what happened at the house, feeling foolish as Nick remained completely silent until she ended with, "and Taylor and I would appreciate it if you or one of your men would come and check out the house to make sure no vagrants are there."

"Did you see any signs of someone staying inside?" Nick asked.

"No, but something strange has been going on. Both Brad and I have felt something."

"Let's be sure there's nothing amiss. I was going to leave for lunch, but I'll swing by the cottage instead. Do you want to meet me there?"

"Okay. I'll ask Taylor to come with me," Dani said. "Thanks. We'll see you at the cottage in a few minutes." She ended the call and faced Taylor, who'd been hovering nearby.

"I need you to go with me, Taylor, even though I know you don't like being at the house."

Taylor let out a long sigh. "Okay, I'll do it for you. It'll give me a chance to see Nick in action."

Dani studied her sister. "Do I detect special interest there?"

Taylor's cheeks turned a pretty pink. "Maybe."

"Well, then, we'd better go," said Dani, amused by Taylor's reaction to her teasing. Maybe after writing all those sweet romances, her sister was going to find a hero of her own.

When she pulled up to the house, she noticed Brad's truck in the driveway where it had been earlier. The sheriff's black patrol car was parked next to it.

She pulled up behind the truck, and she and Taylor got out.

Nick emerged from his car looking strong and capable in his uniform. Knowing he'd look out for them, Dani felt more comfortable being back at the cottage.

"Hello, ladies," Nick said pleasantly. "Let's see what if anything I can find. You unlock the front door for me and stand outside. I'll go in and check things out."

"Thanks, Nick," said Taylor. "We'll all feel better if we're sure it's safe."

He grinned at her. "You don't believe in Mrs. Maynard's ghost, do you?"

"I'd prefer to think ghosts don't exist, but I'm open to the suggestion," said Taylor. "I know it seems silly, but I just don't want to deal with a ghost."

"Fair enough," he said, walking with them to the front door. "I'll make sure there are none."

Dani opened the door and stepped back. "Holler if you need me," she said bravely, heading down the porch steps to stand by Taylor who hadn't made any pretense of coming closer.

While they waited on the front lawn, Dani studied the house. With a fresh coat of paint and the interior renovated, it would be a gorgeous part-time home for her and her sisters.

As minutes passed, Dani began to grow concerned. How long should it take Nick to look around?

When he finally appeared on the front porch, Dani let out a breath she hadn't realized she'd been holding. "Everything, okay?" she called to him.

He walked down the steps to her. "I went through every room, every closet, and even the attic and found nothing of concern. It may be as Brad thinks, and he simply tripped. It can happen to anyone."

"Thank you for doing this for us. We want to be able to start renovating as soon as possible. I'm still working on initial schematics, but once those are agreed upon and electricians and plumbers have approved my plans, we can draw up the blueprints for everyone involved."

"Seems like you're going about it in a professional way," said Nick, looking impressed.

"GG knew we'd want to do it that way. The house itself deserves it," said Taylor.

"It's a relief to hear that," said Nick. "It's been a landmark at the lake for years."

"Please wait while I lock the front door, and we'll walk back to your car with you," said Dani, trying to hide her wariness. She couldn't forget the sight of Brad tumbling down the stairs.

CHAPTER TWENTY-THREE
TAYLOR

Standing beside Nick, Taylor observed his broad shoulders, the way his dark hair curled at the nape of his neck, and his long stride. She memorized each thing she liked about him because he was book material—a perfect hero.

"Are you going to lunch?" Nick asked her.

Flustered, she said, "With you?"

He shrugged. "Why don't the two of you join me at the café? It's quick and easy. I can ask Dani more questions there."

Taylor glanced at Dani.

"Sure, I can do that. I appreciate your help, Nick," said Dani.

They got in their cars and drove to the center of town. After living in New York City, Taylor loved the ease of getting to places so quickly. And there were so many interesting people to get to know in a town this size. Especially a certain sheriff.

CHAPTER TWENTY-FOUR
DANI

Dani was just returning from a walk with Pirate when she noticed the silver Mercedes parked behind Brad's truck in his driveway. Rachael's car. She'd seen her driving it around town.

Not wanting to be seen, Dani hurried toward her house. Living next door to Brad had seemed an ideal situation. Now, it made her uncomfortable. She didn't want him to think she was spying on him. He was free to do as he wanted, see who he wanted.

She was crossing her front yard when she heard someone call her name and turned.

Rachael waved to her and walked closer. "Thanks for helping Brad this morning after his fall. Both he and I appreciate it."

Rachael's tone and air of proprietorship irritated Dani. She barely managed to hide her frustration. "I was happy to do it."

"Yes, that's what good neighbors are for," said Rachael beaming at her. "Though Brad is taking it easy, I've brought him some soup."

A *good neighbor?* Dani forced a pleasant look on her face. "I'd better go. Time to feed Pirate."

Pirate, who was normally overly friendly, had stayed right at Dani's side, much to Dani's amusement. Dogs have a way of choosing which people to be with.

Dani went inside the house, closed the front door behind her, and leaned back against it. She had to get her complicated feelings about Brad under control. Just because she felt a connection between them didn't mean he experienced the same thing. In time, she'd get over her infatuation. She was glad Taylor was upstairs in her office and couldn't see the disappointment threading through her. Time to stop dreaming, Dani told herself.

The next morning, as agreed, Dani pulled up to the cottage for a meeting with Aaron. His silver truck rolled up behind her, and she breathed a sigh of relief that she wasn't alone. Common sense told her there was nothing to be afraid of, but then she'd seen what had happened to Brad.

She and Pirate got out of the car. She waited for Aaron to finish a phone call before he emerged from his truck. A little taller than Brad and with dark straight hair and deep-brown eyes, he was as handsome as his younger brother. His smile softened his sharp features.

"Let's hope I don't fall down the stairs like Brad," he quipped, and she laughed.

"Nick checked out the place yesterday and gave the house an all-clear verdict." She shrugged. "But I'm glad you're here. I wanted to go over spacing and plumbing and electrical ideas with you."

"No problem. I'm curious to see what you have in mind." He stood and studied her a moment. "Brad has told me how much your friendship means to him. He appreciates being able to talk openly with you about everything. He's coming out of his shell a bit more, and it's because of you."

Dani blinked in surprise. "Thanks. He's a special guy."

Aaron stared into space and turned back to her. "Just so you know, this thing with Rachael isn't going anywhere."

"Oh, but ..."

He held up a hand to stop her. "Trust me on this. Now, let's get to work."

They walked up to the front door. Aaron lifted the large key ring attached to his jeans and used one of the keys to open the door.

Dani waited until he stepped inside the house and then she followed him and looked around. Everything seemed peaceful.

Aaron held up a finger and then in a loud clear voice said, "We bring no harm."

In the quiet that followed, Dani whispered, "I didn't know you believe in ghosts."

"Spirits are a part of living whether we choose to recognize it or not. They are memories of people from the past. But my mother taught me to respect them. She was a descendent of the Abenaki tribe."

Dani had heard the story of his past and nodded. Two years older than Brad, Aaron had been just ten years old when his mother, dying from cancer, had dropped him off at the Collister's household, where neither his father nor anyone else had known about him. The family considered him a special gift, especially Brad because with two younger sisters, he was desperate for a brother.

"I like the thought that we respect those who came before us," said Dani, seeing him in a new light. No wonder Taylor had had such a fun time with him. They'd be perfect together. Not that she'd mention it. Taylor was presently mooning over Nick. There was something about a handsome man in a crisp uniform that was irresistible.

"Well, let's get started," said Aaron.

Dani handed him a set of the schematics she'd created. "I want to mark where electricity and plumbing should go. Then we'll be able to bid the work out."

"You'll probably want to use one of our sub-contractors for

the best price. Plus, we'll have them fit you into their schedules by working with them on the timing of projects at The Meadows."

"Perfect. We want the house completed before winter."

"Agreed," said Aaron.

In each room, they discussed the best places for electrical outlets, lighting, and switches, then drew up requirements for plumbing.

When they reached the door to the attic, Dani stood behind Aaron, as if he could protect her from Mrs. Maynard or another ghost who might remain in the house.

Aaron opened the door and stepped back as a rush of air swept past them.

"It's okay to go up," he said and climbed the stairs.

Light from the two windows filled the space, giving them a chance to see its possibilities. Dani hoped it would serve as a special area where she and her sisters could congregate – a family room of sorts. The view through the windows was spectacular, like a window on the world, she thought whimsically.

They took more measurements, discussed electrical requirements, talked about heating and cooling the space, and agreed a bathroom could be installed but at an added cost that might not be included in GG's budget.

"What is GG's budget for this?" Dani asked Aaron.

He shook his head. "Sorry, I can't tell you. It's a confidential agreement between Ms. Wittner, Brad, and me. It's how she wants it for now."

"Okay, I understand," said Dani, wondering why GG wanted to keep it a secret. She knew GG would have enough money set aside to cover all costs and didn't want them to cheap out anything. She and Taylor had intended to visit GG earlier to talk about Mrs. Maynard and were distracted. But this afternoon Dani vowed to make it happen.

At home, Dani placed the marked-up plans on her table in the kitchen and went to see what was in the refrigerator for lunch. She couldn't keep spending money on eating out every day.

She selected a container of yogurt and sat at her workspace eating it and thinking about what she'd need to do to update the plans. She liked putting together a plan layer by layer to make sure she wouldn't miss anything.

Taylor walked into the kitchen. "Did you have an interesting morning with Aaron?"

"Yes, he's such a cool guy. I really like him. After we walked into the house this morning, he spoke a message to the house, to settle any memories that might still be there."

"Really? How interesting," said Taylor. She pulled a chair over to her and sat down. "What did he say?"

" 'We bring no harm.' Isn't that a perfect thing to do? He doesn't believe in ghosts, but he honors the memories of other people."

Taylor grinned. "I love that. He's such an interesting man."

"More interesting than a certain sheriff?" teased Dani.

Taylor laughed. "There are so many intriguing people I'll have writing inspiration for several books."

"We didn't make it to see GG the other day, but let's do that now. I'll call her and see if it's a convenient time."

A few minutes later, they were on their way.

As she drove to The Woodlands, Dani thought of GG and wondered if her memory would continue to guide their family. Certainly, GG would always be a part of her, but would any children of hers know GG through her? Dani supposed they would if she talked about her. More than that, GG had done so many generous, unexpected things for people granting them wishes that her spirit extended far beyond the family.

She parked in front of the main building and walked with Taylor suddenly anxious to hug her grandmother.

When Dani walked into GG's room, GG was sitting in a chair dabbing at her eyes with a tissue.

"What's wrong?" Dani cried, rushing toward her.

GG looked up at her. "It's only a movie on television. I've always been a sucker for a sweet romance."

Dani bent down and kissed GG's cheek. "Glad it's not something more than that."

"Me, too," said GG, smiling at her and accepting a kiss from Taylor. "Now what are you two up to?"

"We're here to talk about Mrs. Maynard," said Taylor taking a seat on the couch next to GG.

Dani sat in a side chair facing her grandmother. "An incident with Brad took place at the cottage. At first, he swore someone pushed him down the stairs, then he said he tripped. But, GG, something weird is going on there."

"We had Nick walk through the house checking for vagrants, and he said there's no sign of anyone living there," said Taylor.

GG sat quietly for a moment. "Well, you know I don't believe in ghosts, but I don't discount stories of other people seeing them. What do you want to know about Mrs. Maynard? Any story that she might be a ghost is just town talk, nothing more. It was horribly sad that she died outside the house alone, but there was no foul play or anything beyond natural causes to make people suspect it."

"But what about her family? Why was she alone?" asked Dani.

"After Addie Maynard's husband died, she had to leave the

manse the local church had provided them so a new minister could move in. I offered to have Addie and her daughter, Rita, stay at the cottage. By then, I'd decided to live in the owner's apartment at the Inn, and the house was empty."

"Mrs. Maynard had a daughter Rita?" Dani asked. In all the folktales about Mrs. Maynard she'd never heard about a daughter.

"Yes," said GG. "That was another sad story. Her daughter ran away one night and wasn't seen again. Rumor had it she was pregnant and left to go find her boyfriend."

"If that is true, maybe that's why Mrs. Maynard's ghost is there," said Taylor wide-eyed.

"There are no ghosts, remember," said Dani. She didn't want to continue the rumor. It was trouble and she knew it.

"How are things going at the house?" GG asked.

"Fine. I asked Aaron about the budget, but he said it was a confidential matter between you, Brad, and him."

"That's right," said GG, her eyes twinkling. "I appreciate his keeping it to himself."

"Is it so we won't be foolish about spending money or that we won't skimp on anything?" Dani asked.

GG laughed. "Both. I want that house to be everything you want but to be practical too. By not knowing, I hope you'll choose how things are done based on what you want without worrying about affording it."

"Aaron is a very interesting man," said Dani. "We were talking about spirits. His mother has taught him to respect them."

GG glanced from Dani to Taylor. "Aaron and Brad are two wonderful young men from a hardworking family. I've watched them grow up and know how genuine they are."

"I told Dani this town is filled with a lot of intriguing people. It's a source of inspiration for me."

GG laughed. "Disguise those characters well. Enough people have lived in the area long enough to decide for themselves who one might be."

Later, after sharing tea with GG, Dani drove to her house feeling better about the cottage and her job with it. Underlying all the work was the message of love GG was giving her and her sisters.

CHAPTER TWENTY-FIVE
DANI

Dani wasn't used to doing a lot of cooking, but she'd learned to take bottled marinara and spice it up by adding fresh garlic, mushrooms, and seasonings. The sauce over noodles with freshly grated parmesan cheese on top made a filling meal. Served with crisp garlic toast, a fresh green salad, and a glass or two of a nice, dry Italian red wine, it was a perfect dinner.

She'd offered to make it for Taylor, but she'd already made plans with Aaron after she'd called him wanting to know more about spirits. He'd offered to take her out to Chica's, a restaurant outside of town known for their Mexican food.

After going over the pros and cons of calling Brad, she decided to see if he was at home. He may not be boyfriend material, but they were friends, and she wasn't going to shun him because he didn't see her in a romantic light.

Nerves fluttering like butterflies in her stomach, she punched in his number.

He picked up the call right away. "Hi, Dani. What's up?"

"I'm making spaghetti and wondered if you would like to come to dinner. It's a simple meal, but it's tasty."

He chuckled. "I'm sure it will be. I have a meeting with Rachael this afternoon, but I should be through in time for dinner. Okay if I call you later?"

"Sure," Dani said. If it didn't work out with him, leftover spaghetti sauce was always handy to have on hand.

She got out the ingredients and prepared the sauce the way

she liked it. At the last minute, she added an ounce or two of red wine and set the sauce to simmer.

While she worked, the scent of garlic and tomatoes filled the kitchen prompting her to consider putting in a small garden at the cottage. It was too late for lettuce and peas, but fresh tomatoes were a favorite of hers. Summertime sandwiches of sliced tomatoes and mayonnaise on soft white bread was another favorite.

She was working on a plumbing and electrical plan when her phone rang. *Rachael.*

Frowning, Dani clicked on the call. "Hello?"

"Dani, this is Rachael. Brad told me he's having dinner with you tonight. What's that all about?"

"It's about being a good neighbor."

"You know I'm interested in Brad. Why would you do this?"

Dani took a calming breath. "Brad's wife died, and he doesn't like to eat alone. I'm just offering him a meal. He's not ready to start dating seriously."

"Maybe not with you, but I'm pretty sure he's serious about me. Or will be if given a chance. I don't want you to destroy those chances."

"Look, Rachael, I'm not getting into your personal life, and I don't want you in mine. It's a small town, but I'm certain we can all get along by living our own lives as we see fit. I won't speak for Brad, but as far as I'm concerned, I will invite him for dinner whenever I choose."

"You don't seem to understand I usually get what I want. And right now, I'd like a fair chance with Brad. We'll see who comes out the winner of this one."

"Rachael, this isn't a competition. I just want to get along with everyone. Like I said, it's a small town."

"About to become a bit smaller where you're concerned," said Rachael before ending the call, leaving behind a disturbing silence.

Dani stared out the window at the beauty outside and took several deep breaths. She couldn't let Rachael's bullying stop her from doing what she wanted. She didn't intend to hurt anyone, but she wasn't going to let Rachael dictate who her friends were.

When she got a text from Brad asking what time he should arrive for dinner, she texted him back and suggested six o'clock.

Dani stood back and studied the kitchen table she'd cleared and set for dinner. On a whim, she went outside and cut some pink roses from Margaret's rose garden, placed them in a cut-glass tumbler, and set it in the middle of the table. She'd always appreciated her mother doing things like this and often matched her examples even when eating alone.

Brad arrived promptly at six with hair still wet from a shower and carrying a bottle of wine. "Thanks for having me for dinner," he said, handing the bottle to her. "I didn't think I could manage another meal at Jake's again. It's convenient, but not home cooking."

"Don't get your hopes up," said Dani smiling at him. "This is just a simple spaghetti dinner with a salad and some garlic toast. I'm not a great cook, but I do have a few favorite meals that others enjoy."

She gripped the bottle and led him to the kitchen. "I opened a bottle of red wine earlier to let it breathe. Would you like a glass?"

"Yes, please," said Brad. He walked over to the kitchen table and studied it. "You've made it fancy. I like it."

"My mother always liked fresh flowers on the table, and I do too. It makes any meal festive."

He grinned. "It's nice."

"Let's go out on the patio," said Dani. "That way, I can keep an eye on Pirate." She handed him a glass of wine and took one for herself.

Outside, the sun was lowering in the sky, and the hush of early evening settled around them as they took seats in the Adirondack chairs on the patio.

Brad lifted his glass and grinned at her. "Thanks for saving me from another business dinner with Rachael."

"Business dinner? I thought you were dating her. She thinks you're dating, anyway. She was furious I'd invited you to dinner."

"Really? I've tried to make it clear that I'm not ready to date," said Brad. "What are you talking about?"

"She called upset that we were having dinner together."

"Seriously?"

"It's not something I'd be confused about."

"What's wrong with her?" He stared into the distance and turned back to her. "Working on the inn is important to the company. After doing The Woodlands project, we think the job at the inn will give us the long-term credibility we need. That's why I've been so careful in my dealings with Rachael. But that will have to stop. She's crossing the line with that behavior."

Dani remained quiet. It wasn't up to her to tell him how to deal with Rachael.

"Sorry. Let's not ruin the dinner by discussing this," he said. "I'm here to relax and enjoy the time with you."

"Me, too," said Dani. She lifted her glass of wine. "To friends."

He grinned. "What's going on with your grandmother? Anything new on recouping some of her funds? She told us all about what happened. From what I read about it in the newspaper, even though they've caught the guy hiding out in the Caribbean on a sailboat, it'll be some time for things to be straightened out. Nobody will get all their money back. But hopefully the 'investors' can recoup some of their losses."

"When I heard about it on the Boston news, I had no idea GG was one of the people he ripped off. My grandmother has been generous to others her whole life. It's so wrong to have someone do that to her. Others, as well."

"Your grandmother is still doing nice things for people. I'm happy you're here because having you and your sisters close means so much to her."

"Thanks. How are things coming at The Meadows? I still haven't had a chance to take a tour."

"Join me tomorrow morning," said Brad. "Because it's a Sunday, the crew won't be on site until later, if at all. I'll pick you up at seven."

"Okay," said Dani. She welcomed the thought of a private tour of the development and more time with him.

They talked about their day's activities, some of their business hopes for the future, and the annual 4th of July celebration. Collister Construction was sponsoring a float in the parade, and Crystal was in charge of it.

Later, while Brad rested on the patio, Dani went inside to start cooking the pasta. She already had put together a salad and stored it in the refrigerator. All she had to do now was toast the garlic bread and dress the salad with her favorite balsamic dressing.

She pulled the baking sheet with garlic bread out of the oven, filled water glasses, tossed the salad, and was just dishing up the pasta when Brad came into the kitchen.

"Just in time. Here's your plate. Go ahead and help yourself," said Dani.

Brad took the warm plate from her and ladled sauce onto his pasta before heading for the table. "Just the way I like it," he said, waiting for her before taking a seat opposite her.

"Nothing fancy, but tasty," she said, pleased by his enthusiasm.

They ate quietly for a moment and then Brad began to talk about life with Patti, how she discovered the cancer, and the long days and months that followed.

Dani listened, realizing he was speaking of Patti more and more in the past as if talking was helping him to work through his loss.

As usual, when he got through talking, he thanked her for listening. "You're a kind person, Dani. Some guy is going to be very lucky to be more than a friend to you."

She was uncertain how to take it. Did that mean he had no serious interest in her now or in the future?

"Dessert?" she asked him, still confused.

"Sure," he answered.

She served him a large scoop of her favorite Rocky Road ice cream, and then dished out a smaller scoop for herself.

They sat in comfortable silence for a while, enjoying the treat, and then Brad said, "Guess I'd better go. Early morning and all."

Dani's surprise turned to understanding. It was close to ten o'clock. They'd talked for hours. "I'll walk you out."

"Need help with the dishes?" he asked.

"Thanks, but no. There aren't many."

At the door, Brad faced her, his gaze boring into her.

Dani's pulse picked up speed.

He leaned forward and hugged her, squeezing her tight. "Thanks for this evening."

He stepped away, gave her a wave, and left the house.

She watched him go and once again reminded herself they were just friends. Wanting more, she sighed. Sometimes you don't get what you want.

CHAPTER TWENTY-SIX
DANI

The next morning Dani awoke just before her alarm went off. She took Pirate downstairs and put him out in the back yard to do his business. There was no time for a morning run. Later, she'd try to fit it into her schedule.

She fixed a cup of coffee and carried it outside. The morning was gray. There'd been a promise of rain, and it looked like the weather forecaster might be right this time.

She fed Pirate and went upstairs to shower and get ready to meet Brad. She was thrilled with the opportunity to see the development at this stage. It would help her try to figure out how she could help Brad and Aaron, as well as their customers. Flexibility in designs was a must for selling custom homes.

At seven o'clock, Brad knocked on her door, holding a cup of coffee from Beans, the coffee shop downtown. "I figured you for a latte. Am I right?" he said, holding up the cup.

"Perfect," Dani said. "It's a treat."

"If you're like me, having that first cup of coffee is the only way to start the day," he said. "We'll go in my truck."

He'd pulled his truck into the driveway. Dani climbed in it. While the truck wasn't tidy, it was clean.

"Sorry, you can move the papers to the back," he said, placing a roll of paperwork behind his seat.

She stacked the papers and put them beside the blueprints before settling into the passenger seat.

Brad slid behind the wheel and turned to her. "My truck is

like my traveling office."

At his apologetic look, she grinned. "Not a problem."

They headed to the far end of the lake, and fifteen minutes later they drove into The Meadows. Land had been cleared for several homes. Two were under construction. Roads and streetlights were in place and lots carefully delineated. A trailer sat near the entrance and was clearly marked "Sales Center."

"Who do you have as your realtor?" Dani asked.

Brad chuckled. "Guess."

"Someone working for Melanie Perkins," responded Dani, smiling.

"Bingo. She's the best around, and I swear she knows everyone living in New England," Brad said. "We're happy with Kellie Yates, the young gal working for her. She's engaged to one of the plumbers who's a subcontractor of ours, and she's eager to make sales."

"It's all like one big family, huh?" Dani said, realizing how everyone in the area seemed to know one another and work together.

He grinned. "Something like that. And it works for everyone. C'mon. I'll show you the two houses we're working on. The first one is done and partially furnished." He parked in front of the one closest to the entrance with a big SOLD sign in the front yard. It was a two-story log contemporary in a beautiful setting of tall trees that softened the clean lines of the house.

Dani got out of the truck and followed him, eager to see inside.

She noted Brad's look of pride as he opened the door for her and stood aside to allow her to enter.

A tall entrance hall gave way to an open living area on the right with a stacked-stone gas fireplace. The room backed up to a small family area off the kitchen that held a couple of overstuffed chairs. On the left of the entrance was a room designed to be an office, with shelves on one wall and double doors to a closet. Beyond that was a half-bath and then a laundry/mud room accessed from the three-car garage. The kitchen, which ran the length of the back of the house was the focal point of the first floor with cherry cabinets, green-granite countertops, and gleaming, top-brand stainless-steel appliances. Bar stools at the center island welcomed people to sit and watch the cook at work. Away from the workspace, a kitchen table had a pretty view to the backwoods through double French doors that led to an outdoor screened-in porch.

"I like what I see," said Dani, glancing around.

"But?" he asked, surprising her.

Dani returned his grin. "Okay, I noticed places where storage could easily be added. There's never too much storage space for active families today."

"Fair enough. What do you like best?" he asked.

"The trim and finishing wood touches are superb. I'm not sure what you're selling the houses for, but those additions are important at the higher price ranges."

"I'm glad you feel that way. It adds cost to the house, but both Aaron and I believe it's important to have them. After you see the upstairs, I want your opinion on what we've done there."

"I'm happy to give it, but you understand I'm taking a quick glance at things, not doing an actual inspection of detail."

"Yes, of course. We'll have you study the blueprints and see what, if any, improvements can be made for the next few houses. We've gone slowly with the construction, waiting for contracts on the first two houses before moving ahead. But now that they're both sold, and we have two new orders, we can add more."

He motioned for her to follow him, and she climbed the stairs to face a little seat built into the wall, with bookcases on either side and a drawer for additional storage underneath.

"A reading nook. How lovely," Dani exclaimed.

He led her to the two large bedrooms to the right with a sizeable bathroom between them.

"Now for the best," said Brad.

Dani stepped into the master bedroom and let out a soft gasp. A king-sized bed faced the doorway. To the right of it was a sitting area and a French door to a balcony overlooking the back yard. Above the bed a skylight allowed sunshine to wash the room with a lemony yellow.

To the left of the bed, a fireplace opened to both the bedroom and a spa tub. Closets on both sides of a small hallway led to the bathroom with double sinks and a shower for two.

"Well?" said Brad.

Dani couldn't stop smiling. "It's gorgeous."

"I think so, too. We talked to a lot of people, did an on-line survey to find out what people would want if given the choice."

"Who's your interior decorator?" Dani asked.

"A woman from Boston," said Brad. "She has a summer home here in the area and is super reasonable to work with because she wants the business. We're showcasing her style. Any storage suggestions?"

Dani laughed. "I'll have to think about it."

They stood smiling at one another and then Brad said. "I want you to see the other house. It's quite different."

"I'm excited to see it."

They left his truck and walked next door to a one-story, gray-clapboard house whose front entrance held a bench and a built-in wooden rack to store boots and shoes.

Inside, she walked past a powder room on one side of the

hallway and a small den on the other to reach the open kitchen and living area. A stone fireplace opened to both areas. Off to the right of the kitchen/living area was a wing that held a master bedroom with ensuite bathroom at the back of the house looking out to the woods. Two other bedrooms that shared a sizeable bathroom, and a small office sat in that wing at the front of the house. Beyond the living room was a large screened in porch that could also be reached from the master bedroom. An outdoor spa sat outside the screened porch along with a fire pit.

"I love this," Dani said. "It's perfect."

Brad grinned. "I thought you'd like this best. It's my favorite too."

Dani opened the sliding glass door and stepped out into the summer morning glow. She'd noticed that behind this lot and the house next door, lilac bushes had been planted at the edge of the woods. She gazed out at the scenery and drew a breath of satisfaction.

Brad came up behind her. "Penny for your thoughts."

She turned to him. "This is such a lovely spot. You and Aaron have done a beautiful job with the houses. I'm proud of you." She paused. "Wait, I didn't mean to sound as if I was judging you. It's just that it's perfect."

Brad smiled at her and drew her close. "Do you know how adorable you are?"

They gazed at each other, liking what they saw. Sexual tension between them hung in the air between them. Dani leaned forward to meet his lips when an irritating cry rent the air.

"There you are."

Dani stepped away as Rachael came into the house. "I thought we had a date for breakfast, Brad."

He shook his head. "No, I don't remember agreeing to meet

with you."

Rachael placed her hands on her hips. "What are you doing here with Dani? You have time for her, but not me?"

"What I do with my time is my business, no one else's. If you must know, this is part of a business meeting with Dani, our architect."

"Well then, you can take me to breakfast," Rachael said. "Remember, I'm your client."

Brad let out a sigh and shook his head. "This is not how Aaron and I run our business. First of all, we didn't have an appointment. We're happy to meet with you and your partners to discuss business on a schedule we all agree to. If you feel it's necessary, and if you have something important to discuss, we can call Quinn and ask him and Liam to meet us at the Café. Otherwise, I'm continuing my tour with Dani."

Dani hid a smile. She could see that Rachael was torn trying to decide whether she should have a breakfast with others or no breakfast at all with Brad.

"All right," Rachael said. "I'll call them now."

A few minutes later, she entered the bathroom where Brad and Dani were inspecting the plumbing. "Okay, it's set. They'll meet us there."

Brad turned to Dani. "You're welcome to join the meeting. It might be helpful,"

"Thanks, but no," said Dani. "I really need to do some work. I'm meeting with plumbers and electricians this week."

"Okay, Rachael. I'll meet you and the others at the café," said Brad reluctantly. "It had better be important."

Brad walked Dani to his truck and after holding the door for her, climbed in behind the wheel. "Sorry about that. As inconvenient as it can be, I need to keep open communications with Quinn, Ross, and her for the business. Rachael thinks she can make the relationship a personal one, but she can't. I've tried to be upfront about setting things straight, but she hasn't gotten the message. I'll bring it up at the meeting."

"She's used to getting her own way," said Dani.

"She's very annoying. That's for sure," said Brad, shaking his head.

He pulled up in front of her house. "Thanks for coming with me to see the development. I wasn't kidding when I said I'd like to make up for this unexpected change in my plans. Will you allow me to take you out to supper tonight?"

"Yes, of course," said Dani, surprised but pleased.

"I'll pick you up at six. There's a restaurant and bar outside of town that sells delicious lobster dishes and fried and steamed clams. You up for that?"

She grinned and patted her stomach. "I certainly am. See you then."

After she got out of the car, he gave her a wave and drove off.

Inside, Pirate greeted her with whines, barks, and tail wagging as if she'd been gone days, not hours. Chuckling, she rubbed his ears. "Where's Taylor?"

She walked into the kitchen and saw Taylor sitting on the patio with a cup of coffee.

Dani grabbed a cup of coffee and went outside to join her.

"You were up early," said Taylor.

"And you were home late," teased Dani.

They laughed.

"Aaron and I had a fun date. As you've mentioned, he's so interesting. If he asks me, I'm going to go out with him again. It takes a while for him to be comfortable talking about himself, but when he does, I see a sensitive, beautiful side to him."

"I like Aaron," said Dani.

"As much as Brad?" Taylor teased.

"Maybe not," replied Dani feeling heat rise to her cheeks. "I thought Brad was going to kiss me, then Rachael showed up. She's after him for sure."

"She can't measure up to you," said Taylor.

"I'd like to think that's true, but I know it's not. She's playing the client card, and he's trapped by it."

"Hm-m-m. I understand how difficult that could be. The project on the inn is important to their business. Aaron was very open about that."

"That's the problem. But Brad is taking me out to dinner tonight." She grinned. "And as far as I know, it'll be just the two of us."

"Sweet! So, it isn't all one-sided," said Taylor, giving her a high-five.

"Maybe not," said Dani, crossing her fingers.

CHAPTER TWENTY-SEVEN
WHITNEY

If Whitney never got an Emmy or an Academy Award, it wouldn't matter. She'd already proven to herself that she deserved one as she remained focused and pleasant while filming the last couple of episodes of the television series. Zane had made a grave error when he'd verbally attacked her for breaking up, proving once again how much he'd changed from when she'd loved him. But even before she came to LA to find work, she'd promised to be careful of drugs and the other sordid sides of the business. She'd been very grateful for her prominent role of "Hope" on the show, but after reassessing her life, she knew she could leave it behind if she had to. Being back in New Hampshire, seeing her grandmother and her sisters, she knew her decision to break up with Zane was the right one.

Now, on the set, he taunted her during romantic scenes by being extra demanding. She knew he was trying to get a rise out of her, but she wouldn't give him that satisfaction. Already rumors were floating about his drug use on the set and in some of the sleezy, grocery store newspapers. And though she wouldn't comment on them, others were only too glad to do so. She knew rumors of his sexual activities wouldn't be far behind, and as she'd told him, she wanted no part of it.

Her agent, though supportive of her decision to end her so-called relationship with Zane, was pressing her not to leave California, telling her she already had a script for Whitney to look at. But when Whitney saw the movie was about a woman struggling with drug addiction, she wasn't excited to take it on.

CHAPTER TWENTY-EIGHT
DANI

Dani dressed in jeans and a light sweater for the casual evening out with Brad. She wondered if she was being realistic about ever having a real relationship with him. He'd been devastated by his wife's death, maybe more unable to move ahead at this time than people thought. One thing she knew—she didn't want to compete with the ghost of the woman he'd deeply loved.

He pulled his truck into her driveway at the appointed time. Pirate barked and wagged his tail as he stood by the door watching Brad approach.

Smiling, Dani watched them both.

Taylor joined them. "Hi, Brad. Nice to see you."

"Thanks. Are you going out with Aaron again?"

"Not tonight," said Taylor. "Later in the week." She held onto Pirate's collar as Dani and Brad walked to his truck.

Once they were under way, Brad turned to Dani. "Glad we could have this time together."

"How did the breakfast meeting go?" she asked.

"Pretty well. We were able to agree on a schedule for the tear-down of the wings. The owners of the inn have also agreed to keep as much of the flavor of the main building as possible and are having new plans drawn for it. I think you'll be pleased."

"Great news. I think GG will be pleased as well. Even though she knew she couldn't keep running the inn, she hoped new owners would respect what she'd created."

"A lot of her guests were repeats, which was a big factor in helping the owners to change their mind on the design."

"Speaking of design, as I said earlier today, I loved the two houses you showed me. I'm certain they'll be well received by the Boston and New York City markets. I think you're going to do very well with the development."

Brad grinned. "Thanks. That means a lot coming from you. We were hesitant to take the risk but it's already paying off."

He pulled up to a rustic, wooden one-story building sitting next to a narrow stream. A colorful metal sign tacked by the front door advertised seafood and craft beers. Above the door a carved wooden sign said "Stan's." Dani guessed from all the trucks in the parking lot that this was a local hang-out not known to many tourists.

"This is a great place to simply relax," Brad said. He too was dressed in jeans. The golf shirt he wore with them matched his green eyes and showed off his muscular torso.

Dani climbed out of the truck eager to enjoy this evening.

He took her elbow and led her to the door. "Hope you're thirsty. They've got great beer."

Inside, a bar lined one end of the room. Most of the bar stools in front of it were filled. The rest of the space held several four-top tables with plastic, red-checkered tablecloths adding to the casual atmosphere.

"Let's grab a table while we can," Brad said.

They found one in the far corner of the room and sat down in the wooden chairs there.

A waitress wearing tight jeans and a red halter top came over to them. Her name tag said Jenn. "Hi, there. What can I get you?" She poured water into their glasses and placed two menus on the table between them.

Brad looked at Dani.

"I'll have a whatever beer you're having," Dani said.

Brad ordered a handcrafted local IPA for them both.

When Jenn came back with their beer, she said, "If you want steamers, you'd better order them now. They're going fast."

"How about the fried clams?" Brad asked.

"No problem there," said Jenn.

"Can you hold an order for steamers for me?" Dani asked. Steamed clams with a buttery garlic sauce were one of her favorite things to eat.

"Okay, I'll tell the chef." She turned to Brad. "You ready to order?"

"Not yet. I want some time with my date," said Brad.

The waitress grinned at Dani and walked away.

"I'm sorry we were interrupted this morning. Rachael is a problem. I'm doing my best to handle it without bringing it up to Quinn or Ross."

"She certainly is determined," Dani commented, wanting to stay away from talk of Rachael.

Brad lifted his beer. "Here's to us spending some quality time together."

Dani clicked her bottle against his. "To us."

After they each had taken a sip, Brad said, "Nothing like a cold beer on a hot, summer day. I limit myself to just a couple, but this is refreshing."

A husky bearded man approached the table.

Brad got to his feet and shook hands with him. "How're you doing, Jim? I want you to meet Dani Gilford, one of the owners of the cottage on the Lilac Lake Inn property." He turned to Dani. "This is Jim Kirkland, a plumber who works with us. He's engaged to Kellie Yates, our realtor."

Jim grinned and held out his hand. "Nice to meet'cha. Can't wait to work with you on that cottage. I've got you marked down for a meeting next week."

"That's right," said Dani. She liked this friendly, burly man with a reddish-brown beard that matched his hair.

After Jim left, Brad explained that he and Jim had gone to school together, but instead of going to college, Jim had gone right into business with his father and was doing well.

They talked about some other members of the crew, and then it was time to order. Dani waited with anticipation for her steamed clams to arrive. Steamed and fried clams, mussels, or lobster were special meals when she'd spent summers with GG. She still loved them.

Brad had opted for broiled scrod, a sweet white fish whose name was the source of many kids' jokes as in the pluperfect tense of screw. But the fish was delicious.

They ate in comfortable silence, and then conversation resumed about the new houses to be built in The Meadows. Having support from Brad and Aaron meant more than Dani could say after constantly being challenged in her office by her male counterparts or having her concepts stolen.

After they completed their meal, Brad said, "Want to take a stroll around the area? There are walking paths along the creek and even a couple of benches. It's a favorite place for birdwatchers."

Dani patted her stomach. "I need a walk. The dinner was delicious, and I ate everything, even the French bread they served with the clams."

He grinned. "I like it when people enjoy their food. My mom is a great cook. I can't wait for you to meet her. Her favorite thing in the world right now after the family is her pet pig, Pansy."

"A pet pig? How adorable! I hear they're nice pets, very clean," said Dani. She noted the look of love that filled Brad's face when he talked about his mother. An important sign of character.

They left the restaurant and walked down a well-worn path beside the creek whose moving water seemed to caress the larger rocks as it flowed over and around them, forming small ripples and eddies that burbled softly in the evening.

She listened for the chirps of birds and heard the familiar song of a cardinal. She stopped and studied the trees and soon saw a flash of red as the bird took off.

"It's so beautiful," said Dani turning to face him.

"*You're* beautiful," Brad said softly and drew her to him. "May I?"

Her heart pounding in anticipation, Dani nodded.

His lips met hers and desire swept through her. She remembered his earlier kisses and knew now that the feelings he'd aroused in her then were the real thing.

Caught up in their kiss, they didn't hear people approaching until a voice said, "Sorry to disturb you. Don't worry, keep on doing what you're doing. We'll walk on by."

Dani couldn't hold in her laughter. Brad joined her and they stood holding onto each other chuckling happily.

"Guess it wasn't as private as I thought," said Brad. "Let's go back to my house." He took Dani's hand, and smiling broadly, he led her to his truck.

Holding his hand, Dani's pulse still sprinted from the kiss. Brad made her feel so treasured. She realized she'd become jaded about men because of her office experiences, but Brad was as honest, kind, and sexy as anyone she could conjure up in a dream. She glanced at him and smiled when he winked at her.

Brad opened the door to his house and ushered her inside. Dani hesitated for just a moment and told herself not to be foolish. Patti was a memory and no longer had a real presence in the house.

"Would you like something to drink? Water, coffee, beer?" Brad asked.

"Ice water would be perfect," said Dani following him into the kitchen.

Brad fixed two glasses of water and said, "Let's get comfortable in the living room." The look he gave her sent her pulse racing. She knew what he wanted. She wanted it too.

They settled on the couch and faced one another.

"As I told you earlier, I like you and want to get to know you better. We've agreed not to rush into anything, but you're the first woman since Patti that I'm truly comfortable with, enough for me to keep seeing. I meant what I said when I told you that you were beautiful. And I don't mean just in looks."

"I haven't been truly interested in a man in a long time. I'm excited to get to know you better as long as you're sure about it. I don't want you to rush into something you're not ready to commit to emotionally."

Brad's gaze rested on her, softening his features. "I'm very sure. I've been thinking a lot about it. You've made me accept that it's time to move forward."

He reached for her, and Dani happily went into his arms.

His lips touched hers and she lost herself in the whirling emotions of desire, pleased that he wasn't rushing, but was taking his time to get to know her.

They snuggled together on the couch. When it became apparent it wasn't enough for either of them, they stretched out. Making love, they learned how to please one another.

Later, Dani traced a scar on Brad's shoulder. "What happened there?"

He grinned sheepishly. "Fell off a ladder when I was just a kid and broke my collar bone. Been on ladders most of my life since then."

She continued trailing her fingers over his body, learning

the shape of him. "When did you know you wanted to get to know me?"

"That's easy," said Brad. "It was when I saw you at the inn for the first time. It rattled me a bit, but after seeing how kind you are with everyone and the care you took with the family photos at the inn, I knew I was right. That maybe we could share something special."

"I was interested from the beginning, but considered you unavailable," she admitted. "But I'm really happy you're comfortable enough with me to take this step." She lifted her face and they kissed again.

Sometime later, Brad walked her to her front door, kissed her goodnight, and headed back to his house, leaving her to stand on the porch a minute, telling herself it hadn't all been a dream.

CHAPTER TWENTY-NINE
TAYLOR

Taylor was sitting on the couch watching television when Dani walked inside. She turned to her and after studying her, smiled. "Looks like it was a successful date."

Dani sank down on the couch beside her. "I'm in love. I fell for him a while ago, and I know why for sure."

"Wow." Taylor grinned at her. "I'm so happy for you."

"There's something so special about him, what we have together," Dani said, and could feel her throat choke up. She knew that what she and Brad shared didn't often happen.

"I'm glad things are working out between you. Aaron told me he thought you were perfect for Brad."

"Thanks. I think so too." Dani got up and stretched. "I met the plumber we'll be using. Another competent guy. He's engaged to Kellie Yates, the realtor at The Meadows. Have you seen the development?"

Taylor shook her head. "Not yet. But I hope to go there soon. Aaron has told me about it."

"I'm going to bed. See you tomorrow," said Dani.

Taylor gave her a little wave and turned back to the television wondering if the time would come when she'd fall madly in love. She'd met a lot of interesting guys in the area, but so far none of them made her feel the way Dani looked when she talked about Brad. But then, she hadn't really given them enough time.

CHAPTER THIRTY
DANI

Dani awakened and lay in bed thinking about Brad. Their lovemaking had been something precious, a sharing of souls and deepest desires. She wondered what lay ahead for them and decided to be private about their new relationship so Brad wouldn't feel pressured to move forward any faster than he was comfortable with.

She got ready for the day and went downstairs for breakfast. She was sitting outside on the patio watching Pirate when her cell rang. *Brad.*

Smiling, she clicked on the call. "Hello."

"Good morning," he said cheerfully. "I just wanted to start my day hearing your voice. Do you need me to come to the cottage with you to meet with Jim to go over the plumbing contract?"

"That would be helpful," Dani said. "I don't want to miss anything, and two sets of eyes on the drawings and on a contract are so much better than one."

"Okay. Jim mentioned he was going to meet with you at ten. I'll see you there."

"Thanks again for dinner and all," said Dani.

"You're welcome. Especially for the 'and all', said Brad.

Dani chuckled even as her cheeks turned hot. "See you soon."

After she ended the call, she was still smiling when Taylor joined her on the patio.

"'Morning," said Taylor. "You're bubbly this morning. Did

I overhear you talking to Brad?"

"Yes," said Dani. "He's going to be at the cottage at ten for my meeting with the plumbers."

"I'm going to take GG to the dentist this morning," said Taylor. "She called last night, and I'm happy to do it. I suppose it's smart for the three of us grandchildren to get to know professional help, like doctors and dentists, if we're going to stay in the area."

"You're thinking of moving here permanently?" said Dani, surprised.

"At least for part of the year. During winter months, I may go south to warmer weather. I can do that easily because I can write most anywhere."

"True. Wouldn't it be something if all three of us moved here," Dani said.

"Heard anything more from Whitney?" asked Taylor.

Dani shook her head. "In her case, I think no news is good news."

They sat with their cups of coffee and stared at Pirate trotting around the yard. When Dani got up to leave, Pirate raced to her side.

"Time for breakfast," she said, rubbing his ears before leading him inside.

As she fixed his food, Dani thought about the possibility of having her sisters living in the same area and decided she liked it. They were different enough that they shouldn't be in one another's business.

As if she conjured her, Whitney's name flashed on her phone. She lifted it and read the text message: *Getting close to returning to Lilac Lake. No matter what you hear about me, it isn't true. Xo.*

Dani went outside to show the message to Taylor.

They looked at each other and shook their heads.

"What a life," said Dani. "No wonder she wants to leave California."

"There's plenty of room for her and Mindy right here," said Taylor. "Let's hope it's sooner rather than later."

As Dani pulled up to the cottage, she was glad to see Brad's red truck and a large white truck beside it. She parked and got out and let Pirate go free before she walked around to the front of the cottage.

Hearing voices, she walked inside and called to them. As she waited for someone to appear, she realized she was nervous about seeing Brad after their lovemaking last night.

Brad emerged from the kitchen and strode toward her. "Hey, there. How are you?" he asked before giving her a tender kiss.

"Fine," she said, smiling at him. Out of the corner of her eye she saw what looked like sunbeams sparkling in the background and felt as warm and bright as they.

"Jim already has some suggestions," said Brad leading her into the kitchen.

When they walked into the room, Jim looked up at them. "Glad to see you, Dani. You've done a great job of drawing up plans for plumbing, but I've got a few things to add. And, by the way, you're lucky. Copper pipes were used when this house was built in the '60s, but in some instances, we'll want to use different plumbing parts to handle more modern appliances and needs."

They spent time going over the plans and talking about changes.

"I'll try to get back to you within a couple of days with quotes on labor and materials," said Jim. "I'll give you a discount because of our work with The Meadows and Brad's connection to it, but the cost of supplies is constantly on the rise, so it will be important to consider that."

"Thanks for your honesty," said Dani. "We're still getting cost estimates from other resources and will be able to make a decision then."

"We're meeting with electricians tomorrow," said Brad.

"Okay, I'm done for now," said Jim. "Gotta take off, but glad we had this time to go over things."

He left, and Brad captured Dani's hand and slid his thumb across her palm. "I've been thinking about you."

At the sexy look he gave her and his sensual touch, Dani filled with heat. "I've been thinking about you too. I want to keep this thing between us growing."

"Me, too. I'm ready. I just have to get through next week when my sister-in-law makes a visit as she's done every year since Patti died."

He stepped forward and took her in his arms. "I've fallen hard for you," he murmured into her ear sending goosepimples racing up and down Dani's back.

She turned and met his lips with hers. Their kiss, tender at first, deepened as hunger built. Dani was so lost in the feelings he created in her that she didn't feel a cool breeze behind her until the kitchen door slammed shut.

Startled, she jumped back and saw those sparkling lights that Brad's kisses always made her imagine. She smiled to herself, pleased by the chemistry between them.

Brad wrapped his arm around her, and they walked to the front door and stepped onto the porch.

"No need to lock the door," said Brad. "Some of my crew is going to leave work at the inn to come check on this house. Seeing the "before" of any project is exciting. Aaron will show them the house and the plans, and then lock up."

"Okay, I'll go home and work on modifying the plans. I'm waiting for Garth's figures. Maybe I'll go say hi to Bethany and see if she has any updates on them."

"I'm glad you like Bethany. She's a sweetheart," said Brad. "She and Patti were close." He waited until she got the dog into the backseat of her car and then said, "See you tonight?"

"Sure. Come for dinner. I'm not sure what we'll have, but I'll come up with something."

"Anything will be fine as long as you're there," said Brad. He kissed her. For a moment Dani thought he might linger, but he pulled away. "I'm late to get to The Meadows. See you later."

As he walked to his truck, Dani studied him, loving the man he was.

The drive to the Beckham Lumber Company didn't take long. Situated halfway between the town of Lilac Lake and The Meadows development, it was an impressive sight. In the front close to the entrance sat a red barn that housed offices and the gift store. Buildings storing lumber and other supplies were behind it, along with a loading area serviced by all kinds of equipment.

Dani noticed the sign on the door that welcomed dogs and let Pirate out of the car and hooked a leash on him.

Inside, Dani quickly realized what Bethany had called a gift shop was much larger than she'd imagined. It was filled with a huge variety of gifts from bird feeders to lamps to garden décor. She tied Pirate to a corner for dogs and wandered through the store for a few moments before a clerk approached her.

"May I help you?" the clerk asked.

Dani shook her head. "I'm just looking around, thanks. But if Bethany is here, I'd love to speak to her."

"She's in the office. I'll go get her," said the woman pleasantly. "In the meantime, enjoy looking at all our beautiful things."

Dani had just picked up a porcelain dog dish when Bethany approached.

"I'm so pleased to see you here," Bethany said, giving Dani a quick hug before pulling back and grinning at her. "How's it going with Brad? Garth said he saw him recently and he mentioned you."

"Really? To answer your question, things are going very well between Brad and me." Dani couldn't hide the smile that crept upon her face.

"Ah," said Bethany grinning. "I thought you two might hit it off. You were so cute together. I'm happy for both of you."

"Thanks," said Dani. "We're not talking about it until after his sister-in-law visits, then we'll let people know."

Bethany frowned. "If you're talking about JoEllen, you'd better be careful. She's had her eye on Brad ever since Patti died. She once told me she'd give him two years to get over Patti and then she was stepping in."

"Is Brad interested in her?" Dani asked, blindsided by this information. "He's told everyone he wasn't interested in dating until now."

"I don't want to say too much, but you'll see for yourself. She wouldn't be healthy for him. She may look a lot like Patti, but she's very different from her sister. I just want you to be aware of the problems she's about to bring. Enough talk about that. I want to show you around the store."

"I love what I've seen," said Dani. "Such cute things for both outside and inside any house."

"As a customer of Beckman Lumber, you get a ten percent discount," said Bethany glowing with health.

"How are you feeling? You look wonderful," said Dani. She'd hoped to have children one day, and now that she'd met Brad, she wanted that more than ever.

"Thanks for asking," said Bethany. "I feel well overall, a bit queasy from time to time. But Garth and I are so excited about a baby that it's all worthwhile."

"I know from your excitement that a baby will be very lucky to be in your family," said Dani, touched by the way Bethany was caressing her stomach.

"We're excited for sure," said Bethany, smiling. "C'mon, I want to show you everything."

Dani decided it was like walking through a wonderland as her gaze met one delightful gift after another. She already knew she wanted several items for the cottage when it was completed.

After they finished a tour of the store, Dani asked Bethany if Jim was around.

Bethany grinned. "No, but I'll remind him you're waiting for those figures. It's such a busy time of year for us, but I'll make sure he gets that job done." She handed Dani a brass sign for the front door of the cottage that had the initial G in the center. "Here's something for the Gilford women. I'm so excited to think that we'll be seeing a lot more of you."

Dani gave her a quick hug. "I'm glad we're friends."

"Let me know if you have any problems with JoEllen. Hope to see you again."

Dani left the store cradling the plaque. A treasured gift from a new friend.

Dani was drawing in the kitchen when Taylor walked in.

"Hi. How'd it go with GG?" Dani asked her.

"Fine. It was special to spend time with her. After she was through with the dentist, we went to lunch and did a bit of shopping. I got a jean jacket and a couple of knit tops. GG got a couple of summer nighties." Taylor sank into a chair nearby. "And I asked her about that envelope with the baby's birth certificate and the death certificate."

"You did?" said Dani, surprised. "What did she say?"

"She told me she'd forgotten she had the envelope, but that she was just holding onto to it for a friend. She isn't sure where those documents came from and didn't know the story behind them."

Dani frowned. "That seems a little odd to me. But I totally understand. It must have something to do with someone she helped, and that's always been confidential information."

"With my imagination, I already have several stories in my mind," Taylor said.

"I don't know how you do it, make up stories for books," said Dani.

"Sometimes, it doesn't work as well. I've had several starts and stops with this latest book. That's why I've decided to stay for the whole summer. This is a refreshing change in scenery."

"I wonder how Whitney is doing?" said Dani.

Taylor gave her a look of surprise. "You don't know? Last night there was a blurb on a Hollywood news program that she and Zane are back together. It showed a picture of them coming out of a store together."

"That must be why Whitney told me not to believe anything coming out on the news. She must've known something like this was going to happen."

"For all the glamour of her work, her love for her job, Whitney is down-to-earth. And lying is something she hates. So, whatever happened between Zane and her must be serious for her to be so adamant about not being with him."

"That makes me wonder what's going on with her now," said Dani. "It will be so much better to have her here for as much of the summer as she can manage."

"Agreed. By the way, do you have plans for the night?" Taylor asked.

"I've invited Brad for dinner. Do you want to join us?

"No, thanks. I've promised to meet Crystal at Jake's. She's hoping Ross will show up as he mentioned." Taylor grinned. "She's been trying to learn baseball lingo."

"Ross Roberts is hot, but he doesn't strike me as the type of guy to get involved with anyone in this small town. Even though he's retired, he's still making a lot of money through endorsements for various sports brands."

"But he's one of the new owners of the inn," protested Taylor. "I can't believe he won't be spending some time here. He's got a room at the Lilac Lake B&B for the rest of the week."

"How do you know that?" Dani asked.

"Crystal asked him," said Taylor. "One advantage of serving the best breakfast and lunch in town."

Dani laughed. "I'm still not used to this small-town living." A thought came to her. "When you see Crystal, ask her about Patti's sister, JoEllen, will you?"

"Why? What's happening?"

"Brad mentioned he had to get through a visit with Patti's sister, and he seemed a little worried about it. And then when I said something about it to Bethany at the gift store, she said that JoEllen had her eye on Brad. I got the distinct impression that Bethany didn't like her."

"Maybe JoEllen thinks he would be open to her now that a couple of years have passed since Patti's death," said Taylor. "I used that scenario in one of my books."

Dani grinned. "How did that end?"

"Pretty badly for her," said Taylor, smiling.

CHAPTER THIRTY-ONE
TAYLOR

Taylor walked into town, pleased that she could do so when she knew she'd be having something alcoholic to drink. It also pleased her that Crystal had asked for her support. A sweet sign of growing friendship.

She met Crystal at her apartment above the café, and they headed to Jake's together. Ross had agreed to meet Crystal there, and because he and Nick were friendly, they'd all agreed to convene there.

Taylor couldn't wait to get to know Nick better. He was a hot, no, a *very* hot sheriff. His uniform looked made for him. He was the source of a new character in her latest book, and she knew her readers would love him.

"You and Ross have talked about going out?" Taylor now said to Crystal as they walked down the street to Jake's.

Crystal turned to her with a smile. "We've been chatting at the café for weeks and when I suggested we meet up at Jake's tonight, he was all for it."

"Won't it be awkward with Nick around?" asked Taylor.

"No, we're friends now. He's looking for someone new in his life. Sooner or later, he'll realize he's the kind of man who should be married. He likes taking care of people," said Crystal. "The thing is, I don't want anyone taking care of me."

Taylor cocked an eyebrow at her. "How's that going to work trying to find a new man in your life?"

Crystal laughed. "I'm not saying I'm looking to marry again. Now or if ever. I like my freedom."

"I love romance," Taylor admitted. "But it has to be with the right man."

"Well, for tonight, let's just have fun," said Crystal. "Here we are."

They walked into the bar.

Taylor searched for Nick and Ross.

Nick waved from a booth and stood to greet them. Ross slid out of the booth's bench, towering above it. Though Taylor had seen Ross briefly before, she'd never had the chance to meet him. Now, she took in his sandy hair, blue-eyes and boyish grin and automatically responded. No wonder he'd been considered America's baseball sweetheart for a while.

Nick introduced Ross to her and waited while she slid into the side of the booth next to him. Then he turned to her. "You look nice. Thought I'd leave my sheriff's uniform at home."

She grinned. "I'm glad you had the evening off. I'm enjoying getting to know everyone in town. Especially because I'll be here for a few months or more."

"Are you considering staying into the fall?" he asked.

"Maybe living here permanently, with a few periods of time away each year," said Taylor, surprising herself with the ease with which she'd told him. She'd been churning that thought over and over in her mind but hadn't realized she'd already decided.

"It's great when some of the old summer gang decides to return from time to time. To have the Gilford girls here is fantastic," said Nick smiling at her. "Those summers were fun times."

Taylor basked in the warmth of his smile. "It was a little easier for my sisters because being younger, I was sometimes left behind. But as I got older that became less of a problem."

"Dani was a winner at some of the tougher games, and Whitney always wanted to do something like put on shows until we all outgrew them," said Nick.

"We both like acting and singing," said Crystal.

"You used to do duets together," said Taylor, smiling at the memory. She realized how alone she'd felt in New York.

Crystal turned to Ross. "I hope we're not boring you with talk of summer memories. Where did you grow up?"

"In Cincinnati, and my summers were always spent at baseball camps or playing in a league," Ross said. "I still love the sport, even though I can't play professionally anymore because of my injuries."

"That's right. I'd forgotten about that motorcycle accident," said Taylor. "How awful for you."

"Disappointing," said Ross, but Taylor saw how his face filled with lines of pain and understood how devastating that was for him. To make him feel better, she reached over and patted his hand before lifting her bottle of beer and taking a cool sip.

When she glanced at Ross, he was leaning toward Crystal, listening to her talk about some of the plays she'd been in. Taylor turned toward Nick and found his eyes on her.

"Glad we could meet up tonight," Nick said. "Sorry, but I have to leave. That call that came through is important." He patted his cell hooked onto his belt.

Seeing his phone, Taylor realized the shock she'd felt must have come from the ringing of his cell phone right next to her. "Thanks for coming. I think I'll go too."

They both stood.

"Where are you going?" asked Crystal.

Nick explained about his call and Taylor said she thought she'd better go too, keeping her gaze focused on Crystal. She didn't want to interfere with Crystal's opportunity to spend time with Ross.

Crystal gave her a grateful look. "Okay, guys, see you

tomorrow."

Taylor followed Nick out of the bar.

Outside, Nick turned to her. "Sorry about leaving so soon. Say hello to Whitney and Dani for me."

Disappointed, Taylor forced a smile and gave him a wave. "See you around."

It had been a terrible evening.

CHAPTER THIRTY-TWO
DANI

Dani fussed in the kitchen trying her best to put together a delicious meal. She knew Brad's wife had been a good cook, and though she wasn't exactly competing with her, she wanted to prove she wasn't a complete dud in the kitchen. She was used to fixing simple, low-calorie meals for herself, not feeding a hard-working "man dinner."

She'd once made him spaghetti. Now, she was putting together a lemon-chicken casserole her mother had taught her. It was easy to make but looked quite fancy with slices of lemon atop crispy chicken breasts cooked in a sweet and sour sauce. That, rice pilaf, and an avocado salad would make a tasty meal for Brad.

When the doorbell rang, Dani looked up at the clock with surprise. She'd been so busy cooking and setting the table that she'd forgotten the time.

She and Pirate went to the door.

Brad stood there in shorts and a golf shirt, looking perfect as he gave Pirate a pat on the head.

Dani brushed the hair away from her sweaty face. "Glad you're here. The time got away from me but come on back to the kitchen. Dinner will be ready soon."

He held up a bottle of wine. "Thought we could have a glass before dinner."

"Perfect. We can sit out back."

In the kitchen, Dani opened the wine and poured two

glasses. "Looks lovely."

"One of my favorites. Or it used to be."

Dani understood he and Patti must have liked sharing it. "Let's enjoy it outdoors."

The chairs were sitting in shade, and though it was a pleasant summer evening, Dani was glad to sit out of the sun after bustling about in the kitchen.

"How was your day at The Meadows?" she asked Brad.

"Fine. I talked to Kellie about some of the changes we're going to incorporate into the new designs, so when speaking with potential customers, she can emphasize they contain lots of storage space. Aaron liked your comments about never having enough of that."

"I'm glad I could be of some help. You've done an excellent job with the houses already," she said.

"I'll make sure you get a set of all the plans so you can review them. At the price level we're offering, we want them to be as perfect as possible. I'm glad you've decided to move here. It means a lot to me ... us."

They studied one another, smiles playing at their lips.

"Tell me what you meant about getting through a week with your sister-in-law," said Dani.

His smile disappeared. "Patti was very close to her sister. She thought I should marry JoEllen after she died, so I wouldn't be alone. It was something JoEllen wanted too." He shook his head. "But I can't do it. JoEllen hasn't pushed it until a few months ago when the two-year anniversary of Patti's death passed. Now she wants me to follow through on Patti's wishes."

"Wha-a-at?" said Dani.

"JoEllen says going forward with Patti's wish is proof of my love for her. Pretty weird. She says she's coming next week to talk things over."

Dani let out a long sigh. Okay, she was understanding, but the situation was worse than she'd thought. She didn't want to get caught up in a mess like that. Tears stung her eyes and she held onto her stomach, feeling sick.

Brad got up, walked over to her, and pulled her up in his arms. "I don't want anything to get in the way of what we have."

"Neither do I," Dani responded. "And that's why this crazy idea must be put to rest. Immediately."

"I've already told her not to come," he said cupping her face in his hands.

"Hello. Anybody here?" came Taylor's voice.

Dani pulled away from Brad. "We're here." She stepped into the kitchen. "What's wrong? I thought you were going to be out for the evening."

Taylor shrugged and her mouth turned down. "I thought so too. Then Nick had to leave, and I couldn't stay when I'd promised Crystal that I'd help her spend time with Ross. So here I am."

"Do you want dinner with Brad and me?" Dani said, hiding her disappointment.

"Sure, thanks. It smells delicious," Taylor said as Brad walked inside.

Dani gave him a bright smile. "Taylor's going to join us for dinner."

"Okay." Brad turned to Taylor. "I haven't spent much time with you. But I've heard about you and your books."

"And I've heard about you and your new project, The Meadows," Taylor responded smiling.

The three of them moved to the patio and conversation flowed about Brad's new development and Taylor's books. Dani tried not to be irritated, but any time alone with Brad was already jeopardized by the forthcoming visit from his sister-in-law.

When Brad and Taylor complimented her on the dinner, Dani reveled in their praise and decided to continue to do more cooking. It was a way to use her creativity. Especially when it made others happy.

"May I help clean up?" Taylor said when they'd finished eating.

With her plans for a quiet, sexy evening with Brad ruined, Dani said, "No worries. I'll get to them later."

"Okay, then, I'm going up to my room to try to get some work in. Thanks for dinner. Nice to see you Brad," Taylor said and waved to them as she left.

Alone in the kitchen, Brad walked over behind Dani and wrapped his arms around her. "Sorry, but I'd better go. With the sun coming up sooner each day, we like to get an early start on the houses. And tomorrow, the men should show up to tear down the wings of the inn."

Dani turned to face him. "I wish you could stay, but I understand."

"Tomorrow, come to my house for dinner. We won't have any interruptions there."

She looked up at him. "Perfect."

He lowered his head to kiss her.

Dani closed her eyes, loving the feel of his lips on hers, the fresh lime smell of his aftershave. This, she thought, is what I've waited for all evening. We can't let JoEllen or anyone else ruin what we have.

When they finally pulled apart, Brad settled his gaze on her and smiled.

"Thanks for dinner. Tomorrow, my house."

"Deal," she said, accepting another kiss from him, wanting even more when he pulled away with a sigh. "I'd better go while I can."

Dani glanced up at the stairway, heard Taylor working on her computer, and nodded.

She walked Brad to the door and watched as he crossed the front lawn to his house, then waved before he went inside.

Disappointed at the way her plans had changed, Dani closed the door behind her and headed to the kitchen where dirty dishes awaited her.

The next morning, Dani drove to the inn to see the demolition of the guestroom wings. Rather than use any explosives, the contractors had brought in pieces of heavy equipment: a crane with a wrecking ball, an excavator, and a bulldozer. Huge dump trucks stood by waiting to be filled with debris.

As she watched the buildings turned to rubble, sadness clutched her heart. The inn had meant so much to her family, and it had been her own summer escape. But new, more modern buildings would be erected. So, all was not lost.

Aaron saw her and walked over to her. "Hi. How's it going?"

"Fine," said Dani. "I've met with Jim about the plumbing for the cottage and am meeting with the electricians today."

"They're a talented group," said Aaron. "Brad asked me to get plans to you. I'll deliver them to your house later today if that's all right."

"That will be fine. If I'm not there, Taylor will be."

"Okay. Gotta go check on these guys. Hate to see buildings torn down, but the new ones are going to be awesome."

Dani was grateful that GG had enlisted help from the Collisters. It made working on the cottage so much easier.

She climbed behind the wheel of her car and drove to the entrance of the long driveway leading to the cottage. She stopped and stared at it wondering if there was a way to dress up the entrance without encouraging people to travel down the road. She supposed a different gate that required a security code to be entered might be the answer.

She pulled up next to a yellow truck with a logo for Wilson's Electric Services. She checked inside the truck, but it was empty.

As she walked around to the front of the house, she saw a man standing on the front lawn staring out at the lake and called, "Hello!"

He turned and lifted a hand to greet her. "Hey, there. I'm Harry Wilson." He was a tall, thin, middle-aged man with a thatch of brown hair escaping his Red Sox baseball hat.

They approached one another and Dani shook his hand. "I'm Dani Gilford. Both Brad and Aaron Collister have said nice things about you."

"They're two of the best in the business. Pleased to meet you." His brown eyes shone with friendliness. "This is such a beautiful spot. No wonder you're anxious to get the place fixed up. I have the electrical schematics you sent me."

"Let's go inside and look around to be sure we haven't missed anything. I always like to be careful and am open to any suggested changes."

Dani went to the front door, glad that Harry was right behind her. She knew she'd have to get over her initial fear of entering the house. But until the house was truly theirs, she supposed she and her sisters would feel like intruders.

Inside, the house was still, almost eerily silent. It remained that way as she and Harry went from room to room, checking and marking where outlets and switches would be placed. They talked about recessed lighting, added outlets in the kitchen and outdoors for any future sunporches, and covered all the questions on Dani's list.

An hour or so later, Harry said, "I think we've taken care of everything. Replacing the old wiring with new makes sense especially when you're going to replace interior walls. Let's see how everything goes. There are always a few surprises in renovation work."

"Thanks for coming," Dani said. "How soon can you get the cost estimate to me?"

"By the end of the week, I promise. This is a busy time for me, but I'll have my wife work on the numbers for me."

"Okay, thanks," said Dani. She'd thought it would be easier to put everything together for GG, but she didn't want to push her subcontractors too hard.

As she was ushering Harry to the front door, Brad arrived. "Am I too late? I tried to break away earlier but couldn't."

Harry looked at her for a response.

"I think we've got everything under control, Brad, but thanks. Harry had a couple of interesting comments for me, and he'll get the cost estimate to me by the end of the week."

"Glad to hear it," said Brad. He shook hands with Harry. "Thanks."

Harry tipped his hat and left them.

Brad faced her. "How are you? I was sorry our evening was cut short. Hopefully, tonight we'll have privacy." He moved closer, cupped her face in his broad hands, and kissed her.

Dani wrapped her arms around his neck and kissed him back, loving the taste of him, and wondered what it would be like to share kisses with him every morning.

When they pulled apart, Dani stared at the sparkling lights floating around them and closed her eyes. Brad always made her feel as if his kisses were magical. She opened her eyes and found Brad smiling at her.

"Yeah, I feel it too, that ... I don't know ... that magic." He drew her close and she nestled against him, sure of her love for him.

A few moments later, Brad said, "Guess I'd better go see what's happening at the inn."

"Let me lock up and I'll follow you," she said. She was interested in seeing the work there but even more anxious for private time at Brad's house that evening.

After working diligently all afternoon, Dani showered and dressed for her evening with Brad. Their one session of lovemaking had proved to her that their relationship was founded on more than lust. She'd been rocked to the core by the giving, the desire to please one another, the meeting of souls they'd shared.

Dani wore the new, lacy pink panties and bra she'd ordered under a pink sundress that was both flattering and easy to wear. She spritzed light, summery perfume on her wrists and put a little extra between her breasts and at her neck. Putting one last coat of shiny lip-gloss on, Dani considered herself ready.

She went downstairs, took the bottle of white wine out of the refrigerator, and headed for Brad's house. She debated whether to walk in and decided to ring the bell.

A few seconds later, a blonde woman opened the door and frowned at her.

Dani staggered back a step. "Who are you?"

"I should ask the same of you. What are you doing here?" The woman studied her with a suspicious look.

"I'm Dani Gilford, a friend and next-door neighbor of Brad's," Dani said, relieved when Brad approached them.

"Hi, Dani," said Brad. "Come in. I see you've met JoEllen Daniels. She surprised me with a visit a couple of days early."

"We haven't had time to exchange names, but I told her mine," Dani said, still standing on the porch. JoEllen most definitely didn't want her inside.

Brad reached in front of JoEllen and opened the door for Dani. "Come in and let's have a glass of wine together before I take you both out to Fins for dinner."

Dani shot him a questioning look and handed the bottle of wine over to him. "I thought you might like this."

"*I* thought it was going to be just you and me here for dinner," said JoEllen. "Besides you know I like only certain foods."

"I'm sure we can find something you like at Fins," Brad said, showing remarkable patience.

They went to the kitchen, where Brad opened the bottle of wine and poured three glasses of it.

"Let's go outside," said Brad, leading Dani and JoEllen to the patio without giving them a choice.

The three of them sat in a circle.

Dani waited for Brad to give a toast and when he didn't, she followed suit and took a sip of her wine.

JoEllen pointed to the back corner of the lot. "I see you haven't started on the gazebo yet."

"No, I've changed my mind. I'm going to do something different," said Brad.

"But it's what Patti wanted," JoEllen said.

"It's been two years, Jo," said Brad. "It's time I made my own choices."

JoEllen studied him, ignoring Dani. "Does this have anything to do with Dani being here?"

Brad turned to Dani with a determined look and faced JoEllen. "Yes, it does."

"You do know that Brad has more or less committed to marrying me," JoEllen said to Dani as if the matter had been settled.

"I'm not about to get involved with family squabbles," said Dani, setting down her wine glass. "You'll have to speak to

Brad about that." She stood and faced him. "I'm sorry, but I think it's best if I leave."

Brad jumped to his feet. "Please, don't go."

"I can't stay," said Dani, knowing the situation would only get worse.

"Okay, I'll walk you out." Brad took her elbow and they headed for the front door.

"I'm sorry, Dani. I didn't know she was going to show up today and, obviously, we haven't had a chance to talk," said Brad. "I thought it might be easier on her if she saw how happy I am with you. But she hasn't changed. I don't see why Patti could ever believe JoEllen would be a good match. Patti never saw her sister as others did."

"I'm sorry too. Neither of us was prepared for her visit. She certainly has the wrong impression. But I leave this problem up to you to settle quickly." Dani hesitated and then blurted, "I love you, Brad."

A smile lit his face. "Love you, too." Brad leaned forward to kiss her.

"So, this is how it is?" said JoEllen as she walked toward them. "I've given myself one week to change your mind, Brad, and do the right thing by Patti."

Brad stepped away from Dani and faced JoEllen. "We need to do some serious talking."

"See you later," said Dani, exiting the house, her emotions racing in circles. She'd made it clear how she felt about him. Now it was up to Brad to set things straight.

CHAPTER THIRTY-THREE
WHITNEY

Whitney stared at her photo with Zane on the entertainment news website and gritted her teeth. She'd been tricked into meeting him at a well-known store on Rodeo Drive when he told her he wanted to talk to her about a rehab center, which turned out to be another of his lies. When she'd arrived, Zane was there, smiling as he handed her a fancy gift bag. A perfect PR shot. Zane was suddenly everywhere: in magazines, on talk shows, in both sleazy and acceptable newspapers discussing his trying to win her love back. But Whitney knew it was simply to save his reputation and his career. Drugs in Hollywood were no surprise to anyone, but the inkling of him abusing women was worth fighting against.

She'd done her share to help him by remaining quiet, but the time was coming when people would find out the extent of his problems and realize his addiction to drugs and sexual games were ruining his looks and talent. Some might call her a prude for caring so much about her own reputation, but she wouldn't do anything to hurt her parents or GG. Despite all he'd put her through, she'd offered once again to help Zane find a discreet rehabilitation facility, but she knew now he had no intention of ever going to a rehab center.

The producers had agreed to write her out of a couple of upcoming episodes, but if the show was optioned for another season, they wanted her to come back. By then, Zane would either be cleaned up or kicked off the show. They were tired of trying to help him understand the need to change his behavior.

Whitney continued to sit at the kitchen table with Mindy in her lap and stared out at the bright sunshine. No matter how sunny it got in LA, the sky could never be as blue as in New Hampshire. She couldn't wait to leave.

Mindy reached up and kissed her cheek.

Laughing, Whitney patted the dog. "You're so sweet. The best thing to happen for me in a long time." She picked up her cell to call Dani. She couldn't wait to hear how the cottage was coming along.

CHAPTER THIRTY-FOUR
DANI

Dani's spirits brightened when she saw who was calling her. She hadn't talked to Whitney in a while, and it would be reassuring to hear her voice.

"Hi, Whitney," she said smiling. "I saw your picture with Zane on the cover of a trashy magazine. You told me not to believe anything we heard or read. What's the deal?"

"Zane is a mess and getting worse by the day. He's due for a big fall, and I don't want to be part of it. I once more offered to help him get into a rehab program, but he refuses to listen to me or anyone else."

"I'm sorry. I know how much you liked him when you started working with him," said Dani.

"It was more than like. I truly loved him before he began to change," said Whitney softly. Her voice strengthened. "How are you? And Taylor?"

"I've been better," said Dani honestly. "I'm in love with Brad and he loves me, but he's dealing with his ex-sister-in-law who claims they agreed to get married to honor Patti, his deceased wife. She's here now, staying in his house for a few more days. He's moved in with Aaron until she's gone."

"It's like a spicy Hollywood story," said Whitney. "What are you going to do about it?"

"Me? Nothing. Brad will have to work it out. I told him I wanted no part of a family squabble."

"I like Brad. He seems like a straight-up guy. I'm sure things will work out," said Whitney. "And now that I think about it, you're right to have him work out his problems. That way, you can be sure of his intentions."

"Yes, I agree, but JoEllen is very determined," said Dani.

"How's Taylor?" asked Whitney.

"Fine. She seems to be writing and jotting down ideas for books. I think it's healthy for her to be in Lilac Lake. She said she might move here permanently as long as she can spend time away occasionally."

"It'll be so much fun to be together. I'd forgotten how treasured our times were at our summer retreat," said Whitney. "I'll get there as soon as possible. In the meantime, I'll send some stuff along. I've been packing up clothing and a few personal items to have in New Hampshire."

"No problem. We'll have your boxes waiting for you," Dani said. It would be better to have Whitney at the house with Taylor and her. As the oldest, she'd always been their natural, benevolent leader.

She ended the call, pleased Whitney agreed with her decision to step away from Brad's family issues.

Taylor walked into the kitchen. "Any coffee left?"

Dani pointed to the coffee maker on the counter. "Help yourself. I just talked to Whitney. She's boxing up some of her things and sending them to us."

Taylor grinned. "An encouraging sign. How are things going for her?"

Dani relayed their conversation to Taylor.

"It'll be healthy for Whitney to get away from L.A.," said Taylor. She studied her. "You were pretty upset last night. Are you okay?"

Dani grimaced. "I just have to let things play out."

Taylor got her coffee and headed upstairs.

Dani got up from the table and stepped outside. Pirate was stretched out in the sun. He sensed her immediately and opened his eyes.

"Nice day, huh?" she said taking a seat in one of the patio chairs.

Pirate got to his feet and came over to her for some attention.

She rubbed his ears and was thinking of going back inside to work when she heard a voice coming from next door. She couldn't hear what was being said, only angry tones.

Sighing, she returned to the kitchen.

Later, Dani was working on her drawings when her cell rang. She saw the name of her former company and frowned, wondering what they wanted.

She clicked on the call. "Hello?"

"Hi, Dani. This is Herb Watkins."

Dani held her breath. Her old boss. "Hello," she said crisply.

"I want you to know we've let Frank go after discovering his misrepresentation of your work as his. The client in Rhode Island is asking for you to supervise the project. I've told him I'd do my best to see that it happens."

"Oh, I see," said Dani. She'd wondered how long it would take for her co-workers to realize that Frank was not only a sleazy man, but a lazy one as well.

Herb rushed on. "I'm serious about wanting you on board for this project. We'll give you a new title, a hefty raise, and a chance to become partner ..." his words trailed off.

Grinning, Dani raised her right hand in a triumphant fist.

"What do you say?" Herb said, his voice full of confidence.

That tone, the confidence that she'd come crawling back did it. Dani drew a deep breath and let it out slowly, telling herself to be careful.

"Thanks, Herb, for thinking of me. At this time, I must turn down your offer because I have commitments in Lilac Lake."

"I'm certain those commitments don't equal the prestige of the project we're handling for this client. Can I get you to reconsider?" Herb's voice wasn't as confident as before.

Dani thought of how excited Brad and Aaron were to have her on their team, how flexible they were, how creative she felt.

"Thanks again, but I can't leave clients in the lurch. I'm also working on something for the family."

"Okay, how about if you work part time for us on this project?" asked Herb, a little more hopeful this time.

"I doubt you could afford me," said Dani, relishing this role.

"Try me," Herb said.

Dani named a price double her usual rate certain Herb would laugh at her and maybe, just maybe, understand how frustrated she'd been at the firm.

"I think we can do that," said Herb. "This client has worked with you before and trusts you."

"Okay, I'll come into Boston sometime tomorrow and we can talk specifics," said Dani. It would be a perfect time to leave Lilac Lake. The cost projections hadn't come in for the house, and with JoEllen in town, Dani would be out of the way.

Dani ended the call, let out a whoop of joy, and did a little happy dance in the kitchen.

"What's going on?" asked Taylor entering the room.

Dani giggled. "It seems my old firm can't get along without me. I'm going to be paid an outrageous sum to work part time on a project. Don't worry. It won't keep me from overseeing the cottage."

"Congrats! You've been underrated and unappreciated there for years," said Taylor, giving her a high-five.

"I'm going into Boston tomorrow for a couple of days to discuss it with the firm and my client. With JoEllen here, it's an ideal time to leave town."

"While you're gone, I'll keep an eye on things. Isn't that what sisters are for?" Taylor lifted her hand for another high-five.

Laughing, Dani met it with a loud smack.

Dani called Brad and left a message that she needed to talk to him and asked if he would meet her at the cottage as soon as possible. Excited by all that was happening, she put Pirate in her car and took off for the house.

GG called her, and Dani pulled over to the side of the road to give her the latest news.

"It shouldn't interrupt work on the cottage," Dani explained to her.

"That's great news, Dani. It's about time people at that firm recognized your ability for not only the work you do, but the way you handle clients."

Dani pulled back onto the road and drove to the inn, down the driveway to the cottage, and parked in front of the garage next to Brad's empty truck.

She let Pirate out of the car and went to find Brad.

Not seeing him on the lawn or the front porch, she wandered down the slope of the lawn to the sunning rock.

Brad was there, sitting and staring out at the water.

Dani called his name. Seeing him like this, she was reminded of past summers where she, herself, had sat on the rock contemplating life.

As she approached, he turned and smiled at her.

Dani took off her sandals and waded in the shallow water to reach the rock. Then she climbed up and sat beside him.

"Hi," she said as he put an arm around her and pulled her closer. "How are things going?"

"Being with JoEllen has brought up all those awful memories of Patti being sick and me standing by, helpless, as I watched her slowly fade away."

Dani reached for his hand and gave it a squeeze. "I'm sorry. I understand how painful that is for you."

"Yes, but I've decided not to take a step backward but to keep moving forward. I've told JoEllen that the relationship I have with you is serious, that I want you in my life."

"And?"

"And she says I'm breaking a promise I made to Patti and her. She has plane tickets to fly back to her hometown outside Cleveland in five days. I've told her I won't kick her out of the house, but I expect her to leave then. Aaron is being a good sport about me staying with him."

"I understand how much she wants to be married to you, but I didn't see any signs of real affection between the two of you," said Dani. "Surely, she wants more than that."

"She's not getting it from me," said Brad. "JoEllen hasn't had successful relationships in the past. She thought moving in with me would be simple. That's how shallow she is." He stared out at the water, watching a couple of ducks swim by toward the end of the lake.

"I'm going to Boston tomorrow for a couple of days or so," said Dani. At his look of surprise, she explained the job offer from her old firm.

"Does this mean you have no intention of staying in Lilac Lake?" he asked, his eyes boring into her.

"No, it means I'm going to help with this job on a part-time, one-project basis. I'm happy working with you and Aaron. We haven't made a formal contract between us, but I want to because I'm sincere about it."

"Okay. When you return from Boston, Aaron and I will sit down with you and write up an agreement," said Brad, pushing fingers through his sun-bleached hair.

He drew her close again and settled his lips on hers. "M-m-m," he murmured, deepening his kiss.

Dani responded, and her fears about their relationship disappeared.

CHAPTER THIRTY-FIVE
DANI

That evening, after returning from a visit with GG and talking on the phone with Brad, Dani sat with Taylor and Crystal in her kitchen sharing pizza and salad.

"This is such a treat for me," said Crystal. "I work with food every morning and into the afternoon, but I would never put pizza on the menu when we have such a successful pizzeria in town."

"I think your work schedule is smart," said Dani. "Closing the café at four gives you time to clean up and then have an evening for yourself."

"Yeah, but I have to get up at five o'clock," said Crystal. "But I've made a success of it, and I'm proud of the café's reputation."

"You should be proud," said Dani. "I remember how it was in the old days."

"You mean how poor my family was?" Crystal said with a soft laugh. "I'm grateful my mother lived to see my success before she died. As a single mother with an abusive ex-husband, she wanted my sister, Misty, and me to be strong and have a better life."

"What's Misty doing now?" Dani asked. She remembered Misty as a competitive, athletic, blonde girl.

"She lives in Florida and teaches girls softball at a high school outside Orlando," said Crystal, smiling. "Talk about tough."

"Is that why you like baseball?" Taylor asked Crystal.

"I'm learning to like baseball because of a certain guy named Ross Roberts. But, Taylor, even after you left Jake's the other night, Ross wanted to know more about you. I think he's going to ask you out. I don't mind."

Dani nudged Taylor with her shoulder. "There you go. A chance to get to know him."

"Maybe I can get some information from him for one of my books," said Taylor.

"Come on, there's a better reason to date him. He's just not for me," said Crystal.

Taylor gave her a sheepish look. "I really hoped to get to know Nick better."

"Yeah, well, I think he's always had a thing for Whitney," said Crystal. It didn't seem to bother her to talk about her ex this way.

Dani saw the disappointment on Taylor's face and reached over and gave her hand an encouraging squeeze. "Maybe you should spend some time with Ross. He seems to be a nice guy."

"Maybe I will," said Taylor.

The next morning, as Dani was loading her car, Brad drove up in his truck, got out, and trotted over to her.

"Have fun in Boston but don't forget to come back. We need you here."

She beamed at him. "I'll only be gone a couple of days. Hopefully, by the time I return, JoEllen will be gone. That should make it easier for all of us."

"I hope so," said Brad. "Aaron has refused to have anything to do with her, and Crystal took me aside and told me she'd shoot me if I didn't send JoEllen packing."

Dani laughed. "Crystal can be very outspoken, but she's right. I hear JoEllen hasn't made friends here with her attitude of thinking she's better than everyone else."

Brad sighed. "She's promised to leave as planned this weekend." He kissed her and then straightened. "I've got to go, but you have a safe trip. Okay if I call you while you're gone?"

"I'd like that," said Dani suddenly wishing she didn't have to leave. "I'm going to miss you."

Taylor came outside with Pirate on a leash. "He wants to say goodbye to you."

Dani hugged Pirate and gave him several loving pats on the head. "Sorry you can't go with me this time. I'll be back soon."

He whined and gave her a mournful look.

She kissed his head. "Later, Pirate. Be good for Taylor."

Dani slid behind the wheel of her car realizing how much her life had changed.

She backed out of the driveway, waved to Taylor, and headed back to her old life with a sense of triumph. But no matter how much of an ego boost this job was for her, she'd already come to love her life in Lilac Lake.

Being back in her condo seemed strange to her as Dani rushed around to get ready for her visit to the office. She'd become used to wearing jeans and shorts and found the dark skirt, heels, and crisp white blouse constraining.

But as she entered the office, she was glad she'd taken the time to look professional.

"Glad to see you back," said the receptionist.

Thanks," Dani said headed for Herb's corner office, returning the smiles and waves sent her way.

Herb was standing by his door ready to greet her. "Glad to see you. Come inside so we can talk. Mr. Albono will meet with you tomorrow morning here at the office."

"All right. I assume you have the contract between me and

the firm ready for me to sign," said Dani. She wasn't going to do a bit of work until that was done. She'd learned her lesson with this firm.

Herb ushered her inside, and she sat in the chair he offered her in front of his desk. "I was hoping you'd reconsider your rate for this project. It's rather steep."

"I know it is, but it's a huge disruption to my new life, and I wouldn't consider doing it except it's Mr. Albono's project. So, no, I won't reduce my price. Is that going to be a problem for you?"

A look of frustration crossed Herb's face. He shook his head. "Mr. Albono won't work with anyone but you," said Herb. "He was going to take his business elsewhere if you didn't agree to take on the project. Frank almost ruined Mr. Albono's relationship with the firm."

"Frank knew Mr. Albono was a client of mine." She gave Herb a steady look. "So did everyone else. As I said, I'm here because of my client."

"I understand," Herb said, sliding some papers across his desk to her. "Here is our standard sub-contractor agreement. I've taken the liberty to insert your rate and made it clear it was for this project only. If we can convince you to come back it will be at a lower rate."

"Of course," said Dani, content that wouldn't be a problem. Just walking into the office after a couple of weeks away, her stomach had clenched with memories of how she'd sometimes been treated. She was content in New Hampshire with the opportunities that awaited her there. She'd already spoken to Aaron about designing a clubhouse for their new development.

Dani rose. "I'll go over the contract in the conference room and if I have any questions, I'll come to you. Fair enough?"

"Yes," said Herb. "I think you'll be pleased."

On her way to the conference room, the receptionist approached her. "You look terrific, Dani. Healthy, tanned, and happy. I'm so pleased for you. I've missed you."

"Thanks. I'm here for just a couple of weeks on a part time basis," said Dani. "We'll do lunch one of these days."

"I look forward to it," said the older woman beaming at her.

In the conference room, Dani took the time to vet the contract carefully. Seeing nothing to alarm her, she made a change to the available dates she'd be able to work and headed back to Herb's office.

He agreed to the new time constraints and signed the contract. Dani smiled. It felt so freeing to be in control for once.

That evening as she sat with two of her girlfriends in a restaurant at The Boston Harbor Hotel, Dani listened to all the gossip about who was dating who and thought of Brad. Funny, just as she'd decided not to worry about dating anyone seriously, she'd met him. Now, listening to the conversation, she felt truly lucky they'd clicked from the beginning. All the dreaming in the world wouldn't work without that initial attraction.

"So, tell us more about Brad," said one of her friends.

"Show us a picture," the other one said.

Dani found a picture of Brad she'd taken on the lawn of the cottage. He was standing in the sun smiling at her.

"Wow," said the friend who'd asked her for a photo. "He's really hot. And look at the way he's smiling at you. You're one lucky woman."

"Thanks. I think so too," Dani replied, anxious to see him again.

CHAPTER THIRTY-SIX
WHITNEY

Whitney took a last bite of her lettuce and put her fork down, remembering the delicious food in Lilac Lake. She didn't plan on going crazy eating everything in sight when she returned to New Hampshire, but she was going to enjoy herself. For the first time in years, she wouldn't be forced to eat a meal like this. Or for photo ops with Zane.

"Thanks, Whitney, for understanding how important this is to me," said Zane. His hands were shaking from withdrawal from the drugs he was denying himself until he was off the set. "Your announcement that we were through almost ruined my career."

"Hey, let's get something straight. *You* almost ruined your career. Now that we're pretty sure the show isn't going to be picked up for next season, we can all get on with our lives. I, for one, will be grateful for that. I hope you, Zane, will make those changes we talked about."

When Whitney had first met Zane, she'd been as star-struck as any woman her age and found herself falling in love with him. It was unsettling, painful almost, to have that deep tender feeling changed to one of disgust.

"You guys going to be ready for your love scene?" asked one of the assistant directors.

"In a short while," said Whitney. "I have to get my makeup touched up."

Zane stood. "I'd better get ready too."

Whitney gave him a steady look. "Brush your teeth and take a shower before you go for makeup."

Zane gave her a little salute and walked away.

Whitney knew of all the performances she'd given this would be one of her strongest—pretending she loved someone she now detested.

CHAPTER THIRTY-SEVEN
DANI

The next morning when Dani walked into the office and saw Anthony Albono, she hurried forward with a smile. When he saw her, he held out his arms, and she rushed into them. She knew it wasn't the most professional way to greet a client, but Anthony was special. A short, thin, bald man with a fringe of gray hair and weathered features, the seventy-six-year-old matched her height. His small size didn't diminish in any way the sense of power he exuded. His hazel eyes seemed to miss nothing as he observed her with approval. But rather than be annoyed with his frank appraisal, Dani knew him well enough to understand he was assessing her in a nonsexual way. More like a parent or a grandparent seeing a child after some time.

"So, how's my girl?" he asked. He shot a look at Herb and said to her in a gruff voice, "They tried to pawn off a nitwit to work with me. I trust you, Danielle. You proved your honesty to me. Something I don't forget in people."

"Thank you, Anthony. It's important to me too, which is why I tell you if I think something won't work or something else will work better."

He grinned at her and turned to Herb. "See why I like her? Bet not all your people are so honest."

"I'm glad we could proceed with this project," said Herb. "It's an interesting one. I'll leave you to your discussion about the project."

Dani led Anthony to the conference room. She'd brought

along her leatherbound notebook. She'd learned early on to talk to a client to learn what he or she envisioned beyond a building and to discover what was truly important in their lives.

Anthony, she knew, had many interesting family members in Providence. Some were called unsavory, but Anthony wanted to do things for others. For this project, he'd proposed to build apartments for the underprivileged. Something that balanced things out for him, he'd told her, after amassing a small fortune in real estate.

She was eager to help him.

Dani took careful notes while sitting and talking about how he foresaw the project, what things he wanted included, and how they could save money but provide an excellent product. She'd worked on another building of his, so she knew what styles pleased him. She'd draw up comparatively simple plans to show the various government agencies for approval before the real work would begin.

"Are you prepared to return to Providence with me to check out the site?" Anthony said.

Though surprised, Dani replied, "Of course. I can drive down there this afternoon."

"Why don't I pick you up in my limo? You can stay at my house. My wife would love to see you again, and then after we've taken care of business tomorrow, my driver can deliver you back to Boston." His eyes twinkled with mirth. "That way, you don't have to worry about traffic. My driver will."

She chuckled. "Thanks. If she didn't know Anthony and his wife, Bella, she wouldn't consider it. But they were like another set of grandparents to her.

Later, sitting in the back of the limo, Dani was thankful the driver and not she had to cope with the traffic. She'd become used to the lack of city traffic.

"So, tell me what's new, Dani?" Anthony said, sipping on a glass of champagne from the bottle he'd opened for them both. "Still interested in having me introduce you to one of my nephews?"

Dani laughed. "No, thanks. I wasn't going to mention it, but I've been seeing someone in Lilac Lake. He's a really nice man who's in the construction and development business."

"Ah, it's time you settled down," said Anthony giving her a thoughtful look.

Dani set down her glass and grimaced. "Now you sound like my mother."

He laughed. "Bella will want to hear all about it. She thinks so highly of you. Too bad we never had children together, but it was not to be."

"Your nieces and nephews adore you," said Dani. "I remember how it was at your wedding anniversary party."

His lips curved. "I knew Bella was for me the first moment I saw her."

"You look well. Is she well too?" Dani asked.

"We're both getting older, but we're okay," said Anthony. "Not that getting older is easy."

Dani finished her glass of champagne and put it in the glass rack behind the front seat of the limo. She noticed that Anthony was getting tired and took that moment to look out at the scenery, giving him the chance to fall asleep.

At the sound of soft snoring from him, she turned. She thought of him as someone who had entered her life for a reason. They'd always hit it off. His support now meant the world to her.

They pulled into the driveway of his home a short while later.

Anthony roused. "Easy, peasy drive this way, huh?"

"The best. Thank you," she said, studying the large, center-hall Colonial in Wayland Square. She'd seen the house before on a previous visit but looking at it now after Anthony's comments about children, she sensed how awful it must be for them to live in such a huge place with no family to fill it.

Bella greeted them at the door. A small, round, older woman with a pleasant face, she beamed at Dani as she embraced her. "Well, look who's here. Tony called me to tell me you were coming. He was excited about it as I am. Such a darling girl."

"Thank you for having me," said Dani. "Anthony wants me to inspect the site for the new building he wants to put in place. And when he mentioned seeing you, how could I refuse a stay here at the house?"

Bella chucked Dani's chin. "So nice to see you, sweet girl."

Feeling about twelve years old, Dani returned her smile. A little pampering was in store for her, and she was ready for it.

That evening after a delicious meal of some of Anthony's favorites— an antipasto, spaghetti Bolognese, and veal piccata, Dani did her best to turn down dessert. But when a piece of tiramisu was placed in front of her, she enjoyed every bite while telling herself it was just one night of eating like this.

Later, she lay in a high-post bed feeling like a pampered princess in her lovely surroundings. She knew some of Anthony's family history and thought how different members of any family could be. She wondered when she'd have the chance to spend time with Brad's parents. It would tell her so much about a future with him and what moral support his family would give them. Living in the same town wouldn't always be easy.

Her cell chimed. *Brad.*

She clicked on the call. "Hello. I was just thinking about

you."

"I can say the same about you," he said, and she could hear the happiness in his voice.

"I'm in Providence at Anthony and Bella Albono's house so I can go with him tomorrow morning to inspect the site and talk more about his plans. You won't believe the dinner I had. Delicious."

"Sounds like a nice break for you," said Brad. "Just so you're ready to come back. I've missed you."

"Is JoEllen still there?"

"Yes, just a couple of days more and she should be gone," said Brad. "I can't wait until she leaves. I talked to her mother today and made it clear that though I loved Patti, I wasn't going to marry JoEllen."

"I'm glad you did that," said Dani. "It was a twisted idea."

"I agree," Brad said. "JoEllen had told her mother I was all for it, so she was surprised when I called. Patti was a special person, but it's time for me to live the life I want, and that includes you. I can't wait to see you again, Dani."

Happiness wove warmth through her. After seeing Anthony and Bella so happy after all their years together, she could envision the same sweetness for her and Brad. Dani was even more content to think of a life with him. If the day arrived when he asked her to marry him, she knew her answer would be yes.

The next morning, Dani followed the aroma of coffee to the kitchen. When she walked into the room, Bella looked up at her. "Good morning, sweetheart. My famous sweet rolls just came out of the oven, and coffee is ready."

"Thank you. Everything smells delicious," said Dani pouring herself a cup. She took a sip of the steaming liquid and sat at the kitchen table.

Bella joined her. "Tony is a little slow in the morning and I'm glad. It will give us time to talk. I want you to know that Tony wasn't planning on constructing another building, but when he called your firm to talk to you about it and that Frank person at the office told Tony he'd do better to work with him, Tony was furious. That's when he decided to go ahead with the project. He called your boss and told him he wanted you to be in charge, and if you weren't, he'd take his business elsewhere."

Tears stung Dani's eyes. "He did that for me?"

"Absolutely. He was aware of how you had been treated at the office and decided to do something about it. Nobody messes with Tony when he's watching out for someone's welfare." Bella crossed her arms and gave her a steady look. "Me either."

"Oh, Bella, you and Anthony are so sweet. I admit I was having a difficult time at the office. That's one reason I decided to move to New Hampshire. I wanted to do something that people appreciated and to enjoy my work again. Tony's project is special, and I feel honored to help him."

"Help me do what?" Anthony said, entering the room.

"I'm thrilled to be able to help you with the building," said Dani. "Your loyalty means a lot."

"Yeah, well no guy is going to cut you out of the deal because he thinks he's better than you. Especially, when I know he's not." He went over to Bella and gave her a kiss on the cheek. "'Morning."

She smiled up at him.

"I'm naming the building the Bella Apartments," said Anthony taking a seat at the table as Bella got up to serve him.

"How perfect," said Dani, still in awe of what Anthony had done for her. "We'll make them beautiful."

"I told him he'd better," said Bella, and they all chuckled.

Later, standing with Anthony studying the building site and its location in the downtown neighborhood, Dani was pleased. She and Anthony worked well together and were able to discuss ideas freely. The building they had in mind would be attractive and functional for families.

"Let's go back to the house. I'll ask my nephew to drive you back to Boston," said Anthony.

"Your nephew is your driver?" said Dani.

Anthony grinned. "Great-nephew. Family sticks together. He's a good kid."

Dani climbed into the limousine with Anthony and couldn't help staring at the driver. Broad-shouldered, with black curly hair and dark eyes that missed nothing, he seemed dangerous. In her presence, he'd remained quiet, vigilant. She had the feeling that beneath his jacket he carried a gun. It wouldn't surprise her.

At Anthony's house, she retrieved the overnight bag she'd brought, kissed Bella, and gave Anthony a hug. "Thank you for everything."

"Tony told me about you and your young man in New Hampshire. If you end up marrying, don't forget to invite us to the wedding," said Bella, winking at her.

Dani laughed. "I promise."

Back in Boston, Dani met with Herb and told him about the meeting with Anthony.

"I'll do the drawings in New Hampshire. I have a workspace set up, but I need more supplies from here. When the initial plans are ready, I'll return to help with the permitting process, if Anthony needs me. The building will be much like the building I worked on earlier with him."

"I'm pleased you're off to an excellent start. Keep in touch and let me know when you'll be in Boston again. I'd like to spend some time with you," said Herb. "I'm glad you were able to work on this project."

Dani made a face. "Anthony told me what Frank tried to do."

"A very bad mistake on his part," said Herb shaking his head. "I knew Frank was ambitious, but I didn't realize he was dishonest. I'm sorry."

"As it turns out, it's a good thing for me," said Dani, unable to hide a note of satisfaction.

They shook hands, and then Dani gathered supplies and left the office.

CHAPTER THIRTY-EIGHT
TAYLOR

Taylor wasn't surprised when Ross asked her if he could take her out to dinner. Crystal had told her he would call. Still, the excitement of seeing him and getting to know him better surged through her as she ended the call.

The night she and Crystal had met up with them, she'd been so focused on Nick that she hadn't paid much attention to Ross. But then, there were many people her age in town interested in getting to know each other since they'd be living in the same area for the foreseeable future. She thought of it as similar to the first days at a summer camp, where kids were getting to know one another and deciding which ones would become friends.

After living a comparatively solitary life in New York, Taylor was glad for new friendships. But as she got dressed for dinner that night, she knew she wanted to find more than friendship. She wanted to find love. After hiding out following a few disastrous dates with men who'd denigrated her for writing sweet romance stories, she was ready to try again. Lilac Lake was full of interesting and more-accepting people.

Taylor looked into the mirror trying to appraise herself fairly. With straight dark hair and dark-brown eyes, she looked very different from her sisters. As a small child she'd questioned whether she was in the right family but then had to look to her father, her sisters' stepfather, to see the truth. Still, people were sometimes surprised to learn that, with their lighter hair and blue eyes, Dani and Whitney were her sisters.

Tonight, she approved of the way her hair met her shoulders and the sundress she wore. She hoped Ross did too. No doubt, he was used to glamorous women. He was often photographed with them.

The doorbell rang and Taylor hurried to the front door to answer it, beating Pirate by only a few seconds.

Ross stood on the porch smiling at them. "Nice dog," he commented as Taylor opened the door. Pirate nosed Ross's outstretched hand before he stepped back and allowed Ross to enter.

"He's my sister Dani's dog. She's away for a couple of days."

"That's the sister who's the architect, right?" Ross asked.

Taylor nodded. "She's working with Aaron and Brad but is doing a part time job for a client in Rhode Island."

"I hope you're hungry for seafood. I thought we'd go to Fins for dinner," said Ross.

"A favorite place of mine," said Taylor. "We can walk from here if you'd prefer."

Ross's eyebrows shot up. "I'd like that. I haven't been getting enough exercise. Too much time spent at the inn and dealing with the contractors."

"I sit most of the day writing, so I need a walk," said Taylor. "I'll be ready to go after I get Pirate settled in the kitchen. He's a good dog, but we don't want to give him any opportunity to get into things while we rent this house."

"I heard you and your sisters were going to move to Lilac Lake," said Ross as they left the house moments later.

"We are. At least for part of the year. Until the cottage at the inn is renovated, we'll rent space. We were lucky to find the rental we did."

"I've bought one of the homes in the new development Aaron and Brad are creating. My plans for the future are unsettled at the moment, but I like the thought of putting down roots here."

"Yes, I've come to that conclusion too. But I'm not giving up my condo in New York. Even though it's small, I could never replace it with one as attractive for the price."

"A wise decision," said Ross as they walked into town.

Taylor never tired of comparing the town center to the bustling city of New York. She loved the city but was excited to try "country" living. Here, people strolled along the wide sidewalk enjoying the sights, stopping to peek in store windows, or maybe enjoy an ice cream cone. Most of the store fronts had colorful awnings and were well-maintained. Large pots of flowers sat by their doors, adding more texture and color.

With a sweep of his hand, Ross said, "Charming, isn't it?"

"Oh yes. Years ago, when my sisters and I spent summers here, the town was pretty but wasn't gentrified like it is today. This scene could be in any Hallmark commercial."

Ross chuckled. "Well spoken."

They reached Fins, and Ross ushered her inside to where Melissa Hendrickson's mother, Susan, greeted them. "I'm so pleased to see you again, Ross," said Susan beaming at him. She turned to her. "And how are you, Taylor? Still writing those books of yours?"

Taylor smiled and shrugged. "Trying to."

Susan led them to a table by the window. "Your waitress will be here soon," she said, handing them each a leather-bound menu. "Please enjoy your meal. We're pleased to have you here."

Their waitress, an older woman with a pleasant face, approached with a pitcher of iced water. "We can offer you our local water or imported sparkling water."

Ross and Taylor exchanged looks and then Taylor said, "I'm fine with the local water, thanks."

Ross nodded at the waitress. "For me too. But I'd like to see a wine list, please."

"Of course," she said pouring glasses of water for them. "To help you decide, our specials for tonight are baked scrod with a lemon-herb panko coating, broiled swordfish with a beurre blanc sauce, and roasted Cornish hens with garlic and rosemary."

She left and a wine steward came over to the table. "How may I help you?"

"Do you prefer a white or a red wine?" Ross asked her.

"My favorite is a light red wine. Maybe something from Chandler Hill Wineries," said Taylor. She'd dated a man who once told her she should be specific.

Ross said, "Okay, let's see what we can do. Any thoughts on your main course?"

"I'm going with the swordfish," Taylor said, her mouth anticipating the taste of it.

"And I'm going with the scrod. So that makes it easy," said Ross, turning to the wine steward.

After discussing choices, the wine steward left and returned a moment later with a bottle of wine to show Ross.

Taylor watched as Ross went through the motions of smelling and tasting the wine. "I think you're going to like this," he said to Taylor. "It's as close to a Chandler Hill one as we could get."

The steward poured wine into her glass before filling Ross's and gave a quick bow. "Enjoy."

Ross lifted his glass. "Here's to a pleasant evening."

Taylor raised hers. "It already is wonderful."

"So, you write novels for a living," Ross said.

"It's much more difficult that anyone would think. With all the marketing involved, writing the book is only part of the business."

"What kind of books are they?" asked Ross.

Taylor drew a deep breath. This is the question she disliked most. Many of the men she'd dated thought romance books were trash. "I write uplifting, happy-ending stories about women finding purpose and love in their lives."

"Ah, my mother loves books like that. I'm an avid reader but usually read science fiction or fantasy novels." There was no condemnation in his voice.

Taylor perked up. "So, have you read the Son of Orion series?"

He blinked with surprise. "Yes, it's one of my favorites."

"The basis of the story is a lovely romance."

Looking surprised, Ross said, "Hadn't thought of it that way, but you're right."

Taylor's pulse sprinted at the way he was smiling at her.

CHAPTER THIRTY-NINE
DANI

Dani drove into the driveway of the house she rented with Taylor and let out a happy sigh. Lilac Lake never seemed more like home.

Taylor came to the front door and let Pirate out to greet her.

Dani laughed as Pirate sprinted to her, his tongue lolling out of the side of his mouth. She opened her arms and he rushed into them, almost pushing her to the ground in his enthusiasm.

She stroked his silky dark fur and talked softly to him watching as Taylor approached.

"Welcome home," said Taylor. "We missed you, but I'm pleased you had such a successful trip." They'd talked earlier in the day.

"It was an ego boost, that's for sure," said Dani. She looked across the lawn at Brad's house and noticed the driveway was empty. "Has JoEllen left?"

"Not until tomorrow," said Taylor.

"I think I'll call Brad and see if we can meet for lunch," said Dani. "He didn't phone as usual last night, and I missed his call this morning. There's so much I want to tell him."

"Things next door have been pretty quiet." Taylor leaned forward. "Crystal said JoEllen has been hitting the bar scene at night. Alone."

"I almost feel sorry for her," said Dani, realizing it was true. It was sad and creepy to think of a person waiting around to try and fill her dead sister's shoes or, in this case, her sister's bed.

As soon as Dani had settled her things in the house and had her "office" set up in the kitchen again, she phoned Brad.

"Hey, great to hear from you," he said. "I tried calling you this morning."

"I know. That's why I'm wondering if we could meet for lunch to catch up," said Dani.

"Sorry, I can't do that today. But let's get together tonight. I'll take you and JoEllen to dinner for her last night in town. With luck, neither one of us will ever have to see her again."

Dani didn't think that sharing the evening with JoEllen was the best idea but decided to be a sport about it. "Okay, deal."

"My mother is inviting you to Sunday dinner. She tries to get the family together at least once a month. More if we can all make it."

"That sounds like fun. I haven't seen your mom around town, but I remember her famous pies at the annual summer town fair. And those delicious fresh vegetables from the family farm."

"Yes, the farm is still functioning. My parents had to hire people to help them now that Aaron, Amy, and I have left the nest. Poor Becca is left at home while her boyfriend is away in the service."

"I can't wait to see everybody again," said Dani, feeling more at home than ever. "I'll see you later. Thanks for the invitation for tonight."

She ended the call and phoned GG. "Want a visitor for lunch?"

"You bet," said GG. "We eat early so come right away. Can't wait to hear your latest news."

At the sight of GG sitting in her room, Dani's heart swelled with love. GG was about the same age as Anthony and, like him, was still mentally alert. But all the labor of running the inn was beginning to show on her.

GG's smile lit her face. "I'm so glad to see you. Tell me all about your trip to Boston. It must have been a marvelous trip for you. You're glowing."

Dani laughed. "More like gloating. It was so pleasant to be in control for once. Herb was extremely respectful. But then, Anthony Albono made it very clear what he thought of Frank and the company for treating me with so little respect."

"It's splendid to have a champion outside the family to cheer you on," said GG, grinning.

"Anthony and his wife Bella are the sweetest people. I've even promised to invite them to my wedding."

GG's eyebrows shot up. "Do you have other news to share?"

Dani shook her head. "Not really. But I've fallen for Brad Collister. And he feels the same way about me. His mother has invited me to dinner tomorrow."

"Ah, so it's more serious than I thought. Mary Lou Collister's meals are important family events, and for you to be included is a big deal," said GG, beaming at her.

A shiver of nerves crossed Dani's back. She didn't want anything or anyone to ruin what she and Brad had found with one another.

Back home in the kitchen, Dani tried to focus on her work, but her mind kept jumping to the evening ahead. After being away for a couple of days, she couldn't wait to be with Brad. The downside was that JoEllen would be present.

Pirate barked when Brad's red truck pulled into the driveway.

Dani and Pirate hurried outside to greet him.

Brad's smile when he saw her lit his entire face, and the

frisson of nerves that Dani had fought all afternoon disappeared.

He swept her up in his arms and hugged her before lowering his lips on hers.

Sighing happily, Dani sank into his kiss, feeling her insides fill with pleasure and need. Secure with the knowledge that the magic they shared was real, she emitted a soft groan.

When Brad pulled away, he grinned at her. "Glad to know you missed me too."

She chuckled. "It was a successful trip, but I couldn't wait to come back here. I'll give you the details when we're alone. Where is JoEllen? I don't see her rental car."

Brad frowned. "I've tried to call her all day, but no answer. We had another honest talk and she told me she was going to do some errands today before she takes off tomorrow morning."

"Maybe she's purposely avoiding you," said Dani, thinking it would be just like JoEllen to do something like that.

"Let's not worry about that now. While you were gone, the crew took down some of the walls we wanted removed in the cottage. Let's go check it out."

She called to Pirate, opened the back door of Brad's truck for Pirate, and slid into the passenger seat.

"I'm glad the project has actually started," said Dani. "We want to be ready to move in by the fall."

"If we keep working on it every day, it'll happen," said Brad. "The kitchen was supposed to be ripped out today."

Dani was surprised to see JoEllen's rental in the driveway when they pulled up to the house. "What's JoEllen doing here? This is private property."

"She came out to the site yesterday to check the progress. Maybe she decided to come back to see the work on the kitchen," said Brad calmly, but he was frowning.

Dani got out of the truck and opened the door for Pirate. He took off running, glad to be free.

Brad held out his hand to her and they walked together to the front of the house. The door was open and swinging in the breeze.

"I thought the house would be locked up when the work crew left," said Dani.

"Yes. We keep the key under the stone by the stairs. Not original but it works with so many different crews coming and going." Brad climbed the stairs.

Still skittish about the weird feelings she had about the house, Dani stayed behind him.

"Hello?" Brad called.

"Here! I'm in here," came a reply.

Brad and Dani walked into the kitchen and stared at the scene with dismay. Sitting amid a pile of rubble JoEllen looked up at them. It was obvious she'd been crying.

"What happened?" Brad asked, rushing over to her. He pulled a large piece of old wall aside to free her.

"I saw the men tearing down the walls yesterday and when I saw a sledgehammer left behind, I wanted to try it," said JoEllen. "I didn't realize the wall would collapse."

Brad continued to carefully remove debris from JoEllen's body and when enough had been cleared, he helped her to her feet.

"Are you okay?" said Dani, approaching them. JoEllen didn't appear to be hurt.

"Just scared. I didn't dare move for fear of having more stuff fall on me. And I couldn't call for help because I left my phone in the car," said JoEllen. "I know the house is supposed to be haunted. I think it's true. I swear a ghost-like figure appeared just before the wall fell and then it evaporated."

Brad frowned. "Did you bump your head when the wall

landed on you?"

"No," said JoEllen, giving him a defiant look. "I'm telling you the truth." She looked at Dani. "You know what I'm talking about, don't you?"

"I ... I'm not sure," said Dani. JoEllen had done a stupid thing, but did an entire wall normally collapse on someone. It seemed strange to her.

"Well, I've learned my lesson. I'm leaving and I'm not coming back here. There's something weird going on in this house." JoEllen stretched, checking her body, and then she hurried with a slight limp to the front door.

Dani turned to Brad. "I'm scared."

Brad put an arm around her. "No need to be. I'm here."

She looked up at him and as they were about to kiss, she saw twinkling lights in the glow of the sun and relaxed.

That evening Dani sat with Brad and JoEllen in a booth at Jake's. She wished she had Brad to herself, but they had just one more night of JoEllen's presence

Sitting in the booth opposite JoEllen, Dani sipped her drink and wondered what it was about JoEllen that made her so unpleasant. She was attractive, a qualified nurse's aide, and book smart. Why then, did people not like her?

JoEllen turned her attention to Brad. "I have a surprise for you. For both of you, actually. I've taken a job at The Woodlands and will be moving back here full time in two weeks."

The look of shock on Brad's face equaled her own.

"Where will you stay?" asked Dani.

"One of the nurses at The Woodlands told me about the River Run Cabins along Lilac creek. They used to be for campers but now they're used as rentals for locals." JoEllen gave her a smug smile. "They're adorable really. Two bedrooms, kitchen/living area with a fireplace, and a large bathroom. They even have a covered parking area."

"How long have you known this?" Brad asked, looking annoyed.

"For a few days. I didn't want to tell you until I was sure about the cabin. But I like it," said JoEllen. "After seeing how much fun this area is, I decided why not? This way I can keep an eye on things."

Dani bit her lip to keep from speaking, but she wondered what GG would think about JoEllen working at The Woodlands. Dani had already told her about JoEllen's ridiculous idea about marrying Brad.

"You don't have to keep an eye on anything here but yourself. And you do realize that winters here are a lot different from what you call summer fun," said Brad tersely.

"I was here for one Christmas. Remember?" said JoEllen. "I figure by winter I'll have already met someone. That's my goal, anyway, now that plans have changed with you."

Dani didn't need to wonder anymore why JoEllen was unpopular. In a matter of minutes, she'd irritated both Brad and her by talking about keeping an eye on things, insinuating that she had the right to do so.

The waitress arrived with their food. Dani looked at it with distaste, her appetite gone.

Beside her, Brad squeezed her hand and she rallied, wanting to support him.

After the uncomfortable meal, Brad dropped JoEllen off at his house, and drove into Dani's driveway.

"Will you come in?" Dani asked. He was clearly still upset.

"Yes. Thanks. I'm so over JoEllen and all her bullshit."

"I understand," said Dani. "Come inside. How about a cup of coffee or a glass of iced cold tea?"

"A cold drink would be great. I need to cool down," said

Brad. "No lemon for me, please. My stomach is already a mess from holding back my anger."

"Let's try to enjoy ourselves. JoEllen will be out of your house in the morning."

In the kitchen, Dani found a note from Taylor saying that she and Ross were going to a movie and out afterwards so she wouldn't be home until late.

Dani showed Brad the note.

"That will give us some time alone." He stepped forward and took her in his arms. "I missed you when you were gone. I didn't think I'd ever find love again, but with you, I have."

She gave him a teasing look. "So, you're saying you love me?"

He laughed. "I *do* love you, Danielle Gilford. Even with all the interruptions we've had in being alone, I thought you knew that."

"I love you too," she said, lifting her face to his. She craved hearing those words from a man she knew she'd love forever.

When kissing wasn't enough, Dani took hold of his hand. "Come with me."

Upstairs, they walked into her bedroom.

CHAPTER FORTY
DANI

Dani awoke expecting to find Brad beside her. When she saw the space next to her empty, she remembered he'd told her he'd leave early in the morning to see JoEllen off. She had an early flight to Ohio, and Brad wanted to make sure JoEllen left.

Dani rolled onto her back and stared up at the ceiling and emitted a happy sigh. Brad was a wonderful lover—passionate, kind, giving. She was pleased they'd had this time together before she joined his family for Sunday dinner.

After taking care of her morning rituals, she headed downstairs and was surprised to see Taylor sitting at the kitchen table.

"Well, well, the princess awakens," teased Taylor. "I was surprised to bump into Brad earlier. He said something about going to see JoEllen off."

Dani poured herself a cup of coffee and joined Taylor at the table. "JoEllen might be leaving today, but she's returning in two weeks. She's going to be working at The Woodlands and living at the River Run Cabins."

"Wh-a-a-a-t! Why? She doesn't have real friends here. She's antagonized so many."

"She told us she'll be able to keep an eye on things," said Dani. "Brad is done with her nonsense. We're both unhappy that she's sticking around."

"I'm sorry, but I don't think you have to worry about Brad. He adores you. He told me you're invited to his family's

Sunday dinner. That's a big step, Dani."

"I know. I was nervous, but I feel more confident. We're so in love."

"That's all that matters right now," said Taylor. She lifted her coffee cup in a salute. "Here's to you both!"

Dani lifted her own cup in return. Taylor was right. Neither she nor Brad could allow someone to ruin the love they shared.

"How was the movie last night?" Dani asked sitting down. "Is Ross as nice as some people say?"

"Yes. He's a great guy, but we both agree that we're content to be just friends," said Taylor. "I'm not interested in seriously dating a famous baseball star. I'm used to hiding out in my house writing."

"Well, maybe it's time for you to get out into the real world," said Dani, getting up and giving her a quick hug before heading upstairs to get ready for the day.

Later, sitting beside Brad in his truck, Dani got a perfect view of the Collister farmhouse as he drove up the long driveway. The white clapboard, two-story house with black shutters and a wide porch sat among a scattering of sugar maple trees. The driveway extended to a well-maintained, small red barn that was used, in part, as a storefront where customers could buy fresh produce, homemade jams and jellies, and other food items during the summer months. Dani remembered a greenhouse behind the barn where flowers and plants were grown, along with vegetable and herb seedlings.

GG had loved to come here in the late summer to get fresh corn and other treats. Though it was small compared to some farms in the area, every inch of land was put to use and well maintained. No wonder his parents now needed to hire help. It would take a lot of work to maintain it.

Brad pulled his truck into the designated parking space and cut off the engine. Turning to her, he said, "Don't mind my mom. She'll probably go overboard when she meets you. She was very excited when I told her I was bringing you to dinner."

Dani grinned. "As long as you come to my rescue, I'll be fine."

They got out of the truck and headed to the house hand in hand.

Brad's mother, MaryLou, stepped onto the porch and beamed at them. She was a heavy-set woman with pretty hazel eyes and light-brown hair with a few streaks of gray. She wore navy pants and a pink floral top. Dani knew her as one of the most-respected people in town for raising an exceptional family who worked hard together.

"There you are. So glad you could come, Dani. It's been a long while since I've seen you with your grandmother."

"I know," said Dani. "I haven't been to the farm in a long time. I used to come for vegetables with GG, but that hasn't happened for years. Just bad timing, I guess."

As soon as Dani stepped onto the porch, MaryLou threw her arms around her. "Welcome. It's the first time Brad has brought anyone for dinner since Patti died. I'm so glad it's you. I remember you and your sisters as little girls, and I've watched you all grow into fine young women. Your grandmother keeps me and everyone else up-to-date on your activities. She's so proud of you."

MaryLou took a much-needed breath and Dani said, "I'm proud of GG, too."

"What's for dinner?" asked Brad.

MaryLou hugged him. "Some of your favorites. Roast chicken, fresh peas, and a sweet potato casserole."

"Thanks," said Brad. "Who else is coming?"

"Just the family. Amy and Bill and their baby boy, Becca, of course, and Aaron. Hard to get everyone together, but today your father and I are lucky."

Just then Brad's father opened the screen door, letting a small, pink pig outside.

Dani jumped out of the pig's way. "Who's that?"

"That's my beloved Pansy. Don't let anyone tell you that pigs don't make nice pets. She's the best," said MaryLou, leaning over and giving Pansy a loving touch on the head.

"Glad you could make it, Dani," said Brad's father.

In contrast to his wife, Joe Collister was a tall, thin, handsome man with strong features on a weathered face and a head with thick gray hair. Dani could see Aaron's features came from his father, Joe. Brad had more of his mother's blond, finer features.

"Thank you for having me to dinner," said Dani.

He gave her a steady look and then a nod of approval. "We're happy to have you. Right, Brad?" he said, giving his son a hearty slap on the back even though Brad stood taller than he.

"Well, come on inside and meet the youngest member of the Collister family," said MaryLou. "We think he's pretty special."

Dani followed MaryLou inside as Joe held the door for them. In the living room, sitting on the couch holding a baby, Brad's sister Amy smiled up at her. "Glad to see you here, Dani. It's been a couple of years since my wedding and now look what's happened." She proudly held up her baby boy for Dani to take.

Surprised, Dani took the infant and hugged him close to her chest. Looking down into his round face, she wondered if all the Collister babies would be so beautiful. "He's so handsome. What's his name?"

Amy grinned. "We're calling him Will. He's named after my husband Bill." She turned as a man entered the room with her sister, Becca. "This is Bill Blanchard, my husband, and of course, you know Becca."

The baby began to whimper so Dani jiggled him in her arms and cooed to him.

He stopped fussing and held up a hand to touch Dani's face.

"Dani, you're a natural with children. I hope you have lots of them," said Amy.

Dani glanced at Brad and felt her cheeks go red hot.

"Now, Amy," scolded MaryLou, "don't go and embarrass our guest."

"I'm sorry," Amy said to Dani. "I know you and Brad are just dating."

Brad walked over and put an arm around Dani. "It's much more than that," he said giving her a loving look, bringing more heat to Dani's cheeks.

Becca hugged Brad. "Really? I'm so happy for you. I loved Patti, but that sister of hers is awful. She tried to tell me that you and she were getting married. I didn't believe her, but I'm glad to know it's not true. Especially seeing you now with Dani."

"It's most definitely not true," said Brad. "It was an idea she wanted to be true, but it was never going to happen." Dani could tell he was upset by the thought of JoEllen spreading such news.

Will fussed again, and this time Dani handed him to his mother.

"Why don't you come into the kitchen with me," MaryLou said to Dani. "You can help me with some last-minute touches. There are certain family recipe tricks you might want to know about."

Brad winked at Dani and went outside with his father and Bill to greet Aaron, leaving the sisters with the baby.

"Do you like to cook?" MaryLou asked as she led Dani into the big, family-style kitchen.

"Sometimes," Dani answered honestly. "I've been living either alone or with a roommate since college and never did much cooking."

"Well, hard-working men doing physical labor need healthy, hearty food. I'll show you a few tricks to make meals tasty. By the way, you should know, your GG helped us when we were having a bad year with the farm. Such a kind, generous woman. We'll always be grateful to her."

Dani remained quiet, uncertain what to say. GG didn't talk about the people she helped.

MaryLou gave her a quick hug. "I don't mean to put pressure on you, but I see how happy Brad is, and I know your grandmother would be as pleased as us if anything were to come of his feelings for you."

Tears stung Dani's eyes. His parents' warmth toward her meant so much.

"Aw, honey, I didn't mean to make you cry," said MaryLou, handing her a paper napkin.

Dani dabbed at her eyes. "I've never felt this way about any man before. It's happened quickly, but Brad's such a fabulous person."

"He is, indeed. And he deserves happiness. As Brad's mother, I'm relieved to see him like this again. Collister men love deeply and long. Now it's time for Brad to be happy again."

"Thank you for being so accepting," said Dani. "As Brad said, we're doing more than dating. We'll see where it goes."

MaryLou raised her eyebrows and shook her head, a smile playing at her lips. "I already know."

"What are you two talking about?" asked Aaron coming into the kitchen and throwing his arms around his mother's shoulder.

"It's just girl talk, son," said MaryLou beaming at him. "When are you going to bring someone to Sunday dinner?"

Aaron laughed, held up his hands, and backed away. "Who knows? What's for dinner?"

"You'll see. Now leave me to teach Dani a few of my tricks."

He left, and MaryLou pulled a perfectly browned roast chicken from the oven. "We'll let that sit for a minute while I cook the peas and see to the casserole. Dani, pull out the bread from the top oven and slice it, please. Then I'll show you what's inside the chicken to make it taste so delicious—lemon wedges, garlic, and my special seasonings."

And just like that, Dani felt as if she'd found a comfortable new family.

Joe carved the chicken while Dani and MaryLou placed food on the large kitchen table so people could help themselves to servings from heaping bowls of vegetables, potatoes, and salad.

Sitting with the others at the table Dani thought of her own family dinners. Her mother was a beautiful woman who prided herself on serving small, delicious portions of healthy food to daughters who watched their weight. Here, nobody seemed to care.

Conversation centered around family matters, farming, the new baby, and the latest fishing reports. Dani was amused as she watched how Brad, Aaron, Amy, Becca and Bill fought for a time to speak. Even the baby, sitting in an infant seat, seemed to find the talk interesting.

After dinner was over, Dani offered to help with the dishes.

"Thanks, sweetheart," said MaryLou. "You can help Amy and Becca."

Dani helped clear the dishes from the table and then stood by as Amy rinsed and Becca loaded the dishwasher and set aside serving dishes and pots and pans to be done by hand.

Amy filled the sink with hot, sudsy water and tossed a dish towel to Dani. "You can dry. Becca will put everything away."

"Don't mind her, Amy's always bossy," said Becca, giving her sister a playful punch.

Amy laughed. "Can't help myself. Now, Dani, tell us all about you and Brad. He looks so happy. How did you two meet? Give us some details."

Dani grinned. This seemed more like home. Gossiping in the kitchen. "I met Brad at the Lilac Lake Inn my first day here this summer. He's so ...

"Hot? Nice?" teased Becca.

"Both," said Dani chuckling. "Anyway, he and I are working together on renovating the cottage on the property. My grandmother gave my sisters and me the house with the understanding that it be occupied for at least six months of the year. Now all of us have pretty much decided to live here. I've agreed to work for Collister Construction and do other architectural and design consulting."

"What about Whitney? Is it true she and Zane are back together? How does it feel to have a movie star for a sister?" asked Amy.

"An actress and a well-known author for sisters? We're just sisters. We treat each other the same," said Dani.

"I remember you all coming for a brief time each summer when you were younger. I wasn't always able to take part in some of the fun stuff, but the Gilford girls were always part of it," said Becca.

"We used to love coming to Lilac Lake, which is why we're excited about spending more time here," said Dani.

"When Danny gets back from his tour of duty, we're going

to get married and stay right here. He's interested in someday taking over the farm. He and Bill may work it together," said Becca. "That's my hope anyway."

"Bill still hasn't committed to it," said Amy. "But the baby has made him think more about it. Right now, we're both working outside Boston for high tech companies. My mother is really pushing us to make the move."

"I imagine taking care of the farm and the business that goes with it is a lot of work," said Dani, unsure if she could ever do farming for living. So much of it was dependent on the weather and other things out of one's control.

"Time will take care of many things," said Amy. "I haven't told Bill yet, but I think I might be pregnant again.."

"Oh, sis, that's wonderful! Does Mom know?" said Becca hugging her.

"Yes, but she's sworn to secrecy," said Amy. "And if she promises not to tell, she won't. Some secrets are worth keeping until the time is right." She winked at Dani.

"No secrets yet," said Dani. "None that I know of, anyway."

CHAPTER FORTY-ONE
WHITNEY

Whitney spent every moment she could packing up. She'd decided she'd sublet the condo until she was sure of her plans for her future. She'd miss the sunshine and the beach, but it was time to go to New Hampshire and make a different life for herself. If and when the time was right for a return, she'd make it happen. Her agent would continue to look for movies and other projects for her.

Mindy raced around on her short legs sniffing boxes, pulling at wrapping paper, and generally being an adorable nuisance. In the short time Whitney had owned her, she'd become a devoted parent to the demanding dachshund.

When her cell rang, she checked caller ID. *Mom.*

Grateful for the time to talk, Whitney clicked onto the call. "Hi, Mom."

"Hi, darling. I got your text. What's going on?"

Whitney took a seat on the couch and drew a breath. "I've made the decision to move to Lilac Lake on a permanent basis. Or at least until there's a reason for me to return to California. I don't have to work for a while, and I need to reassess my life after all the trouble with Zane. I'm ready for a life with people who care about the same things I do."

"And what are they?" her mother asked, her voice rolling slowly off her lips in the Southern accent she'd picked up after living for years in the South.

"I've earned a nice income and made some good

investments. I've got time to figure out what's next. In the meantime, I want to be outdoors in fresh air, hang around with friends who don't care what I look like, and maybe have a family of my own. Something like you and Dad have," said Whitney, fighting tears. She was so damn tired of her life as an actress.

"Darling, that sounds wonderful. You've maintained a fine professional reputation as an actress who is very down-to-earth. In that environment, it can't have been easy for you. I'm proud of you for that. How soon are you going to make the move?"

"I'm almost finished packing and plan on flying out the day after tomorrow. I've shipped a lot of things to New Hampshire and have rented out my condo."

"No holding back a Gilford woman when she makes up her mind," said her mother with a chuckle. It's something they'd all heard her father say many times.

They chatted for a while longer and when Whitney ended the call, she felt more confident than ever that she was making the right decision.

CHAPTER FORTY-TWO
DANI

A couple of days later, Dani sat outside on GG's patio telling her all about the dinner with Brad's family. "They're delightful people," she ended.

"Yes, they are," said GG "It makes me so happy that they've taken to you. I know how sad everyone was to lose Patti."

"Yes, but they don't like JoEllen and weren't pleased to know she'd be sticking around." Dani took hold of her grandmother's hand. "I want you to be careful what you say around JoEllen, and keep your valuables tucked safely away. There's something about her that isn't right. Brad thinks so too. Did you know a wall fell on her at the house? It was very strange."

"What? Was she hurt?"

"Not really, just trapped by debris, almost as if it was a warning to stay away," said Dani. "She had no business being there to begin with. I didn't think I believed in ghosts, but some eerie things have happened at the house that can't be completely explained. And yet, we've had Nick check the place, and he found nothing to be alarmed about."

GG shook her head. "We'll have Nick check the house from time to time. But we can't let fear of the unknown stop us from doing what is right. And I truly believe the right thing for the three of you young women is to find a new life starting here. I'm convinced of it because you've each shared how unhappy you've been."

Dani rose and kissed GG's cheek. "You're always so

generous. MaryLou Collister told me about how you helped them."

GG's face lit with pleasure. "My father was the one who gave me the idea of sharing our wealth when he gave me the nickname Genie, like the magical creature who could grant wishes. Until recently, I've been able to live my life that way. It's been a true joy."

"You've helped a lot of people," said Dani. "I'm proud to be your granddaughter."

"Thank you. Let's see where the next few months take us. In the meantime, how about a little lunch before you go back to work?"

"I'd love that. Progress is taking place at the house. Right now, we're waiting for the plumbers and electricians to do their work. And I'm working on the project in Rhode Island," said Dani.

Dani followed her grandmother into the dining room and sat beside her, amused when a lot of people came up to them to say hello.

"You're so popular," Dani said softly.

GG grinned. "It's not me. They love seeing you and your sisters here. It's so refreshing."

###

When Dani returned to the house, she saw an unfamiliar car in the driveway. Puzzled, she parked behind it and went inside.

"Surprise!" said her mother rising from the couch in the living room. Dani's father and Taylor had jumped to their feet, identical smiles on their faces.

Dani ran to her mother to give her a hug and turned to her father. "It's wonderful to see you. What's the occasion?"

"I talked to Whitney. She told me she was arriving sometime today," said her mother, returning Dani's hug. "She also told me you were dating someone, and she thought it was serious. I decided it was time to check on my mother and my three girls."

"And I'm hoping to get in some fishing while I'm here," said Dani's father, accepting a hug from her.

"Where are you staying?" Dani said. "I'm sorry but we don't have room here."

"No worries. We're all set at the Lilac Lake B&B," said her mother. "After a day or two, Dad is going to go to his favorite fishing lodge for a few days while I stay in town and relax. I really need to spend time with GG, to make sure she's happy where she is."

"I just had lunch with her. She's already made lots of friends at The Woodlands, and some of her local friends visit her too," said Dani.

Her mother sighed. "That's the problem. She doesn't want to move closer to me."

"We'll take care of GG," said Taylor.

"Yes, Mom, Taylor, Whitney and I are ready to help her," said Dani. She gazed around. "Where's Pirate?"

"I put him outside," said Taylor. "He was getting too excited. Hold on, I'll get him."

"I never thought I'd love a dog so much, but Pirate is so sweet," said Dani laughing when Pirate bounded over to her. She gave him a hug and then said, "Sit."

Pirate sat on his hind haunches and stared up at her.

"Great dog," said Dani's father. "Still a bit of a puppy."

"He's learned a lot," said Dani proudly. "Shake hands, Pirate."

The black lab lifted his right front paw.

"Bravo," said her father, and Dani felt a rush of pride go through her. She patted the dog and turned to her mother. "Would you like a tour of our rental house? It's cute. The owner is thinking of selling it.'"

She walked her parents through the house and then they all went outside to the patio.

Taylor pointed next door. "That's where Brad, Dani's boyfriend, lives."

"I see," said Dani's mother. "Whitney filled me in on some of the details, but, Dani, why don't you tell us more about him. He must be special to put such a happy glow on your face."

Dani chuckled softly. "He *is* special." She told her parents about Brad's partnership with his brother, his family, and how he'd taken care of his wife. "She died much too young. Brad has done almost no dating for the past two years since her death. I'm not sure what happened, but we were attracted to one another the first time we met this summer, and it's grown into so much more."

"They're really cute together," said Taylor. "And so in love."

"I'm eager to meet him," said Dani's father. "One of my jobs as a father is to make sure the man that his daughter loves is worthy of her."

"Dad," groaned Dani. "Please don't embarrass me in front of Brad when you have the chance to meet him."

"How about we all go out to dinner tomorrow? We'll make it a big affair. It's not often the entire family gets together," said Dani's mother. "I'll reserve the private room at Fins."

"Okay," said Dani pleased by her mother's enthusiasm. "And tonight, we can just have a quiet meal here. I'm learning to cook."

"That will be lovely, darling. The important thing is we're here with our beautiful girls."

Pirate started to bark and raced inside.

"Someone's here. I'll get it," said Taylor. "Let's hope it's Whitney."

Taylor returned a few moments later with Whitney

carrying Mindy.

"Yay! You're here." said Dani, standing in line to greet Whitney. Her parents had already rushed forward, so she leaned down to pet Mindy. The dachshund wiggled with pleasure and then stopped and stared at Pirate.

Pirate backed away and sat at a distance staring at Mindy.

Dani hugged Whitney. "Glad you're home. Looks like we have a standoff between the dogs."

Mindy barked and Pirate lowered himself onto the floor and waited while Mindy approached him, touched his nose with hers, and then walked away, leaving them all laughing at the interchange.

"Come sit down," said Dani to Whitney.

"Thanks, but first I want to get out of these clothes and get my bags up to my room."

Her father stepped forward. "I'll help with the luggage."

After Whitney and her father left, Dani let out a soft sigh. "Whitney looks terrible."

"It's a good thing she left California when she did. Whitney has always been sensitive to stress. I think it started when her father and I were married. You were too young to remember, Dani, and thankfully you, Taylor, didn't have to go through all that mess."

"Well, I'm glad she's here," said Taylor. "The fresh air and sunshine and all the friendly people here will help."

"Okay, girls, let's plan a relaxing dinner here," said her mother.

"Yes, but let's keep it simple," said Taylor. "Do you want to invite Brad? He could keep Dad company."

Dani thought of the family dinner with Brad's family and how much it had meant to her. "Thanks. I do."

She left the patio and called Brad, hoping he could make it during this busy time. With it lighter later, the crew often worked until dark.

Brad picked up the call sounding breathless. "Hey, there. What's up?"

"My parents have arrived in town for a few days and I'm wondering if you'd join us for dinner at my house. We'll have a simple meal that will give them the chance to get to know you."

"Okay. I'll juggle a few things around. What time?"

"How about seven? Will that give you enough time to get ready?"

He laughed. "Is getting ready a warning?"

"Not really," she said smiling. "I know they'll like you."

"See you at seven."

As seven o'clock drew near, Dani's nerves tingled with anticipation. Her parents' responses to Brad were important to her. He was the man she loved and she wanted them to see what a warm and kind person he was.

As usual, Pirate heard him approach before any others. Mindy followed Pirate inside and Dani hurried behind them to answer the doorbell.

Dani's heart melted with love at the sight of him. "You got a haircut." She opened the door and kissed him.

"Sorry I'm a few minutes late. I had to take care of a few things, and I'm trying my best to make a good impression with your parents," he said, handing her a bottle of wine. He was wearing a golf shirt that matched the striking green of his eyes and a pair of jeans that fit his body well. But Dani knew his appearance wasn't as important as how he interacted with her family about her.

She took his hand and led him out to the patio. "Mom and Dad, this is Brad Collister."

Brad smiled and bobbed his head at her mother and then

shook hands with her father, who'd risen to his feet.

"Pleased to meet you," said her father, giving Brad an approving look.

"Come sit down by me," her mother said to Brad.

Dani and Brad exchanged amused glances. It was the equivalent of Brad's mother inviting Dani into the kitchen.

"I'll open the bottle of wine," said her father. "Dani, why don't you show me where the opener and glasses are."

Dani knew a command when she heard it. "Sure."

She followed her father into the kitchen and handed him the opener. "Yes?"

"I just want to be sure you're happy. Brad's a fine young man and from all accounts he's as serious about you as you are about him."

Surprised by her father's concern, she studied him. "I'm very happy with Brad. We've been seeing each other for only a few weeks, but I know if he asks me to marry him, I'd say yes. Does hearing that make you more comfortable? It hasn't been that long, but I remember all the stories about how you and mom quickly fell in love."

Her father hugged her. "Yes, I know it can happen. I just needed to be sure. Love you, Dani."

"Love you too, Dad."

After a pleasant dinner, Whitney announced she was going to her room to unpack what she could, and Taylor said to her parents, "Why don't I follow you to town? You said you were tired from the trip, and I promised Crystal I'd see her tonight."

"Are you sure it's not Ross you're going to see?" Dani teased.

Taylor grinned, "He might be there too."

Dani said farewell to her parents and Taylor, and after quickly straightening the kitchen, called up the stairs to tell

Whitney she was leaving with Brad.

Brad was quiet as they headed to his house.

"What do you think about my parents?" she asked, too anxious to wait any longer.

He faced her with a serious expression. "They're very nice. I'm glad we all got along. Your father and I may go fishing together while he's here. I told him I'd make the time."

"I saw you and him off by yourselves talking. That's what it was about?" said Dani.

"That and life in general. I didn't realize his background is performing social support work in the court system. He also told me he likes to do woodworking projects in his spare time, and it was he who got you interested in building things."

Dani grinned. "He's really my stepfather, though he adopted Whitney and me. But one way to win us over was by spending time with us. With Whitney, he went to the movies. With me, it was building a playhouse."

"Your mom is pretty and smart," said Brad, stopping and turning to face her. "Like you."

Dani smiled at him. "You make me happy."

Brad took hold of her hand. "Let's go inside where we can have some privacy."

Dani's pulse raced at the thought of being with him. She was glad she'd left Pirate behind. He might interrupt their plans.

CHAPTER FORTY-THREE
DANI

Brad unlocked the front door and ushered her into the living room.

"Please sit down. There's something I need to tell you."

"What's going on?" she asked, her heart pounding as she lowered herself onto the couch.

He sat next to her and took hold of her hand. "Today wasn't the first time I've spoken to your dad. I called him last Sunday and we had a long conversation."

"You did?"

"Yes. I asked him for permission to marry you," said Brad, taking hold of her hand.

"You did?" she said again, aware she was repeating herself. "What did he say?"

"He told me he'd give me an answer after we met. That's one reason they came to Lilac Lake."

"That makes it seem as if he didn't trust you," said Dani frowning.

"Far from it. He told me he was going to use it as an excuse to go fishing," said Brad grinning. "He and I got along on the phone and it's even better meeting him. I can't wait to introduce your parents to mine."

"Do your parents know about that call?" Dani asked, dazed by the information.

"Oh, yes." Brad got down on his knee and faced her. "Danielle Gilford, I love you. Will you marry me? I felt a connection to you from the moment I saw you walking toward me at the inn looking like an angel with that healthy glow of life around you. You offered me your unconditional friendship at a time when I was lost, giving me a lifeline that I needed almost as much as I now need your love. You are my now, my future, my everything. I promise to try and make you happy and be here for you every step of the way as we move forward together." His eyes grew shiny with tears. "I feel like I've waited forever to find you. I love you so much."

Dani threw herself into his arms, rocking him back onto the floor. "Yes! Oh, yes, Brad! I'll marry you!" She looked down at him sprawled on the floor beneath her and laughed for the pure joy of it as he hugged her tight.

Their lips touched and Dani lost herself in his kiss, a promise as true as his words. When they lay side by side, she said, "There's just one thing. I promised Anthony and Bella Albono they could come to our wedding."

"Done deal," said Brad, chuckling happily. "Anything else?"

"Just that you love me as much as I love you," she said, her eyes filling.

"I'm not sure I can do that," he said caressing her cheek, "because I'll always love you more."

"Then we're both going to be fine," Dani said wondering how she could be so lucky.

Brad sat up. "Don't you want your ring?" He reached into his pocket and brought out a small box. He opened it up to show her a round diamond surrounded by smaller ones set in platinum. "See how it looks like a sun with sparkling stars around it? That's how I think of you—bright and warm as the sun."

He slid the ring onto her finger. "It's something I bought a couple of days ago just waiting for this moment."

"It's perfect," gushed Dani. "I love it almost as much as you."

He laughed. "Keep it that way, huh?"

"Always," she said. "Always."

As Dani talked to her mother, tears of joy blurred her vision. "Brad proposed, and I said yes."

"Congratulations! That's delightful news. Your father and I knew it was going to happen tonight, which is why I've arranged a family dinner tomorrow. He's a wonderful young man. We can't wait to officially welcome him into the family. He and your father get along well already."

"And he thinks you're beautiful, Mom," said Dani, still star-struck by the event. "Brad is talking to his parents now."

"I've already invited them to dinner tomorrow," said her mother. "MaryLou and I talked earlier."

"Do you mean I was the last to know this was going to happen?" asked Dani her voice rising with dismay.

"Oh, honey, it's the sweetest thing ever. Two families who want you together," said her mother.

"What about GG. Does she know too?" Dani said.

"Not yet, but she told me the other day to be prepared for an engagement," said her mother. "We're all excited about it, Dani, because it's time you found someone just as special as you are."

Dani ended the call and sat for a moment. Her mother was right. She'd been so bogged down at work with negativity that she'd allowed herself to think she wasn't worthy of something better in every aspect of her life. Time for more change. Maybe in the future, she and Brad could use those tickets to Paris for their honeymoon.

The next evening, Dani watched Brad's people walk into the private dining room at Fins Restaurant and realized that going forward her life would be doubly blessed.

MaryLou hurried over to Dani and gave her a big hug. "Welcome to the family. Brad approached his father and me the day after our dinner together and told us he was going to ask you to marry him." Trying not to cry, she fanned her face. "He told us how much he loves you and that he never thought he'd find someone like you."

"I want to add my welcome," said Brad's father, beaming at her. "It doesn't matter when you kids decide to have your wedding. As far as we're concerned, you're already part of our family."

"Thank you," said Dani, blinking back tears.

"Oh, no," said Brad joining them. "More happy tears?"

"Yes," said Dani chuckling, "and it's all your fault."

He put his arm around her and hugged her to him. "I never want to make you cry."

Becca, Amy, Aaron, and Bill formed a circle around them.

"Welcome aboard," said Becca.

"Thank you all so much. It means the world to me," said Dani. She looked up as her mother headed their way.

"Hello, everyone," said Dani's mother. "Time to celebrate. It isn't every day I gain a son."

"Funny," teased MaryLou. "I thought we were celebrating because I was gaining a daughter."

Dani's mother looped her arm around MaryLou's elbow. "Lucky us. It goes both ways. C'mon. This calls for a little champagne."

Brad looked at Dani and grinned. "Guess it's all going to work out."

Smiling, Dani held onto his hand and studied the crowd. Her sisters were busy chatting to Brad's sisters, and her dad was talking to Joe, Aaron, and Bill about fishing. GG smiled at her from across the room where a waiter was pouring champagne into a tulip glass for her. Seeing them like this, Dani knew how exceptional this group was. It was almost as if their love was by design.

Later that night, Dani stood outside on the patio with Brad, wrapped in his arms. There was still work to be done on the house, a ghost to settle, and sisters to find love, but the summer was off to a fantastic start.

She looked up at the twinkling stars and felt the glow from the moon touch her heart with a promise of more amazing things to come.

The End

Thank you for reading *Love by Design*. If you enjoyed this book, please help other readers discover it by leaving a review on your favorite site. It's such a nice thing to do.

Sign up for my newsletter and get a free story. I keep my newsletters short and fun with giveaways, recipes, and the latest must-have news about me and my books. Welcome! Here's the link:

https://BookHip.com/RRGJKGN

Enjoy a synopsis of my book, *Love Between the Lines*, Book 2 in the Lilac Lake Inn Series:

Keeping a family promise can be the beginning of a whole new life for everyone in town.

Taylor Gilford is more than happy to accept her grandmother's gift of a cottage on the Lilac Lake Inn's property to be shared with her two sisters, Dani and Whitney. The youngest, she's always felt left out when the sisters got together. Living at Lilac Lake will give her a chance to know them better. More than that, it might help the "writer's block" she's been experiencing and help her recover from a stinging critique by her publisher's new editor, Thompson C. Walker. After a few successful books in her fantasy series, Taylor can't allow her career to end without fighting back. As she struggles, she learns a lot about herself and realizes that reading between the lines can bring a lot of happiness.

Another of Judith Keim's series books celebrating love and families, strong women meeting challenges, and clean women's fiction with a touch of romance — beach reads for all ages with a touch of humor, satisfying twists, and happy endings

About the Author

A *USA Today* **Best-Selling Author,** Judith Keim is a hybrid author who both has a publisher and self-publishes, Ms. Keim writes heart-warming novels about women who face unexpected challenges, meet them with strength, and find love and happiness along the way. Her best-selling books are based, in part, on many of the places she's lived or visited, and on the interesting people she's met, creating believable characters and realistic settings her many loyal readers love. Ms. Keim loves to hear from her readers and appreciates their enthusiasm for her stories.

Ms. Keim enjoyed her childhood and young-adult years in Elmira, New York, and now makes her home in Boise, Idaho, with her husband, Peter, their lovable miniature Dachshund, Wally, and other members of her family.

While growing up, she was drawn to the idea of writing stories from a young age. Books were always present, being read, ready to go back to the library, or about to be discovered. All in her family shared information from the books in general conversation, giving them a wealth of knowledge and vivid imaginations.

"I hope you've enjoyed this book. If you have, please help other readers discover it by leaving a review on the site of your choice. And please check out my other books and series:"

The Hartwell Women Series
The Beach House Hotel Series
Fat Fridays Group
The Salty Key Inn Series
The Chandler Hill Inn Series
Seashell Cottage Books
The Desert Sage Inn Series
Soul Sisters at Cedar Mountain Lodge Series
The Sanderling Cove Inn Series
The Lilac Lake Inn Series

"ALL THE BOOKS ARE NOW AVAILABLE IN AUDIO on iTunes! So fun to have these characters come alive!"

Ms. Keim can be reached at **www.judithkeim.com**

And to like her author page on Facebook and keep up with the news, go to: **http://bit.ly/2pZWDgA**

To receive notices about new books, follow her on Book Bub:

https://www.bookbub.com/authors/judith-keim

And here's a link to where you can sign up for her periodic newsletter! **http://bit.ly/2OQsb7s**

She is also on Twitter @judithkeim, LinkedIn, and Goodreads. Come say hello!

Acknowledgments

And, as always, I am eternally grateful to my team of editors, Peter Keim and Lynn Mapp, my book cover designer, Lou Harper, and my narrator for Audible and iTunes, Angela Dawe. They are the people who take what I've written and help turn it into the book I proudly present to you, my readers! I also wish to thank my coffee group of writers who listen and encourage me to keep on going. Thank you, Peggy Staggs, Lynn Mapp, Cate Cobb, Nikki Jean Triska, Joanne Pence, Melanie Olsen, and Megan Bryce. And to you, my fabulous readers, I thank you for your continued support and encouragement. Without you, this book would not exist. You are the wind beneath my wings.